Critical .

THE GAS

Winner of the James T.

'The novel cannot fail to terrify its readers.'
— *The Austin American*

'A literary marvel . . . a sharp, clever and devastating novel.'
— *El Paso Times*

'A chilling, delicate novel . . . a fascinating experience in psychology.'
— *Pittsburgh Press*

'A first novel of many shades and subtleties. If it makes you feel a bit claustrophobic, you can be sure it was meant to.'
— *Chicago Tribune*

'A first novel of impressive originality and accomplishment.'
— *New Statesman*

'Macabre, well-observed and elegantly constructed.'
— *Birmingham Evening Mail*

'This is a dense and intelligent first novel, full of oddness and technical experiment and glittering with small, clever detail.'
— *The Guardian*

'A clever, witty and marvellously well-written book.'   — *Listener*

'The most skilful first novel by a woman since Iris Murdoch's *Under the Net*.'   — *Spectator*

ABOUT THE AUTHOR

Maggie Ross studied Art and qualified as a teacher before moving on professionally in a form of writing which often has 'a multi-layered content allied to a strong visual style'.

Her first published novel, *The Gasteropod* (Cresset Press), won the James Tait Black Memorial Prize. Her second novel, *Milena*, was published by Collins.

Her work has been published in short story collections (Penguin, Michael Joseph, Macmillan, Hutchinson, etc.) Her stories and plays for radio and television have been broadcast and televised. Foreign translations of her work have brought it to the attention of international readers and audiences.

She worked briefly in television as a drama script editor and was fiction critic for the *Listener*. Born in Essex, England, she has lived mainly in London. She is married to the writer and artist Barry Bermange.

MAGGIE ROSS

The Gasteropod

VALANCOURT BOOKS

The Gasteropod by Maggie Ross
First published in the United Kingdom by Barrie & Rockliff in 1968
First published in the United States by Viking in 1969
First Valancourt Books edition 2025

Copyright © 1968 by Maggie Ross

All rights reserved. In accordance with the U.S. Copyright Act of 1976, the copying, scanning, uploading, and/or electronic sharing of any part of this book without the permission of the publisher constitutes unlawful piracy and theft of the author's intellectual property. If you would like to use material from the book (other than for review purposes), prior written permission must be obtained by contacting the publisher.

Published by Valancourt Books, Richmond, Virginia
http://www.valancourtbooks.com

ISBN 978-1-960241-47-4 (trade paperback)
Also available as an electronic book.

Set in Bembo Book MT

I

I am standing in the portrait gallery looking at myself. In front of me, and covering the entire wall, is a giant picture behind glass. It seems to cover the wall and touch the floor, or nearly so. In the glass I can see myself and everything behind me. It is all a question of focus. I have been standing here a long time. Anyone passing from the gallery on my left would think that I was contemplating deeply the contents of the picture: what they would not realise is that from where I stand the glass is pure black, and reflecting perfectly.

There I am in my newish suit and pristine shirt, nicely polished and nicely brushed for this Day of Days. The ears are cleaned, the epidermis shines, the hairs combed in perfect alignment across my smooth and healthy dome. It is many years since I gave myself such attention, such restoration. All my efforts have always gone towards the care of other things: plants to be pressed, insects pickled, and shells preserved with varnishes. But today I treated myself as I would a specimen, carefully going over myself in order to be, at least for one day, a prime example of the Middle-Aged Man. There is no point, usually, in considering myself as something that can be preserved from Time's toll. I know that tomorrow all this good work will already partially be undone and that creeping age, against which I have waged long years of war, will continue its soft attack. I who have rescued and preserved so many specimens from their disintegration should surely know the best ways in which to present myself to someone used to outward show. I carry a hat—brushed fur-felt—the shoes are lustrous. My tie is neat and pierced by a pearl. I have both richness and dignity. Having toyed with the idea of sporting a cane, I tried one out before I left, but concluded that a free hand was safest when meeting people, not to mention more youthful. I have no wish to appear older than I am. A fine balance must be maintained between buoyancy and dignity. I do not wish to look 'spry' or 'dapper', or any name that the thoughtless give to men of my stature and shape. Height, to me, has always been a problem in situations demanding the lofty approach. It seems to me that no one has ever taken seriously the idea that I am, and have always been, in charge of our collective destinies. But today I will show them what I am—a Man of Means in command of a situation he alone has created, and he alone can control. Here he has been standing for a long, long time, superbly patient, prepared and calm, almost as though he has no real wish for that moment to come when the waiting is over, and he knows the worst.

But so far I am alone in here. She doesn't come. Without distortion I can see the long dark run of the floorboards stretching away from under my heels, the length of the room to the arch at the end. The arch is the entrance to this gallery; that is where I must concentrate if I can. The reflected floorboards are darkly red but if I turn towards the arch they change to yellow with stains on them like the Dun Sentinel. It is strange to find so familiar a place taking on such a multitude of aspects, depending on one's view of it. My mirror gives this room vast areas of shadow which, in reality, it does not possess. The walls and pictures come and go even though the light is good and the afternoon a fair one. The windows are high up and to the right, situated so as not to interfere with one's view of the portraits. But the light itself is the interference, causing so many secondary reflections. There is a certain airlessness in here accentuated by the absence of ropes or latches with which to let in the outer atmosphere. From where I stand the windows are insignificant; they fade, like the pictures, into the wall's surface. I stand enclosed within a shell, nacre-lined, shining mirror-like, reflecting dully its own interior and on whose black exit I must concentrate, shifting neither feet nor gaze until she comes to release me. Surrounded by so many specimens I feel like a specimen myself with only one ability left, the ability to lose myself among the faces and hands in the great, black picture above me.

They overwhelm me, these people perfectly preserved in paint. I stand before them, so close that I must raise my head to see to whom these pink hands belong. Two rows of mighty gentlemen sit at their table and look down at me, their hands stiffly folded across their gowns or lightly touching the tablecloth. I have disturbed their conference. This afternoon when I entered under the arch, unsure where to wait, they watched me walk towards them down the boards and held my gaze until I was confronting them. Now they tower over me, identically clothed in some dark stuff which makes an admirable mirror. They look at me still with shrimpy eyes which, by an effort of will, I eradicate. My eyes are constantly drawn to them; to their scalloped ruffs, pink faces and hands, their geometric tablecloth. Its rich patterning leads the eye, willy-nilly, to the back of the room where the window is: lead-lights and a latch. The window is open but the gentlemen turn away from the view of the courtyard outside. They are unaware that the window, for me, is the secret source of my private knowledge, and why I am here today.

Through the window I can see the sunlight clearly catching another wall on the other side of the courtyard. Another window, tightly shut, is opposite mine. From long experience I know just how to crane my neck to catch a glimpse of what lies beyond the thin foliage of that poor, neglected plant, its roots in cement, no doubt just alive and bound to die in a year or two unless we give it attention. We must endeavour to water it from now on, allowing the leaves their natural succulence now that the need for my peep-hole is gone—or will be gone by the end of today. We will water and plant, giving the courtyard the attention promised it when we first moved to the house. We will make of it a secret garden, which links the rooms instead of dividing them.

It wanders, the mind wanders, watching the adumbrations. I must turn away from the shrimpy eyes; try to keep with the Present.

On my right someone stares with the self-same stare from behind the glass. A young boy is looking at me. Is he doubting? Reproachful? Surely not. He should be glad that I am here. Any portrait that stares at one is merely a portrait. Like 'Kitchener Wants You'. I must be merely amused by this staring boy with the feathered cap, but he makes me wary. Best to be wary of a stare like that, such suggested violence, although he has never harmed me. I have always been wary of Jamie's stare, ready to side-step the sudden lunge or affectionate slap. I never cared for contact. I don't care for his pose: he is still a child but he holds his hand on his hip like a woman, precociously. He stares like a woman, boldly. He wears a fine example of Jacobean costume. He wears it well. The silver becomes his pale, red hair but I do not care for such an early hint of self-awareness. It's almost as though he invented everything—colour, pose, the shape of the frame, the shining glove and captive falcon, the fat feather in his hat. He behaves like some princeling, bound from birth to accept the liege of others. By being defiant Jamie gives no hint of his insecurity. I do not like you my fine bonny boy. I don't like you, and I can never understand you. Your homosexual hinterland has always been strange ground to me, despite the invitations. You have forgotten now the invitations to throw down books and bodies in the summer grass; requests to tell you all my thoughts and how I felt in your enveloping presence. So much honey, then, for tea. Despite your efforts I remained unlured, so you cut your losses early, unable, and unlike me, to wait and wait for what you wanted. Your final release is now in my hands: I am here to push you further away than this thin glass barrier that divides us. Now I have only to move a shoulder, slightly, to be rid of you.

It is all a question of focus. If I let my eyes do as they will, I stare at nothing. Then the ears take over the work. I hear marching feet, as though an army is hidden somewhere deep in the other galleries. The sound comes from no particular direction. It is everywhere. Footsteps are walking wherever I turn to listen. I concentrate. Now I can distinguish from where the muffled marching comes. I believe I can tell how long it will take for them to transmogrify. But my task is made more difficult by the gallery floors. Not all of them are made of board: some are wood blocked. The blocks are the same shade of orange yellow, but to walk on them is different. The feel of the floor alters under your shoes. The sound dulls. Only the boards are hollow to the tread. Over the years I have given this gallery the same minute attention that I have given to every one of my specimens. I know it as well as the spirals and whorls of any of my Wentletraps. Raise the shell to your ear and you hear the sounds of your own disturbance. In here my ears are attacked by footsteps and distant voices as though an army is about to come between me and the subject of my watch. What if she is here already, unable to move because of the crowds or frightened to find me in such a press?

I must be able to see her the moment she enters under the arch, that is if she chooses this gallery. When I first came I was quite, quite sure that here was where she was bound to come. She would come here first, drawn by her memories of this place, finding it necessary to seek out the faces she knows so well. She was bound to choose either here or the Holbeins. She surely needs the comfort of familiar things to give her the courage for this confrontation. Unless she too has forgotten how we used to wander these galleries. Indeed it was a long time ago. Nevertheless she must move with the crowd, if crowd there is, leaving the lift and wheeling automatically through the swing doors that lead this way. Visitors always choose this gallery first, or they turn left to look at the Holbeins: it is a question of convenience. But I'm sure to see her when she enters the arch, even with my back to her. She will not walk, like the other visitors, hugging the walls. Fear will make her brave. She will walk a shade too firmly past each stretch of gallery, glimpsed from the corner of her eye as she searches for a man like me, her Middle-Aged Man with Money. By her very walk I shall know she comes for something other than to pass the time or get out of the sun: how few come here to study Art. Like us they come for secret reasons, unable to spare much of their mind on a frozen past. Rarely does anyone come in here with a real interest in what has been preserved. They sidle along a single wall, ignoring the other three, before fading into the promising brightness of another gallery. Sometimes I question whether they look at the portraits at all, so fast do they move. And they never go back to look again, always forward, fast, as though it is a sort of penance being here at all. And never to be repeated. Advancing, they size up the picture ahead, willing to be attracted by anything that smacks of novelty. During my long wait here I have been the object of much surreptitious attention. I fail to see how I can be of such interest. I have always held the view that preserved specimens were preferable to living ones. I cannot see how people can prefer something that ages, promising decay, to the pure certainty of something that has been fixed forever in a perfect state. There is no immortality for humans, only an approximation of what they are can be retained.

Only portraits and photographs keep for us people as they once were, at some tiny point in Time, while the rest of their lives is swallowed up and lost.

I admit myself I have always watched my wife, her friends, with partial interest, content to record very little of their passing lives. Inanimate objects have always been my passion and pursuit. Until I came to the conclusion that I was in danger of losing the prize of my entire collection. Then there had to be action.

I stand quite still, allowing each visitor to creep up to me to see what glues me to this spot. They look at me, then up at the conference. None the wiser. Perhaps for a minute they stand alongside, waiting. I daren't move for I want no company. I must wait for the performance to end, until they lose interest and pass behind me to the left, and the Hanoverians.

When the gallery opened at two o'clock there was no one here to spoil my view. This room was mine and I enjoyed it. The arch was clearly visible. Then people came. A flight of children entered, cluttering the place, disproportionately shouting. Their laughter echoed long after they were out of sight. Others wandered in to skulk along the walls and block my view. Twice I shifted position in front of my black mirror, because of the crowds. But change altered the reflection and I became aware of too much detail in the painting which pecked a place in my brain. I saw a pattern on the cloth, a fringe of wool. Wood grain. A committee member frowned at me. Colours came: red and brown. They vanished when I stepped aside to regain my original position. A simple move can upset entirely all one's powers of concentration.

At two thirty I began to tire and attempted to walk a few steps along the gallery towards the arch. The committee member frowned at me. He seemed to have a hint of nicotine about the nostrils. So I returned keeping my eyes on the frowning man whose clothing was a massive, vague silhouette. His pink face towered over me and, as I advanced, I began to move upwards inside his body until my head took the place of his. His was the stronger body though, but he had my head. I was doing the thinking for him. I was making the decisions although he thought he was the one in command of this situation. He thought he was the one who had arranged this meeting. I was supposed to be thankful to him for this chance of a new lease of life. 'I'm sure you'll fit her very well,' he said. And I smiled.

It was foolish to attempt a move. I was better off when the parallel lines of the floorboards cut through us both and vanished behind me through the arch. I must be able to see the arch. No sense in being caught unawares at this late stage in the game. With my back to her I must be the one to see her first, to make quite sure she comes far enough in for there to be no escape. I want to be able to turn as she comes, and confront her. I may have to grasp her arm perhaps, do some speedy talking. I mustn't let this one get away—my last and most longed-for specimen. She will be the Left-Handed Chank of my collection if she comes—which she surely must. Then all is complete! Standing centrally here I am the obvious point of anyone's focus. Surely there is no mistaking me. I do not wish there to be a mistake so I carry the red carnation carefully, ready to raise it to my nose, when the time comes. At first I stood breathing in the flower's scent until my arm tired and the nasal passages began to object to the unaccustomed pollen. The flower is the largest one I could find in all that profusion of bloom in the garden. She probably planted it herself and will be drawn to me by its very scent. Unless someone else chooses today to come in here sporting a buttonhole.... A man in a hat, and carrying a stick entered the gallery at two thirty five. He came very close and stood beside me, looking for a spell at my profile. I felt his gaze but saw him look at me in my mirror. Then he faced the picture and caught my eye staring at him in the dark glass. Hastily I tried to look at the painting, ignoring the way his face told me he was up to my trick. I stood very still. He put up his hand to adjust the brim of his trilby hat, transferring the stick to his other hand. He was wearing quite a vivid carnation. He stared first at me, then at my reflection. I bent forward as if I was interested in the brush strokes. Suddenly people came in through the arch, but although we both heard them, neither looked round. Instead we both gazed into the black surface, and watched them enter behind us. He had discovered my secret. With great presence of mind I turned with a start (as if at the noise). He backed away before I could question him. I was going to ask whether he too had been sent here today to keep a tryst. I was going to ask why so young a man should find it necessary to be here at all, to wait for someone as old as her. I was almost prepared to explain to him that both of us had been double crossed. It came to my mind I could offer him money if he would go away instantly, removing the carnation as he went. I may even have opened my mouth to speak. But he'd gone, faded away round a corner, so silently that I couldn't hear the squeak of his step. He never came back. I felt for a handkerchief to wipe my face, then turned to the picture again.

Now I look at myself and see that the sweating has stopped although the top of my head has a slight shine today. This gallery is far too hot. There should be a way to open the windows. Should I put on my hat? I look much younger with it on. Sometimes I feel that my quite youthful face is belied by my lack of hair. I wish to appear at my very best, today. But I must not seem to be in disguise. I came to the conclusion that when we meet she should see immediately who I am. She should see it is me making an effort, for once, to please by my appearance. Today I wear the greenish suit which is like an Abalone shell. The green is completely dissipated by the glass. My white collar vies with the faces and hands, especially his hands. I make an attempt to raise my head to the level of the gentlemen in conference. I reach the old man's forearm. No higher. I cannot really touch him. He hides behind his years, case-hardened as any rhinoceros. If I moved a fraction to the right my shining crown would merely brush the fringes of the tablecloth. I am not a tall man.

I am not a tall man. I told him so myself four weeks ago when he was all agog for information. He could see for himself how tall I was, but he seemed to need a spurious fact on which to base his act as Shadchen.

'Yes, yes,' he said. 'I'm sure you'll fit her very well. She's on the shorter side herself. And somewhat younger too. I think.' He eyed me up and down, as if my years had, like the ladybird, been spotted on to me. 'Delightfully immature, I would say. The product of a sheltered life. Just right for you.' In an instant began my dislike of him.

'Max tells me you're something of a collector. Well, so am I.' He paused. We smiled a collective smile.

'My speciality's furniture. Old, of course. But in perfect working order. I could always give my clients guarantees that the stuff's genuine. That is, if they asked for them.' He began to shift and twist, turning his head as he spoke. 'But they trust me, see. I'm a man of reputation.' The words came and went with each pirouette. 'Satisfaction guaranteed. Ha, ha!' Could I believe my ears? His next turn brought him back to me with a serious look on his face. We were getting down to business.

'This one's a real collector's piece. She has a sort of ... period grace. Mellowed. Elegant. Right up your street. I'm not used to this kind of thing, mind you. But I know quality when I see it. And she's got quality. What better to compare her with than the stuff I know so well?' We performed a minor minuet as I tried to follow his words.

'And of course one has to be careful in a deal like this. Wouldn't do for a man of my reputation to be connected with anything ... untoward. Would it? You can see that now, can't you, dear sir?'

He came quite close and spoke in my ear. 'On my books she is down as *Louis Quinze*.' He winked. 'It pays to be careful. In any communications on the matter, we'll refer to her as *Louis Quinze*. Shall we?' My reply was lost in the complications of a reverse turn that took him to the centre of the carpet. 'I must warn you, it pays to be careful, dear sir. We'd both rather there were no letters in evidence, wouldn't we? No telephone calls. After all, it's a simple matter to fit up a gentleman such as yourself. Hmm? You're young enough, aren't you, Heaven knows? We can settle this thing without involvements.'

I said, 'As you wish. My age is forty-seven.'

'Nothing to be ashamed of there. Nothing at all. Although I would have taken you for slightly older.' He danced up to me and patted my arm. 'Forty-seven is young yet.' Having felt no previous embarrassment at my years, some began to rise. He looked hard at my face and lingered on my hair.

'Look at me,' he said, 'and guess how old I am.'

He looks a badly preserved fifty. He owned to ten years less. I diagnosed excessive alcohol as the cause of his skin's disintegration. The pickling process had not yet reached the epidermis. He smoked too much, inhaling nasally so that his nostrils were lined with nicotine. Unfortunately my height is such that when we opposed each other, I looked straight into the wide, yellow cavities of his nose.

'I keep myself in trim,' he said. 'It's in the mind, one's youth.'

I felt my hair, smoothing it over the skull, glad to be younger than he, but sorry for the skin's exposure. He made me self aware. The years of polishing and scraping other things had left me with little knowledge of myself. His critical frown was a warning that in his world I was the specimen. The exterior needed attention.

He slapped my arm as he always did when being rude. 'But appearances tell,' he said. 'Haircuts and shaves pay dividends. So do baths and a decent tailor. Mens sana in Corporation Street!' I laughed and he looked at me.

When he and I faced each other for the first time he looked at me as if the sight was something vital; as if I must pass his secret test before he could handle this affair. What nonsense. He was trying to suggest that he was doing me a huge favour.

'I've never done this sort of thing before,' he said. 'You must understand this isn't my usual line of business. Hard times are to blame, of course. Rising costs, resources draining—everything a burden to a man like me. Capital won't last forever, will it? Not unless something's done to implement the old income.'

Had I known then of the 'Genuine Antique Furniture Co.' I might have accused him of suppressing facts. In retrospect, he seemed to lie with every breath. A fake, like his furniture, he began to lie from the moment we met. I never told him how I had the edge on his mendacity. How, over the years, I had learned the art of lie-detecting so thoroughly that none, however white, slipped through unnoticed. But his were boorish lies, as boorish as himself, lacking subtlety of thought or composition. Not like some I've heard, that needed a mind like a Geiger Counter to detect them. He lied so carelessly, always playing on the central theme of his honest impecuniosity. With each new variation I heaved a sigh of recognition, receiving it like the Holy Wafer into my storage system.

First of all he said she was big, but changed his mind later. He said that if I liked them big, then 'big and bold' was what she was: an archaic form, I thought, for someone owning to a mere forty.

His eulogy on large females quite carried him away. Among the women that he cited were Lady Hamilton, Mae West and bathing belles on certain seaside postcards. He said Max had told him I liked them large. He lied. Even his suits propound untruths. No one with complete honesty would wear stiff buckram panels in his jacket to hold the figure in. From that I deduced he was a man able to afford an efficient tailor, or perhaps a corsetière. He needs the money for his expensive tailor: he must take a lot of skill in being padded out like that. Being in the upholstery business has obviously affected him; my concentration on years of collecting has made me a careful, patient man with an eye to detail. Perhaps, in his way, he too felt the need for padding against life's shocks. For that I cannot blame him. We all must have some defence, something into which to retire when the waves break.

'Would you like to see a photo of her?' he said. Of course I answered 'Yes', preparing my face with a look of surprise and immediate pleasure, as though I had never seen the photo before. The surprise came naturally at his words.

'Shall I let you into a little secret? Shall I?'

'Please do. Feel free.'

'Well ...' He looked like a man about to make a big decision. 'She's ... related to me. Quite a near relative, in actual fact.'

Being a man long used to keeping to himself life's knocks and shocks, it wasn't hard for me to appear to believe him. I nodded gently, taking the photograph in my hand to stare at with interest. Had I not known the truth of the matter I would have said there was a superficial similarity. They both possess the over-round chin and soft-tipped nose that suggests spinelessness and lack of true direction. They have identical nostrils but hers, thank Heaven, aren't lined with nicotine. Her breath never smelt. I could have convinced myself there and then that they were related. Perhaps even brother and sister. But I knew they weren't.

'Just like me she is,' he said, pointing at the shady hair with his stained finger. 'Dead ringer for me. Lovely nature too. Just like me! Winning ways. Seriously though, she's a real good sort. Lovely dresser. Good cook. Amiable. No bad tempers like some of them.'

I must have raised my eyebrows. 'Of course she has her faults. Find me a woman that hasn't, hmm? Hers has been a tendency to withdraw. If you see what I mean. She's never been one to push herself forward. In any way. Result, lack of friends. And we all need friends now, don't we? Especially a woman at her time of life.' He sighed. 'Kept herself to herself all these years. It's sad when you think of it, isn't it?'

'With such a virtuous woman, yes.'

He was alert in a flash. Why bring virtue into it, he asked. Mine hadn't been questioned, so why question hers? He wasn't suggesting that she was a paragon with a mind like a nun. Far from it. She'd knocked about a bit. She wasn't green. All he was saying was that at her time of life she needed security, the kind of security a man like me could guarantee to a woman like her, with a well-developed taste for the little luxuries that make the difference between having it rough and really living. I wasn't to suppose she wouldn't cost a lot. But well worth the cash to one who had it. And I had it. Didn't I? Yes, I had it to spend on her, willingly.

With reverence he put down the frame and smiled. 'She'll be worth every penny I can promise you that. She's a real lady that one. A queen.' The smile continued. 'The queen of hearts, eh? As opposed to the queen of tarts!' He had a nasty habit of fingering me. He poked me in the ribs to underline his witticism. It was rather late in our acquaintance that I discovered the need to counter-attack. His horny finger scored more points than mine, coming, as mine did, up against hard buckram, not to mention the possibility of whalebone. If I lunged at him with darting finger it was only in self-defence. My prods were always tempered by the fact that I had the advantage of youth.

I do not look my age, therefore this mirror is a liar too. In it I see things far too faintly. Can I rely on it to tell me when she comes? If it takes all colour from me, how can I safely see whether it is her or merely someone similar who, when I turn round, won't have one ounce of red at all? I do not want my hopes raised, then shattered on the turning. Or am I being far too fussy?

Fussiness has been a personal defect. My specimens all suffer from my care. I dust and shine them ceaselessly, then wonder why the colours dim, as if the sunlight is to blame. Now I allow no sunlight to enter my room. I keep it out with blinds. To see the motes dancing in its beams would make me think I lived in one vast dustbin. The suggestion has been made before, but rather in fun than anger. I forgave her. How can a room that has meant so much to me be compared with rubbish? The contents alone are worth thousands: Conches and Cones and Trochidae are there by the score, lovingly cleaned and lovingly labelled. They all rest on shelves or lie in deep drawers made by me over the years. I have built everything—cupboards, cases, storage racks. If anyone came to me and asked for one particular specimen, I'd be able to say, without hesitation or pause, where it was. Acids, brushes, magnifiers, all have their place in that room of mine. They all bear witness to the love I've lavished on it. Nowhere is there a collection more worthy of the name. My shells are my pride; they will always take first place in my affections. I have cared for that room too long to be wooed completely from it now. It is my real home into which I have drawn each item, whether common or rare, to preserve and label it. From time to time I open drawers and gaze at what I have caught. I must be able to look at them, see that the permanence which is so dear to me is visible. I must be able to keep within sight anything I have acquired. Years went by sometimes before I got hold of certain specimens, yet I always knew they would come my way, if I waited. I have always had the gift of true patience. The ability to watch and wait.

If my mirror is so dim that I must turn to see if it is really her coming under the arch, then she will see me simultaneously. This I can't allow. Before she recognises me I must be able to grasp her arm, to draw her towards me and keep her there. She mustn't be able to recognise me from afar and make a snap decision. Or rather, to act. She has never been one to make decisions. The impulse comes first and then the thought. Her life has been full of unconsidered moves and qualifying statements as if she has had to excuse her acts. She has often said that it wasn't her fault. Other people made her do this, and this. If only she had been left to work it out for herself then her path, she has said, would have been less involved. She has waited, like me, but unlike me, has not been inviolate. I put it down to a basic weakness inherent in all her family. They wish to have resolved for them the stresses of living. Like the Limpet they wish to carve out a niche to which to return from their tiny forays. There they twist and settle into the very same grooves that they made themselves. On this fact I rely.

Have I made a mistake in waiting here? Downstairs I might be less conspicuous. Downstairs the revolving doors precipitate the visitors into the hall. They take a second to get their bearings. I could conceivably conceal myself while she spun round, ready to pounce before she could think. If I should hide behind the bust of William Shakespeare I would be too distant. There is no other hiding place. Ten to one she would fling herself across the tiles and up the stairs before I had a chance to speak to her. Finding no one upstairs I should see her descend, her coming as tedious as go o'er. What if she should miss me and Will entirely, flinching herself out of the building, relieved to have got away so lightly? She could say she kept her part of the bargain. Did she not come here as planned? She would be relieved, at this late stage, to be reprieved.

I could not wait for her on the stairs. As she ascended she would raise her eyes to me in horror. How could she acknowledge me and pass a kindly word or two before going on up in search of her mythical man? Or would the meeting stir her memory and she would think it natural to see me there, almost as if I was once more waiting to take her hand and escort her up to the Elizabethans? By now the memory may have left her of how we spent our hours wandering the galleries, having so much to say to each other, so much time to spend looking round for things to take her fancy. She invented games for us to play, to relieve the monotony of serious study. Here we played Spot the Friend or Pin-Point the Enemy, searching the oily likenesses for familiar faces. Dorothea thought she was an expert.

'There's Jamie,' she would say. 'Just the same as ever. Look at him standing there so sure of himself with that smug grin. His smile has an edge to it, don't you think? He is lording it today. He should have the key of the door in his hand. But it's a sword, isn't it? Do you think the falcon was a present for today? I could have given him it, I suppose. It might tear out his throat! No, I gave him the sword, I've decided. With that he could do so much more damage to himself, don't you think?' She amused me then.

'He's so horribly over-decorated. Isn't that Jamie to a T? There's something about him so beastly feminine, have you noticed? He may be big and hairy and ... well ... strong, but under it all he's womanly. He looks so violent. Doesn't he?' She would stand, apeing the pose, hand on hip, staring back at him. The portrait worried her. 'You know what Jamie's doing, don't you? Has it ever occurred to you that he's looking at himself? He's looking in a mirror! I guarantee when the poor Artist Unknown painted him he brought along a mirror to keep our Jamie quiet. Jamie was beastly to the poor man until the mirror came. Then he went quiet as a mouse, admiring himself with that secret smile. How else could he have been persuaded to keep so still? Over-dressed lout!'

Darting like a pretty stoat from frame to frame she would cry out noisily in the humming stillness, causing attendants to peer round corners or half-raise themselves from seats.

'Let's go and look at me,' she said. We always had to look at her. She felt she owned the painting. Tapping the glass with her long nails she would bend as close to the glass as she dared, clouding it with her breath. She examined every painted shred, every pore of the polished face. 'Today she seems a trifle sullen, don't you think? She really regrets being twenty-one. She doesn't want to be grown-up you see.'

'You'll have more freedom.'

'What does that mean, the word "freedom"? Today she looks a trifle pale. But still beautiful. Isn't she?'

'Very.'

'As beautiful as me?'

'No.'

'I don't have pearls and turquoises. She has rubies too. I wonder who told her that rubies are the very best gems for a red-head? Rubies would suit me, wouldn't they? Yes. I'll settle for rubies. They keep their worth. You could look upon them as an investment.'

'Her father was rich.'

'So is yours.' Her finger traced the jewelled cap. 'With all that money you'd think she could look a bit more cheerful. She could have smiled for the painter.'

'Other things meant more to her than money.'

'For instance?'

'Religion.' Dorothea laughed. 'Religion meant more to her

than money. She wanted England to be Catholic. She felt her countrymen were living in mortal sin.'

'What do you know about sin!' She ran her nail across the glass, making it squeak. I was losing her attention.

'She never married the man she loved.'

'I know. Poor darling.'

Leaving a damp handprint on the glass, Dorothea turned away and began to wander down the gallery. I followed. Through the Hanoverians she walked, turning her head occasionally to glance at some thin face that caught her eye. She looked only at men.

'Who are you looking for?'

'Funny, isn't it? Not one portrait of Max in the entire gallery. Have you noticed that?'

'No. I haven't given him much thought...'

'Don't suppose you have. I invented the game, didn't I? But you'd think *someone* would look like Max.'

'There's one in the basement a bit like him.'

'Where? Quick, let's go and see! Who's it by?'

'Singer Sargent.'

'Don't be ridiculous! That old picture? Max would be pleased if I told him he reminded you of a *passé* old man! He's never as much as hinted there's a likeness there. No, we've combed this gallery without finding one Max, anywhere.'

'Who's "we"?'

She briefly hesitated. 'You and I, of course. Look around and see for yourself.'

'What about him?' I pointed at one with a saturnine pout. 'Or him?' An ugly old man with a wart on his chin. 'That one has Max's devilish smile, don't you think?'

Dorothea was not amused. She didn't look. Instead she stared hard at my right ear. It was one of her tricks meant to make me feel uncomfortable. 'How can you say such stupid things? Max's face has great... power. Yes, power. He has an aura about him...'

'Aura?'

'Yes. Aura.'

'Of sex, do you mean?'

She laughed then and asked me what I knew of sex. She said that I had slender proof. Then she ran off down the long gallery, leaving me to stare at a roomful of Hanoverians all with Max's bland and youthful face with the old, old eyes.

Knowing this place as well as I do, it is no wonder I chose it for the rendezvous. When he asked me where it was we should meet, immediately I said: 'The Portrait Gallery'. He smiled approval, showing his ginger teeth.

'She's an Art Lover too,' he said. 'You'll have to make a lot of that. Something there in common.' He picked up her portrait and held it with a large finger and thumb that blocked my view. I remember noting that the frame was too large. The photograph slid under the glass. Beneath her portrait was another one, also a woman, if I could go by the rounded neckline and white skin. Underneath that perhaps there were more photographs; more women of his stable, all sound stock and saleable. He may have kept a set of photographs in the frame, all ready to be interchanged before the arrival of yet another client. I wanted to ask if he laid claim to kinship of the hidden girl with the rounded neckline, but resisted such an impulse, not wanting to infuriate him at this crucial stage in our relationship. Why should I jeopardise his willingness to be a part of Max's plan?

I held the frame for a moment only before he took it from me and stood it on the table. I may have mentioned Max then. Perhaps I said, 'So Max told me,' or something similar. He looked at me sharply, wanting to know what else Max had divulged. His wary look required an answer. I told him Max had said very little, preferring to leave the talking to him. Although Max and I were friends, friends of long standing, there was no great intimacy between us.

'Ah. More buddies,' he suggested. He said that all of us were buddies, bound together for a common cause. Only in the cause of friendship would a man of his integrity become caught up in such a deal. Did I understand?

'Let me be clear. If I took on this little job for you, it's only because of friendship's call. I wouldn't do it for everyone. You understand that? Max, in the past, has acted for me in the spirit of true, lasting friendship. Now I'm in the position of doing something for him in return. As a good friend should. Right?' I agreed.

'Any friend of Max's is a friend of mine too. Ha! Ha! I'll do my best, you may be certain, . . .' Here he lowered his voice a shade, '. . . to produce the goods to suit your rather fancy tastes.' He suddenly smiled playfully. 'And I shall expect a friendly gesture on your part, dear sir. Very friendly!' The finger shot out from the cuff, scoring a magpie on my ribs. When I tried to shake the hand, his smile vanished. 'I can't speak more plainly, can I?' he said.

A long silence followed while he stared at me. It took time to grasp the nature of what he had said. I was slow to appreciate this couched request for remuneration.

'Will a cheque suffice?'

'A cheque?' He began to blink quite rapidly. Unusual in a man like him such nervousness. He seemed insecure in his role as middleman. I knew he wished he had greater control over the merchandise. 'Cheques aren't usual in such circumstances, dear sir. Or so they tell me.' He raised his hand to his inside pocket, protecting his fountain pen. 'Wouldn't we both rather deal in cash? I'm sure we would. Just as we would both rather the goods were considered as furniture. Wouldn't we?'

'Just as you say.'

'Then, my dear sir, I say "cash" for the *Louis Quinze*.'

'From whom am I supposed to be buying this antique?'

'The Genuine Antique Furniture Company, of course. I own a bona fide business.' My question had shocked him. 'They're hard to come by, gentlemen like you with money to spare for indulging. But friendship is friendship. I shall require cash.'

'I never carry large sums. Two hundred is all I have on me now. Will that do? On account?'

'And the rest?'

'In cash, one hour from delivery. I shall bring it to you in person.'

'You'll have the lady with you . . .'

'Ah, yes. I was forgetting. She shall stay outside in the taxi.'

'One hour from delivery. Why one hour?'

'I must have time to check the goods. I must have time to see if the *Louis Quinze* is cabriole legged!' My joke did not appeal to him. 'If I don't arrive within the hour, then you'll know the goods were faulty.'

'And the two hundred pounds?'

'The two hundred pounds will belong to you. But only the two hundred. You'll get no more.'

'That seems a fair arrangement.'

As I handed over the notes to him he rubbed his fingers and breathed deeply. I had to wait while he counted them, listening to his desultory questions. It was Max's part that bothered him most. He worried the problem like a hungry dog. 'Max a great friend of yours, eh?' The counting continued. 'If Max is all that much of a friend, how come *he* couldn't get you fixed up?'

'We're not really friends. Known each other a long time, that's all.'

'Surely someone like Max could find something suitable?' He had reached one hundred and twenty one.

'Max told me you had good taste, when I asked.'

'Ah!' The pile was rapidly growing. 'So has he.'

'His tastes wouldn't be quite the same as mine, would they now? His tastes lie in a different direction, wouldn't you say?'

'Nevertheless . . . fine fellow, Max.' The last of my pounds was counted out. 'Known him long?'

Being a careful man I have seen to it that my loss will be a mere two hundred (if loss there is), the cost, say, of one silk-lined cabinet, or a decent Murex tenuispina. But the thought remains that I am not used to losing specimens. In the long years of my collecting, little of worth has passed me by. If today fulfilment is achieved it will be due to years of patient planning in an atmosphere devoid of foolish hope. Always, in hope's place, there has been the ability to think the long-term thought, so the years have seemed much shorter than they really were. If she doesn't come he will have a great loss. Expecting, as he does, to collect some thousand pounds from this brief introduction, he stands to lose a sizeable sum, despite Max having subtracted his own personal fee. The persuasions he used were surely weighty ones. He would not risk the loss of so much currency. Both Max and he would surely see that the risk of her not coming was made infinitesimal. She will come to me, contract in hand already signed and witnessed.

With such a property in their care, will they allow her to come alone? Surely someone will escort her on this crucial journey. Never has she had to act alone, without someone's support, however marginal. Now, more than ever, will she look for an arm on which to hang as she comes through the arch.

Who will she bring? Who will come with her—if she comes at all? Alternatives are drab enough for her to choose this easy way, but my uneasiness is still with me. Let me now concentrate on the lines of the floorboards and set my mind to waiting.

2

As I handed him the notes he almost sniffed them like a dog. One can always tell real money lovers by the way they handle it. He had the whole two hundred safely underneath his palm before he gave me all his attention. 'I like these notes,' he said. 'Been used before. Can't go wrong with used notes. None of the numbers run consecutively.' I had noticed this, and could have pointed out how easy it would have been for me to take a note of them. But he must have been fully aware that in his line of business some risks were unavoidable. I was such a small risk compared to some I'm sure he'd had to face. And he looked altogether a careful man. The lateness of the hour at which we met was entirely due to him. He chose an hour when no one would be likely to note my arrivals and departures.

That evening when I entered his flat the blinds were lowered and quite dark. The lamps in the forecourt had all been dimmed. Traffic still sounded from a distant road, increasing our isolation.

But not the first time. It must have been earlier, our first appointment, for the windows were glowing, so was the room as though a gay party of people had just left. There was the smell of smoke in the air, a slight perfume about which set me wondering. So this was his home. I couldn't have chosen a more likely place for this man in grey to inhabit. If I had first seen him out on the street and had been given the task of setting him, I would have chosen for him exactly that place with its low lights, mirrors and cut glass decanters. He gave me a drink and led the way across the parquet to stand before the Venetian blind. Had he, from long experience, known that I could barely distinguish him standing there? Light from the orange street lamps striped his face and pushed the massy body into shadow. I drank and let him size me up. We must have drunk a lot that night.

'She's not tall,' he said. 'Just right for you. Bet you like her on sight. Told Max you will. "Max", I said, "he'll like her on sight." Who wouldn't with a face like that?' Since the portrait wasn't in focus and his hand covered most of it, I could do no more than gaze at his finger. Underneath it, I knew, she was standing with one hand on her hip, smiling slightly.

'Kept herself to herself she has, this one. She's always been slightly reserved. Lovely woman. A real beauty. Kept herself to herself.'

'So you said.'

'She's a redhead too. What you wanted, isn't it? A redhead? Not one of the bottled kind either, but real. Lovely colouring.'

'You've seen her then?'

There was a pause. 'Seen her! Of course I've seen her. My dear good sir, what are you saying? Haven't I told you that she and I are distant relatives?' He tapped the glass too harshly, to emphasise his lie. The photograph shifted slightly. He gave it to me. I took out my reading spectacles for a closer look. In the white face her lips showed black. Without colour there was a hint that she might be related to him. Under some circumstances I suppose one human looks very like another, given two eyes, a nose and a mouth.

'She's younger than you,' he said. 'She looks very much like that. The portrait's quite recent you see. Taken last summer, I believe. She said it was taken last summer.'

She had lied to him. The photograph was taken in 1957. I made a note of it in my diary, cursing the luck that had prevented me from taking it myself. Max had posed her against the rockery, making her stand facing the morning light which filtered through the rain clouds. He hadn't wanted to take her photograph at all, giving in reluctantly to her pleading, making her go to my room herself to fetch my camera. I was willing to do the job, but she had to make Max do it. He stood on the lawn and watched her with a secret smile while she floundered among the flower beds at his directions. First he wanted her under the trees which dripped on her hair. Then he sent her a long way away, over the borders among the heather where her shoes were muddied terribly. He complained a lot about the quality of light, said he needed a lens hood, said they should wait until noon for the stronger sun. The forecast for that day was rain later. He probably knew. Finally he chose the rockery, which meant she had to climb between stones like a mountain goat, with the risk of grazing her ankles. The rockery spreads from the base of the lawn like an Alpine field until two hedges intervene. She did much damage to tiny plants before she was correctly placed, as Max wanted her, tucked away between two boulders. She narrowed her eyes against the bars of light. He told her to pose with one hand on her hip. She stood rigidly smiling while her feet sank into the soft earth. I told him to take the photo soon for she was in danger of sinking. 'Good,' he said. He spent much time elaborately shouting directions as to the set of her head and the way her arm should be angled. My camera he carelessly tossed from hand to hand before holding it up to his eye. With a sudden snap he took her photograph.

'Hadn't we better wait for the sun?' she shouted. But the shutter had already closed, transforming her words into a slight smile. Max tossed the camera back at her and returned to the house at top speed.

'Who was this taken by?' I asked.

'Now, that ... I don't know. Wasn't me though! Lovely, isn't she?'

'Yes. Very.'

A suspicious look at me, a punch on my arm, then a loud laugh. 'Ha! Ha! Good job Max warned me about you. Otherwise I might have taken the needle! What did he say you were ...? Whimsical? No. I know what he called you. He said you were dry. "Don't mind what he says. He's inclined to be a bit dry." That's what Max told me. And so you are. Good job he told me, eh?

'What I like about Max is that he's straightforward. Always lets you know where you stand. You may not like it at the time. May even hold it against him. But you thank him afterwards, don't you?

Done me plenty of favours in his time, Maxie has. Not that he hasn't expected something in return. But that's only human, isn't it? That's why I'm willing to do this for him. You scratch my back ... hmm? You've found the same thing, haven't you? With Max, I mean?'

I did not choose to expound to him my belief that Max has been, and will always be, a slight mystery. Having known Max since I was twenty there is still, even now, much that remains outside my range of understanding. Many times his behaviour has seemed to me not only excessive, but incomprehensible. If I had told him the truth—that basically Max is more of a stranger to me than himself—he would have dismissed the idea as rubbish. When I told him that I could only describe the shell of Max, he laughed, expanding the yellow nostrils.

'Describe Max,' he said.

'There is the eternal brown suit, of course ...'

'Excellent beginning. Great powers of observation. What else?'

'He has a high-bridged nose, or rather, did have.' Confusion sets in here, for recently Max has undergone plastic surgery.

The other day, while I was working at the long bench in my room to remove the last traces of a Conus' outer covering, he walked in, went over to my desk and turned off the table lamp. When I said 'Good morning' he merely nodded, waiting for me to notice his face. He had two black eyes. He seemed much paler, and thinner than when we had last met. 'Your eyes look bloodshot,' I said. On my desk were two neat rows of shells which he began to play with, shaking them like dice in his hands. Since this seemed to be one of his usual moods I continued with my work at the bench. The Conus responded extremely well to my treatment, revealing great brilliance of colour in its patterning. Having finished its preparation I could now turn my attention to the inventory. I heard Max sigh.

In silence I busied myself with my notebooks and pens, while Max sat gloomily at the darkened desk. He watched me open the Mollusc drawers at the point where the count stopped yesterday. He sighed again, with exasperation.

'For God's sake stop it!'

'Stop what?'

'Counting, damn you! Is that all you can find to do? Count? When I left you were at it.'

'Two weeks isn't long for work like this. You've only been gone for two weeks.'

'Nice of you to remember.'

'An inventory of this nature takes a long, long time. Even so I must hurry if I want to get it finished in time. I really hate to hurry it. A mistake might be made, inadvertently.'

'You make a mistake! Dear, dear, dear! Better be careful. Do nothing at all. Like you always do. That's much the safest.' He shoved my shells aside with his arm and began to play with the pots and jars that stood on a shelf above my desk. I heard him sigh several times. When I looked round to see how much havoc he was causing, I saw him pick up a brush. He licked it.

'That brush has been in acid.'

He rushed to the sink with a cry of horror and made a great fuss of spitting out streams of saliva and gargling loudly with his face under the tap. With unnecessary noise he plunged about the floor groping for the towel. I gave it to him.

'Well. What do you think?' he said. His eyes were very red.

'I think you'll live.'

'Come on you bastard, you know what I mean. What do you think of it?'

The light above us resembled that of a self-service store where all the goods are on equal, shadowless display. It showed up the yellow contusions on his pale face. Basically he looked no different: the high bridge was gone but not the look of superiority; something disdainful I had always equated with the high-bridged nose. Surgery cannot remake a person's character. I told him he hadn't changed.

He leapt for the mirror and peered at himself, twisting his head, altering the mirror's angle in an effort to profile. What he saw seemed not to displease him. He walked about the room, chin up, stroking his bruised face. 'Look at me properly. Look at the profile. You can't honestly say it doesn't notice? It looks superb. God knows I'm going through enough agony for it.' His walk had become stylised. He was a model treading the cat-walk, toes turned out, tiny steps, drooping shoulders. The imitation was perfect. 'Aren't I the beautiful one?'

'What made you do it, Max?' He was disdainful. 'I thought you were joking.'

'Some joke! Trust you not to see the point. Everyone else understands perfectly.'

'About your nose . . . ?'

'Simple, I would have thought. A new life. A new nose. A nice dramatic start.'

'Dramatic?'

'Trying to explain to you about drama is like trying to get through . . . cotton wool. Look, my dear fellow, don't try my patience when I'm feeling so poorly. I've always been terribly fond of the hooter, it's given me good service and all that, but we needed a change. Now we all start afresh. Hooter and all. Understand?'

'It looks very sore. I believe they use hammers, don't they?'

'Yes. But it wasn't like All-In Wrestling. They put me under for it.' Max was easily irritated by me. Today his tone was unusually mild. He asked me how I was. How I was bearing up under the strain.

'The same as ever, thank you.'

'God save us all from your ready wit!'

'How unlike you, Max, to ask how I am. Sure you're feeling all right?'

'Nasty! I suppose you're going to say that Middle Age is showing. Aren't you? I was feeling fine till I came in here, so it's all your fault. This room and you together are enough to give anyone the creeping greys. Walking in here is like coming into a bad dream.'

'I have heard that opinion expressed before. Both Dorothea and James have suggested it.'

'Only because I said it first. And it's true. You think you're awake, then you open this door . . . I had a dream once. I got into the darkest hole I have ever seen . . .'

'How could you see it if it was dark?'

'Shut up!' Such was the banality of his dream that the exact sequence eludes me now; the gist of the dream was that the hole became a gloomy room full of hisses and clicks and nasty smells. He said a huge creature lived in it, but although they conversed he never saw it. He thought it might have been a Hermit Crab. They had a long, and very boring conversation about the merits of Chanel and Dior (or some such dress-making person). He accused the crab of being a spy for a foreign country—so he said—where everybody had been frozen, or were marble blocks, or suchlike. Then he pleaded with the crab to let him go free, and the crab told him to wait. I busied myself with the shelves of Molluscs while he finished the tale to his satisfaction. I think it ended happily. After that he seemed more cheerful. He came over to see what I was doing and picked up a Red Whelk quite carefully.

'Admit you're excited.' His hands were fluttering. 'Doesn't the prospect of a brand-new start give you a thrill? Not a tiny thrill?'

'For me it may not be such a pleasant start. We must wait and see.'

'Wait and see! God save us, man, is that all you can say! Isn't there the *tiniest* thrill rising in your tiny frame? Sure you haven't been at the formaldehyde?'

'We must wait and see.'

He took a very close look at my face. 'Not a flicker, you bastard. After all our planning, not a flicker. What does it take to get you going?'

'You talk like James . . .'

'I wonder whether you've been worth all the effort.'

'Are you joking, Max?'

'I've worked bloody hard.'

'If you aren't, I must remind you again of who's doing the favour for whom.'

'Whom! Wow!' He raised both hands to ward off the word and started towards the door. 'Don't throw the grammar at me! And don't be so bloody pessimistic, that's all I ask. Everything's arranged. I've done all *I* can, now it's up to you. Right? Best bib and tucker would help a bit. And get there early. Be prepared to wait. Understood? After that, you've got it made.'

'We shall see.'

'Well we haven't long, have we?' Max laughed as he went out, banging the door behind him.

From the beginning he treated my room with familiarity, coming and going as he pleased, as though the house was his. Dorothea had introduced him to the habit of walking in on me without warning, although his footsteps could usually be heard approaching across the hall and under the arch. Max had a need, from the very first, to know where I was and to see me there so reassuringly busy. He continued to visit me long after my wife had ceased to concern herself with what I did, hidden away all those days and years, when left alone with my specimens. Max was curious once. He asked me questions about my work; asked to see books which he took away and never returned. He wanted to know how the shelves were built, how the microscopes worked, what sort of camera I was using. If I had let him he would have redesigned the room. He wanted to know how I ate my food; how I slept. Finally he accepted that I was there, and there to stay, content with the state of things. But Max was always the wary one. He always came in without knocking, on his face a slightly defiant look which settled over the years into one of disdain.

But the first time he came, he came in disguise. His was the playful face, the joyful satyr peeping round the door to catch me unawares doing mischief. 'Got you!' he cried.

I hadn't heard their footsteps in the hall, only the slight click of the doorhandle as they gently opened it. What did they imagine I was doing up there, up on my desk beneath the circular window? Lucky I had the duster in my hand; lucky it was large and yellow. They saw it. I had been removing the dirt from the window ledge. They could see at a glance I had been dusting. Dorothea could see that whatever went on in the rest of the house at least I kept my portion tidy. She stood behind Max in the doorway, shielded by his arm. She gave me such a pleasant smile that I immediately suspected her intentions. Whenever Dorothea smiled like that the worst could always be expected. Max was smiling too, his body hiding Dorothea's. I could see her fingers at his waist. She was pushing him in.

'Meet our new lodger.'

In unison they shuffled over to the desk and smiled up at me like children, pouting a little. Max has woman's lips, full and red. They are unattractive in a man. He has them still.

'Hello Max,' I said. 'So you've come to join us, have you?' I could see Dorothea's face relax. I saw the eyebrows sprouting from her forehead, the pale red hair. When viewed full-face Dorothea has hardly any eyebrows. Her colouring is fair. She is pale-skinned with a wash of freckling like a Cowrie. Her limbs look smooth, but there is with me still the memory of a kiss placed on her arm from which came the tingling sensation of tiny hairs grazing the lips. To lie close to her and see the bare skin is to gaze at the worked surface of a painting: it was like discovering the hidden structure of a Gainsborough not visible unless one looked with care. The skin was composed of single brush strokes regularly applied in all the permutations of pink and yellow to form the mass. My memory is not exact, but there seemed to be a hint of blue in the underpainting which gave added translucence to the skin. The blue would have been Cobalt, perhaps Prussian, subtly complementing the overall red.

'If you'll have me,' Max said. 'Not disturbing you, are we?'

'Not at all. You're welcome. Not often I have visitors. I was doing a bit of tidying up. Dust settles quickly in here.'

'What a room this is! Like a mausoleum!' Max began to make himself at home, wandering over to cupboards, peering in. The size of the place appealed to him. 'My dear old chap do you know what you've got here? A salon, a perfect salon. Lucky fellow. Perfect proportions, perfect light. I could show a collection in here to knock 'em cold. These days elegance is at a bit of a premium, and here are you with a place like this. Those windows are simply crying out for velvet. I could make St. John's Wood quite the latest thing in the fashion world. They'd flock from miles away for a bit of elegance.'

'This used to be the grand drawing room in my father's day. They used to have velvet everywhere. I suppose in its way it was a sort of salon then. He used it for all the grandest balls. Parties for me were always thrown in here.'

'Of course! I remember. I came here on your twenty-first. When your dear old Dad (God rest his soul) gave you the key. Well, well, well. How the old place has changed. What a party that was! Jamie and I got horribly tight for some reason or other. Ah! Yes, I was being a bit beastly because it was my twenty-first too, and I was feeling a bit underprivileged. God knows why. So we knocked back the champers. Jamie got violent because I absolutely insisted on drinking it out of Dorothea's shoe. Remember? Didn't he knock up the furniture?'

'Yes. But the troops continued the work. The house became an army billet. They behaved more like animals than human beings. What they couldn't chop up for firewood and burn, they ruined in other ways. No wonder you didn't recognise it. Even the banisters were missing. Everything had to be renewed. Now it still has the air of a barracks with all the plaster and brickwork like that. I suppose you've shown Max the alterations, Dorothea?'

'No!' they both said together.

'Oh no, dear chap.'

'He's just arrived. Haven't you, Max?' They stood looking up at me to see how I was accepting their first collective lie under my roof. My smile was reassuring. I asked Max if he was satisfied with his quarters. He assured me they were excellent. He said he wouldn't need them for long. 'Only until I get myself organised with a decent workroom and decent staff. Staff shouldn't be hard to get, with everyone being demobbed. I've already started to put out feelers. It's the premises that are the biggest headache. The West End's taken a bit of a pounding. And the City looks like Hell; just a rubbish dump. The damage is unbelievable. Somewhere I've got to find myself a place that won't fall down about my ears the moment I'm installed!'

'Max can stay here indefinitely, can't he?' Dorothea assured him we had plenty of room. She said he wasn't to feel forced to move. Our house was large enough for the three of us.

'You were lucky coming back to this,' Max said. 'Army damage or no. At least you've got a roof over your heads. My flat was flattened!'

'Where have you been living since you got out?'

'Oh here and there, you know. Round and about.' I saw Dorothea flash him a glance. 'With friends, mostly. They've been terribly kind. The returning warrior, and all that! Now I've got to find my feet back in the trade. Times are still tight.'

'And James? What about James? Is he still waiting?'

'James? Oh yes! He's waiting!' Max laughed at my joke and nodded. 'I think he's going Italian. Some smart little place in

Greek Street or environs has just opened up. Has to find a boater and striped vest to serve the customers in! I suppose the usual will happen—he'll lose his temper over some triviality, then the job.'

'And what about you?'

'You know me. Ambitious as ever. I wouldn't fancy being an employee. Doesn't suit the temperament. Just like Jamie in that respect.' Max wandered over to the newly built section and began to pull at an unfinished drawer. Dorothea watched him. He spoke about the house again, telling us how lucky we were to have a home. Dorothea said it wasn't like home to her. Perhaps his arrival would cheer things up. She said it seemed more like a prison. What the house needed was someone with an artistic eye, who could disguise the clinical look of the plaster-work. She wasn't used to the size of it. She didn't like the discomfort, and the way all the decisions had been left to her concerning the furnishings. I had left her to worry about the house, knowing that while her mind was occupied she was less likely to feel the disruption. Dorothea transplanted with difficulty. The move had been a strain. Max told her sharply not to complain while she had a roof over her head.

'He spends all his time refurbishing in here,' Dorothea said.

'I have plans for this room, Max. Sinks over there. Double partitioning, plenty of cupboards and specimen drawers. With enough left free for future expansion. I have great plans. How do you feel about joining me in the work? Good are you at painting and decorating? Skilled workmen are scarce.'

'Hopeless, dear chap. Except with the needle. I ply a lovely needle, but the rest's not my cup of tea. Is it Dee?'

'Max is an artist, not a plumber's mate. Fancy asking him such a thing!' Dorothea was embarrassed for me. 'We should ask his advice on the things that matter, not your beastly old room. We should ask him for help with the colour schemes. Let him decorate a few of the rooms.'

'Perhaps he won't want to . . .'

'Steady on. Steady on, both of you!' Max laughed. 'My time is pretty full right now. I have my career to put into motion. I'm supposed to design dresses, not interiors!' Seeing Dorothea's face he added hastily, 'Otherwise I'd love to help. Nothing I like better than the challenge of creating.'

'Yes, of course Max dear,' Dorothea said. 'We understand. But what a waste to have you here and not make use of your marvellous talent. You will advise me a *little*, won't you?' He smiled. 'And how could I possibly *dare* to decorate when I know that you're around with that critical eye?'

'You expect too much of me,' he said.

'Then I shall give you an easy task to begin with. Advise me on how to create an exotic atmosphere in the bedroom! I know you'd be marvellous at something like that.' The exchange of looks seemed to settle the matter.

I asked Dorothea whether, in view of the fact that she'd have more time, she would like to help me with my room. But she didn't answer. She had gone over to where Max stood, and was trying to see what he was looking at. He was looking at nothing really, merely picking up tools at random, tossing them down, poking at shells. He moved along the benches slowly, with Dorothea behind him. When he reached me standing on the desk he stopped and touched my feet. 'Why don't you come down from there?'

'I like it up here. I like to look down on you.' He snorted and took hold of both of my ankles, firmly. Then he braced himself, gripped me hard, and lifted me clean off the desk and on to the floor. I had the sense to keep straight knees.

'And I like you better down here,' he said, 'where I can see you properly.' Before I could dodge, he had patted the top of my head.

They stayed a little longer while Max continued his wandering around my room, prying into every corner, looking out on to the desolate garden. He wanted to know why I used screens, and I told him about the draughts. I gave him a resume of my plans for central heating, while Dorothea tapped her foot by the desk. 'I love a warm house,' Max said.

'Like a good hostess,' Dorothea muttered. She stood with arms folded, adding nothing more to the conversation. I told Max how she had seen to it that his rooms upstairs had been heated in readiness for his arrival. They'd been ready for days. He was pleased to hear of such attention. 'Magnificent!' he said. 'Nothing I enjoy more than a bit of comfort. Haven't felt such a V.I.P. since the army. When Jamie and I used to stroll the town we'd play "collecting salutes". He kept count of how many I got, and paid me sixpence a piece. Then I'd treat him to a meal on the loot.' Dorothea's impatience to leave cut short his reminiscences. He would have told me more about his army days, but she lured him away with the promise of food, which I was not invited to eat.

'Describe Max,' he said.

There is the eternal brown suit, of course. He has worn one ever since I have known him. Often I couldn't tell whether the suit he was wearing was new, or the same old one, retailored. He was very clever in cutting cloth, and sewing it too. The clothes he wore were always the long and narrow kind, built to accentuate his build. Max is thin, and very tall. He likes his height. His face is tall with a high-bridged nose which he has had remodelled recently by a method known as Rhinoplasty. All the same, he will continue to grow old. His nose will continue the same slow process of disintegration as will the rest of his face. Yet he suffered considerable pain both in nose and pocket, which suggests a great, deep-rooted vanity. I am only just beginning to understand the way in which such a transitory thing as one's appearance can mar one's life. Had I been born taller, fatter, more robust, should I have become a different person? The question begins to bother me. Others may have been quicker to appreciate my many merits. I may not have had this long fight to preserve what is rightfully mine, if I had been more outwardly attractive. Had anyone bothered to see below my surface scaling they might have been surprised to find me there, so interesting a specimen. It isn't a pleasant thing to think that others may have been the cause of my being what I am. I can hardly bear to think it; that lack of interest in what I was, caused me to develop compensatory interest in others. There must have been a time, once, when I didn't collect people. But I can't remember it. Max fascinated me. He still does. Yet we have things in common.

Like me, Max has thin, grey hair. It is a decent grey, touched here and there by strands of white. He doesn't dye it any more as he did when he was in his thirties. Then the colour would fluctuate alarmingly from week to week, but as his sight worsened the colour of his hair ceased to bother him as much, and he let it grow as it would. Not that he was ever anything but careful of his appearance, a phenomenon found, I believe, more in the short-sighted than in other men. Max is short-sighted. He hides behind thick, white lenses which seem to have a life of their own; they are two blank white moons and Max has no eyes at all, or in certain lights they are startling circles drawn on his face. When he looks down at you you can see yourself in miniature reflection, doubled and flattened like a microbe. Beneath the glass Max's skin has always been pale, as though it has been continuously denied some vital vitamin, like grass beneath stones. On his nose he used to have the bright red bite of his spectacles. Without them the distance between us seemed narrower, for I could try to guess what his eyes meant. I have seen him rub the stigma until it shone with inflammation. His operation has removed the scar, but he never likes the defencelessness of being without his spectacles, so the scar is bound to return.

We exchanged confidences once; when we were twenty-seven. I told him how my lack of height made me self-conscious. He told me he had fooled the army about his sight; had they been stupid enough to turn him down, they would, in his opinion, have prolonged the war by months. His mood was buoyant.

I told him I feared his height would make me look ridiculous at the ceremony, especially since it was customary for the best man to stand quite close. He offered to bend slightly at the knees, if that would help to get the whole thing over. He couldn't guarantee to remain like that for long, only until the organist had finished the march, and the vicar had begun his speech. My suggestion that he stand slightly behind me, instead of at my side, met with refusal. He said that he could always be relied upon to do the correct thing, and this occasion was one at which he would be the object of much attention. He'd invited many of his own friends. Did I wish to make him appear ridiculous? He went into great details about the risk of a fall if he stood too far away. The last thing he wanted to do was to turn somersault in the aisle, and end up on his knees beside Dorothea. He said churches always confused him; put 'too much demand' on him. The very idea of a wedding made him shudder. He said he would be there at my side only in the line of duty. Agreement was reached when I complied with his request to put on my thickest soled shoes, and wear my hair *en brosse*. And there was to be no rehearsal. I hadn't wanted Max at all as my best man, I'd wanted James. But the suggestion only met with red-faced silence from my fiancée. We had to wait for Max's leave before we could get married. Dorothea asked him if it was 'compassionate'. I had no real complaints about his behaviour: he saw that everything went as planned, despite difficulties over coupons for this and coupons for that, and the need to go to the Black Market before his tastes could be satisfied. He managed to find someone with champagne to spare, petrol too for the Daimlers. I was directed as to what to wear, and what to say at the reception. He would have liked the bells rung during the nuptial, but the vicar stepped in and said that the sound of the bells meant that the enemy had landed. Max complimented the vicar on the way his church had stood up to the bombing and the vicar showed him the Grinling Gibbons carvings hidden away in the crypt. I heard him tell the vicar the details of our wedding; of how he had arranged for flowers, and how the colour of my tie was going to be the same colour as my true love's hair.

I asked Max why he was going to so much trouble for me. He told me I was marrying a prize. He said I was marrying well. I asked him why he didn't do likewise. There seemed little reason to delay life until tomorrow, when some people's tomorrows had a habit of not arriving. He was amused; he was too careful to die. He said he thought his fellow officers' plans for him didn't include marrying a strange female in self-defence. We spoke as though we were very close. I remember the sirens sounding.

'Describe Max,' he said.

Very well. I will. Max is a portrait after the school of Singer Sargent. He should have been painted by him. He is the tall, aristocratic man, standing stick in hand, in a self-conscious pose. He feels the weight of his own importance and pretends to be unaware that someone is working at his portrait. Although he will owe his future preservation to the artist, he behaves as though he is the one conferring favours: he is allowing himself to be painted. His chill mien defies liberties to be taken with his likeness, unless they err on the side of flattery. For who wants his worst points accentuated? Who pays good money to be reminded of his imperfections? And Max is parting with good money for this work. So let it be good.

He knows how he would like to be seen. There must be a hint of drama in the whole; a generosity of treatment in keeping with the sitter's nature. He would like a slight theatricality to suggest itself in the lighting, in the crudely careless brush-strokes of the background, that throw into relief the fine painting of the face. Let the face tell all. Let its long lines and pallor hint only at past fatigues, byegone boredoms, stoically borne, at the domestic daily snags by which this sensitive man has been so unfairly beset. Let the clothes hint at regained beauty; at the youthful form relaxed under the mohair and wool. Let the grey hair gleam like shot silk against the velvet background which he over-shadows. A luxurious life is ahead. The white hand closes over the lion-headed stick and sports the very best in jewellery. Its gleam hints at a future full of planned enjoyment.

Max will decide the frame himself, as careful in its choice as of everything he does. It will be austere but gold, to offset the limpid brown of his suit. He has already planned where it should hang, reserving a place on the wall of his private office, directly behind the great, gold desk with its myriad telephones. Already he is planning to get his money's worth from the investment. He will let it work for him: it will be the central pivot of his new collection, which he sees in his mind's eye as the grandest he has ever done. Only browns and gold will be employed; the theme will be a life of luxury, personified by the portrait. In their opulent clothes the models will have a varnished look. He knows the collection will be a great success. For its sake he will allow himself to be photographed beneath his portrait, surrounded by the flimsy evidence of his tiny talent. His likeness will eventually appear in rare, selected magazines, the kind that lie on laps in hairdressers'. He will have played his part in making look more ridiculous those who are stupid enough to believe he has their welfare and their beauty close at heart.

The completed portrait will be over life-sized. It will reach from floor to ceiling. It will be an investment.

I gazed at the photograph in his hand and saw a woman. It wasn't in colour. Her lipstick was black, her hair grey. The hazy morning light had given the torso a sculptural smoothness and solidity; to the face a non-existent youthfulness. But the light had not disguised the thin lips and bulbous nose, or the heavy lids: all it had done was to remove the skin's fine lines and blemishes. One could not see the gentle sagging of the surface over the fine framework, nor appreciate Time's corrosion.

Any specimen will fade unless it is treated with more than care. It must be locked away from light, and washed in sea water at least every two or three years. It must be watched. It must be kept on velvet, locked away to lie singly in a dust-free drawer. A slight coating or two of clear varnish can be applied, but nothing more, or the beautiful marking will be impaired. Nothing must mark or injure it. If this happens then the specimen can only be repaired by someone who is a master at the work. Like me.

Her beauty has always been for the specialist, the only one who could appreciate its rarity, and value it accordingly. Not many there are who could respond to such a form as she exposed. She had a full and freckled figure like a Babylonian, only seen to advantage in the water. It was her element. She shone in the sea with such voluptuousness that I held my breath at each wave's fall, watching her rise on crest after crest, until the sea sucked her back and under again. It was never a battle with her, more a returning to something understood and on which she could absolutely rely for comfort. The water took her from us and kept her there for hours. She swam and played whatever the weather, ignorant of any dangers. I pointed her out to Max who sat with me on the rocky beach, while the wind whipped the waves to a fine spray across our feet, and the sun shone. He had his shoulders to the wind, hunching them against the eddies of fine sand that rushed at us across the bay, and blew against the barbed wire barriers which no one had bothered yet to remove. I had to shout before he could hear me against the force of the wind.

'Marvellous? What's so marvellous about her? I call it stupid being out there in a gale like this.'

'The sea looks calm enough.'

'She deserves to be drowned. Look at her.'

'If it worries you, Max, why not go out and fetch her in?'

'No fear. Let her swim in herself. She got out there didn't she? I'm not risking myself for anyone.'

'Wouldn't you say she's in her element? She's always loved water.'

'What a laugh! Obviously you didn't see her neck this morning!'

'Why? Was it dirty?'

'It always is. Haven't you noticed?'

'Be fair, Max. This is a holiday. She's allowed to be dirty on holiday. She's just relaxed. Usually she's pretty clean.'

Max laughed. 'On the surface only, dear chap. Underneath she's inclined to be on the filthy side. You've married a trollop given to wearing her underwear too long at a stretch. It's dirty.'

'How do you know?'

'I've seen it, of course. Haven't you?'

'She's my wife.'

'Then be a little bit more observant. Notice things. You look at nothing but your damn shells.'

'I notice my wife. There she is out there. Look. She's swimming towards that boat.'

'You watch her, dear chap. And that's not the same thing at all as noticing her. And she doesn't like it. She's told me so. She says she's beginning to feel collected too. Like one of your damned specimens. And I must say I see what she means.'

'Has she told you how she thinks I ought to behave towards her?'

'Good God, man! Don't you know that for yourself?' I had to lean close to hear his words through the wind's roar. 'You should be able to think of a way to handle her.'

'What shall I do, Max?'

'Don't ask me. I'm not here to help. I'm here to enjoy a well-earned holiday. God knows I've earned it. It's no fun starting a business from scratch after so long away from it all. Seven years since I had a real holiday. Not like you, you know—hidden away from it all down here.'

'You managed to go on leave quite frequently, I believe.'

'How do *you* know?'

'I mean it wasn't as if you went overseas.'

'There you go, talking from the height of your ignorance. What do you think going on leave was like?'

'Didn't you and James spend a lot of time . . .'

'There was no time at all. Trains were shocking. I ended up a complete nervous wreck.' He stretched himself out on the rocks and rested an arm beneath his head.

Out at sea Dorothea's head bobbed among a line of buoys.

'Max...'

'Hmm?'

'Why did you tell me all that about Dorothea? I mean about her being a specimen. Did she... ask you to come on holiday with us to tell me... what you told me?'

Max sat up. 'Good God, no!'

'Then why did she ask you to come down here?'

'For a holiday, dear chap. Don't I deserve one after defending you stay-at-homes so bravely? If only from the depths of the Quarter-Master's stores!' The wind sent Max's laugh across the water. Dorothea waved.

'This is *our* first holiday together since the war.'

'Implying you'd rather I'd stayed in London? With Jamie, I presume?'

'Maybe. Or brought him with you.'

'How on earth could I have done that? You know as well as I do how Dee hates her brother. And it's reciprocated, I can tell you.' He lay on his side with his back to me so that I could see the small embedded stones which dropped from his skin one by one. The rock we were sitting on was warm to the touch, but I was cold. Right round the bay, as far as the eye could see, were the bleak rocks lapped over by the white spray. There was no one but us three anywhere in sight, only a few desultory gulls seeking footholds on the rusty coils of the barbed wire. Out among the waves I saw Dorothea begin to swim towards us, her arms making tiny flurries with each powerful stroke. As she swam, the current carried her across the bay, finally beaching her on the rocky shore some hundred yards away to our left. I watched her crawl from the water and straighten up, getting her bearings in the new element. Water dripped from her as she moulded the bathing suit with her hands. Then she stepped across the rock pools and came towards us. Max muttered something inaudible. I asked him what he had said.

'I said you'd better start watching her closer.'

'Closer?'

'That's what I said.' As he turned over on to his stomach his words came to me from a great distance, each one carefully enunciated. 'Your wife has been unfaithful to you.' I tasted my salt lips. 'Who with?' I said.

'With me, of course.'

I told him I didn't believe him, and Dorothea came closer.

'Watch her,' he said. He sat up suddenly and put on his spectacles.

Dorothea waded through the pools among the rocks, her reflection cut about by the vortex she had caused with the movement of her legs.

It was late when I left him standing by the door. The money was safely tucked away inside his pigskin wallet. Smoke from the room followed me as I made to descend the first stair. He stopped my departure with another question: 'Are you sure you will know her when you meet?'

'I'm sure to . . . By the photograph, that is.'

'Not good enough, dear sir. Even I, with my eyesight, wouldn't like to chance that face in a crowd. One must be one hundred per cent sure, mustn't one?'

'One must.' I returned along the landing, fearful of shouting my replies down the softly silent corridor. I stood beside him in the doorway, smelling the smoke that drenched our clothes. Our conference had been overlong. 'Then what do you suggest?' He apologised for dragging me back, but a brilliant idea had only just occurred to him. He paid his own price for being such a perfectionist. So that there would be no doubt as to who she was, there must be a distinguishing mark. 'Like the passport says. She must have a distinguishing mark.'

'She has red hair, so you say. Won't that be enough to point her out?'

'Not these days it won't. I can see you're out of touch. Thousands of women have red hair these days. The Henna bottle is in universal use.' He poked me briefly. 'My idea is fool proof. She shall *carry* something. Yes.'

'How original. What do you suggest the lady carries?'

'That, my dear sir, is up to you.'

'A rose, perhaps?'

'Wrong season? I see difficulties there, in the floral department. She may complain about the outlay, and that would be a bad beginning, wouldn't it? We are not all as fortunate as you in the matter of finance.'

'Then I should carry a flower, perhaps? Shall I wear, say, a carnation?'

'Nice touch. Nice touch. A hint of opulence, eh? She should be impressed. Although ...' he hesitated, '... although, if things should go astray, or she isn't suitable, I *may* be able to find something else. I only said "may", mind.'

I thanked him in whispers, aware that the lateness of the hour makes hidden ears keener. I told him, however, that my heart was set on this woman. His fine descriptions of her had done the trick and I wanted only her. He quite understood. Once again he confirmed the place of our meeting. I was to get there early, and wait. He was sorry not to be more explicit about the time of her arrival, but he hadn't been able to pin her down. Women liked to exercise their powers when it came to punctuality. Of course she would be there on Sunday afternoon. 'Day of rest for some,' he said, 'but not for you, eh?' I then suggested that in case there might be a mistake on my part, it would be a good idea if she should be carrying something by which I could recognise her. But what? By her umbrella. He gave me a thunderous clap on the back. 'Good fellow! Yes, she shall carry an umbrella.' 'Let it be red,' I said. 'To match her hair.'

'Masterly, masterly!'

After brief goodbyes he closed his door and left me to descend the stairs alone. I did not usually care for the types of women who carried red umbrellas. They only used them to prop themselves up in narrow doorways. Half-way down the stairs the time-switch clicked, and I continued my progress in the dark.

3

I am standing with my left shoulder to the men in conference. The glass obscures them. I stand on three floorboards, the tips of my toes aligned exactly with the jointing; their lines cut horizontally across my feet. If I look down I see my Abalone suit. If I look up I see the silver boy with the fat feather in his hat. The gallery has emptied. If she comes now she will surely recognise me far too soon. I am standing in the wrong place.

At the sudden sound of distant footsteps I turn and face my mirror. Pink hands and faces leap to view. They must be suppressed if I want to see who is coming through the arch. A woman has entered the tablecloth and her head is rapidly rising above the fringe. In her hand is an umbrella. Waiting, I hear her move slowly across the floor. There is the thud of the foot, followed by the heel's tap. Her umbrella makes no sound: she carries it like a baton. I see her look without interest at the first three pictures on the right hand wall. She stops. She may be looking at the portrait of the queen, but I cannot be sure. From where I stand the angle is too oblique to make certain of the exact direction of her gaze. She may be looking at the queen. She hasn't bent her head to examine details. She doesn't seem to have noticed the colours of her dress. She can't have seen the rounded lids, or the forehead bare of brows. Hasn't she been caught by the cold gaze and the thin lips that rarely smiled? The queen wears strange rings set high on her fingers: there is symmetric strapwork on her dress. Surely these details would excite a fractional interest. Isn't one woman interested in any other so different from herself?

As she moves down the gallery I can see her umbrella's colour. It is brown. She carries it in military fashion, grasping the ferrule beneath her chin. Now she has increased her speed, scarcely giving the portraits half a glance. He can't have sent another one to me. Not this one. I bend towards the corner of my mirror to study the brushwork there. The woman stops before the silver boy. Down comes the umbrella to the floor. She leans on it. I hear it scrape the boards as she turns to look at me. Pink faces meet me as I rise. The old man is looking down on me. His lined face with the hooded eyes is wrinkled and malevolent. There is no indication of the body's shape; all is covered with a voluminous garment out of which the hands protrude. The corpulence of his body suggests he may have on a corset, which could account for the upright posture and pained look. His nostrils are lined with nicotine. I suspect him of having tricked me.

The woman is standing beside me now. She has moved one hand to touch her hair. I risk a glance. But her hair is what concerns her. She is using my mirror to admire herself, making little turns, this way and that, so that she can pat herself into place. With great pleasure her hands run down her clothing, tucking in, adjusting, a little furtively because I am beside her, but she can only see herself. She steps behind me when she has settled everything to her satisfaction, and, looking straight ahead, goes into the Hanoverians. She was a colourless, common type of woman.

Distant galleries are noisier now, with footsteps and faint laughter. What do people find to laugh about? I move my feet gently on the boards, avoiding cracks. I must try to mix more with my fellow beings. I must move away from this spot and try to mingle with some crowd. The feeling of being shut-in in here is stronger now and the heat is greater. No windows are open, although cords hang from them in insignificant loops. The windows are set too high, filling all the upper areas of wall. I look up expecting to see a rush of blue clouds and a touch of sunlight, but the flat greyness of the outer air in no way resembles my idea of weather. Just for once I wouldn't mind a fresh breeze blowing on the face, with a hint of salt in it. I who have always tried to avoid the weather with its changeability find myself, today, longing for its comfort. Melting snows and running rivers bring sudden thoughts of coolness and relief quite at odds with their usual message of disorder and erosion. The light in here is watery. As I move back towards the queen I see her suspended in the isolated clarity of an unreflecting wall. She turns her head to see me come, and, as I approach her, keeps her cheek exposed to my watchfulness. Her hands and face are pale. All her colour has drained into the dress with its enormous sleeves. One must look closely at this dress to see the look it has of watered silk. The pink threads mingle with the yellow: little waves of red curl in convolutions round her body; accentuating the smooth roundness of her arms. Pearls encircle her waist and throat; they cluster on her hair. She has a clear serenity in the way she stands and in her steady, heavy-lidded eyes. Her brows are almost non-existent, but looking down on her I would see the pale hairs sprouting. There was an urchin look to her which belied her nineteen years. The careful waves of her red hair were never orderly for long. She combed it with her fingers and shook the salt from it. She smelt of the sea.

Max was the first to notice that she smelt. I'd told him I'd noticed it too. To me she was like the ocean.

'No, no, no. All red-heads smell,' he said. 'Haven't you noticed?'

'That red-heads smell different? You're joking, Max.'

'I'm telling you, when Dorothea and Jamie get into a room together, they smell. It's like pepper. It gets up your nose.'

'You're saying that to put me off. Well, I'm not listening.'

'You wouldn't! You're so smitten with the girl, she could stink like bad fish and you'd say it was beautiful.'

We sat, isolated from the other visitors by a sea of gingham tablecloths, sipping our tea and eating minute sandwich squares. Even at the back of the tea-room where the shadows were, we could feel the warm air strike. It was going to be a hot summer. With any luck there would be no rain at all.

'I'm offering you sound advice,' Max said.

'Free? I don't believe it! Grandfather Max offering his valuable opinion for nothing.'

He picked up a spoon and tapped the table fretfully. 'Listen. I'm telling you that if you want the girl you'd best be careful.'

'Of what?'

'She's a . . .'

'Max! May I ask you something? Something personal?'

'Go ahead.'

'Have you finished with your sandwiches? I'm partial to cucumber. Builds the body!'

One or two people looked up from their tea as Max threw the

spoon across the cloth. 'Don't be so stupid. What's the good of having a chum if you won't listen to his advice?'

'Given from the height of all his four—is it four?—years' experience of women!'

'Your sarcasm is lost on me, so there. I was only trying to say "beware".'

'I can't think what of, Max. Could it be you?'

Max blushed. Knowing he hated making a bad impression in public, I could go further with my taunts than I generally dared. 'Do you find her smell attractive too? You seem to hang about whenever they're around.'

'Me hang about? *Tout au contraire,* dear lad. I do my best to brush her off. *She's* the one to do the limpet act, but she insists on following us everywhere. Damned embarrassing. Jamie and I don't get a minute's peace with her. What can I do? He's supposed to be my friend.'

'He'd hate to think the matter was in doubt!'

'My problem at the moment is attempting to discover some novel means of enduring this vacation. It promises to be an unusually long one.'

'Why not go abroad? You usually do. Doesn't Paris call?'

'Not this year. To tell the absolute truth, I shan't be going there for a while. Trying to avoid a certain person.'

I never knew whether Max invented half the continental intrigues which he laid claim to. 'Why not get a job?'

'A *job!*'

'James had one last summer as a waiter.'

'Why do you think I took myself off to France? But then, Jamie needs the exercise or he gets violent, with lots of pent-up energies screaming to get out. I'm too lazy by far.' He stretched himself in his chair, tilting it against the wall. 'Therefore I shall continue to make a nuisance of myself until you all entrain.'

'Nuisance is correct.'

'It's not my fault really. I don't want her with us all the time. Neither does Jamie. But she insists. Look at yesterday!'

'I have.'

'Can't you see now what I mean? She has a wandering eye, that girl. Beware.'

'She's mine.'

'Wishful thinking. I've been trying to tell you. She needs keeping an eye on. Didn't you hear her remarks at the timetable?'

'She was skylarking.'

'Oh, I don't mean the hand holding. I get used to that. But do you know what she said? She asked me if I was coming with you.'

'What's so bad about asking that?'

'She was hinting. You don't know how artful she can be. She told me she would far rather it was me going down there, than you. Really she did.'

'You're lying. How can anyone go down there without me? They're my guests. She knows neither of them would be going if it weren't for me. The summer house is mine.'

'Or your dear papa's, rather.'

'He's given it to me. When I'm twenty-one it will be legally mine.'

'What a highly developed sense of property you have.'

'He said so. So will the house in Town. So will everything.'

Flies settled on our empty cups. Somewhere a distant clock chimed. Max patted my hand on the tablecloth. 'Steady, dear lad. No one is disputing your rights. I'm only giving you a friendly warning. Dorothea has preferences. You can do what you will with her for all I care. Marry her, if you're so inclined. I shall be glad for one. Dear Jamie and I might get some peace. At the moment I'm going through terrible times. He snaps my head off if I as much as glance at her.' He leaned forward. 'Do you know he didn't even *introduce* us! She was grinning all over her face, waiting for him to say who I was. I had to ask who she was. Then he had to tell me she was his sister. Didn't speak to me for a week afterwards. As if I thought she was attractive. Me!'

'Well, don't you?'

'You're joking. They do have slight resemblance, I must admit. But she hasn't his power, if you see what I mean.'

'You could come to the seaside with us, I suppose. It might keep James more occupied. They do tend to bicker quite a lot. They did last time, and things haven't improved since, have they? You'll like it down there. Very bracing.'

'No thanks. Must stay in Town this time. Mother insists. I've got some serious persuading to do. She's beginning to wonder whether I'm worth educating!'

'Why not come down later?'

'And see those two at each other's throats? Bore me solid. I can see Jamie in term time without the threat of his sister, thank you. I never ask for trouble. Besides, he's only going with you to spite me. After the last time down there, he swore he'd never go again.'

'We had lots of fun.'

'So he told me! He said you two did nothing but lie around demanding culinary feats from him. Sounded ghastly. No wonder he came running when I sent for him. The poor lad was positively skin and bone. It was pathetic how pleased he was to see me.' At the sound of a cough, Max looked up and waved away the hovering waitress. 'By the way . . .' he said, 'how did you two manage when he'd gone? Get on all right together?' He smiled slowly. 'I presume I did you a great service in recalling him?'

'We managed well enough, thank you.'

'I'm sure you did! Quite remote down there, isn't it? Three miles' walk to get milk. Private path to the beach. Log fires and candlelight, eh? What *did* you do with yourselves in the long, dark evenings? Come on. Tell all.'

'Summer evenings are short. I found my first specimen.'

'I know you did!'

'My first serious specimen—a white-ribbed Cowrie. Have I shown it to you?'

'Many times. Many times. Do you know, your room's a disgrace. It's a wonder there haven't been complaints.'

'I shall take it all home eventually and start again there. Father's quite a collector too. I have plans for the whole house as soon as it's mine.'

'Don't be ghoulish, please. How can you suffer all those nasty bits and pieces? I'd have the place cleaned out in a flash. Don't you ever feel claustrophobic?'

'Why should I?'

The waitress came over with the bill. Max handed it to me. 'You remind me,' he said, 'of a Hermit Crab.' The waitress gave me a second look, then retired behind the urn.

'How original! I have a Hermit in my collection. Imperfect

though. A claw is missing. Dorothea picked it up before I could stop her.'

'Careless girl. Showed *her* your collection, have you?'

'When she came up for the Ball. She was most interested. I told her my plans for father's house.'

'Y-e-e-s. That would appeal to her. Like you she has a strong sense of property. Highly developed in some—the need to acquire.' Max picked up his boater and stood up, waiting for me while I produced a tip to put under the plate. 'I'm the reverse.' I paid the waitress and we crossed into the sunshine of the doorway. 'I need to throw off. I need the luxury of change.' He squinted out at the historic town. 'Don't you feel you'll never grow old as long as you can always give yourself the slip? I do.' Together we walked slowly down the narrow pavement. 'I'd hate to grow old. I shall always be like quicksilver. I shall be a creator of . . . ephemeral things . . . that shimmer for a day. (Must remember that to tell Mother. It'll impress the old girl.) I think I shall probably turn out to be quite wonderful!'

'I want to be a great collector. Greater than Tradescant.'

'Isn't that a creeping weed? The strangulating kind?'

The queen looks out with chill, grey eyes. She gazes past me to my left. Her hands rest rigidly across her stomach, covering the jewelled girdle. She tenses her shoulders and looks ill at ease. The waved red hair lies flatly on her brow under the heavy headdress. She has a taste for jewels, this queen, wearing them lavishly. Pearls are her favourite stones, and rubies. They circumscribe her throat and waist, weighing her down like ballast. She will not move far with such a load. Her face shows signs of paint: the lips are an unnatural red, at variance with the colour of her dress: tiny bulbs of mascara outline the heavy lids, giving her face the doll-like look of an old woman. But she isn't old. Thirty-four is not old to one who has been as sheltered as she. Her only concerns have been her comforts and her pleasures. The freckles gleam beneath the dusting of powder. The eyes move. Now she is not so much looking at me as at the image of herself she carries in my eyes. She knows what I admire in her, and conjures it up for her own satisfaction.

The dress of pink and red rustles as she moves. She wears her clothes too tight, so that her steps are tiny, and lines of strain run across her front and underneath the armpits. She turns her back to me and flexes her shoulder blades. The top of the dress hangs in two pink wings on either side of the zip. The metal tag is stiff; I can move it a bare two inches upward. She kicks the fur rug and tells me to try harder. Threads give way under the strain. I pull again, and Dorothea's speckled skin folds with the constriction. She shrugs her shoulders and sighs. The zip is stuck. Max is lying on the bed, watching the performance. He is enjoying himself. 'Max, can't you do something?' she asks.

'Come here,' he says. She stands obediently before him while he languidly gets up. He turns her round roughly and grasps the silk in his fist. With a tearing sound the zip goes home. 'There you are.'

'Thank you.' Dorothea adjusts her shoulder straps without moving away from him. She runs her thumb inside the neck of her dress and catches her nail on the silk. A thread loops out. 'Dear, dear.' She goes over to the dressing table and takes out a pair of scissors, which she hands to Max. Smiling, he cuts off the thread. Still smiling, he runs the tips of the scissors carefully across her bare shoulder, marking the skin with a thin, bloody line. She winces, but I see her smile. She backs away from him with an effort, her feet caught in the lion rug. 'Now, now, Max.'

'Come here,' he says. 'Come here.'

She is standing now against the purple wall, patterning it like an odalisque. She smiles at me and I admire such handsomeness. 'Come here,' Max says, and goes over to kneel at her feet. He pulls at the hem of her dress. 'It hangs badly,' he says.

'Have I ruined it?'

'I'll make you a new one. Properly. Take it off.'

Dorothea looks down at him for a second, then again at me, questioning. The decision made, she crosses her arms to grip the silk, then pulls the dress up and over her head, showing its yellow lining. The silk crackles as she crushes it. We wait. She stands like a yellow tower, rustling. Muffled now: 'I'm trapped.'

The dress is lowered and Max unzips it neatly as before. I turn to go, seeing in the shining paint of the purple door the faint movements of two shadows removing the garment. Outside I listen for conversation, and hear some sibilance. Then I cross the hall and go under the arch to where my own room is.

The queen is at the height of her splendour. She has everything she wants. She has her own designer who will beautify her with all his arts and skill. As she offered him her house, now she offers him her person. She has now offered herself for eradication, to be re-tailored to his tastes. She has begun the long series of devices with which she must try to tempt him.

The house was the first to go. She spent her time in the beginning in careful search of someone worthy of serving a St. John's Wood heiress. In elegant offices consultations went on concerning the layout of rooms, the allocation of space units, measured lighting, colour schemes. Advisors with impeccable tastes were summoned to the house, which they wandered in search of inspiration, giving her for goodly sums their inestimable opinions. She summoned them to the house in twos and threes, unsure of each one's worth. She was easily swayed by a new arrival's persuasive talk, and would set him one of the rooms to do while his rivals continued their own refurbishings of other rooms. No matter that materials were scarce or labour hard to come by, our house was the terminus. It shook with the violence done to it by the decorators; it rang with daily argument. Fighting went on over the drawing room; in kitchen and halls; up stairs and down stairs. Max wouldn't let them touch his rooms, neither would I let them into mine. Only when I felt directly threatened by the paste and drape mob, did I go to him and ask for help. Unwillingly he gave up precious time to arbitrate, and Dorothea welcomed his intrusion. She said he could have the freest hand he'd ever had. He sent the whole pack packing and told her that her taste was terrible.

So they began again setting the house to rights. Max spent twice the time consulting with my wife than did any of the others; he spent twice the money. Sometimes I was called upon to give my opinion on the merits of various styles. They discussed, at length, the possibilities of knocking down large areas of wall as is the custom in Sweden (so Max said), replacing it with glass. But I was the only one to whom the idea was pleasing. My work was interrupted constantly by one or the other of them agog with the latest Max idea for going Fauve or Regency. It was natural, I suppose, that Max's rooms upstairs were the first to be re-decorated, natural too that they should be turned into workrooms for him. There was less likelihood that way of his being suddenly removed from us to continue his career elsewhere. Upstairs Max would live and work, rent-free, in exchange for his invaluable advice. He built for himself, upstairs, a grand, dramatic setting which, unfolding blackly, changed through the rooms until it became purest white. In this new atmosphere of theatre he took on the role of actor-manager amid the applause of sudden friends. Making friends was a part of his business to which he gave the same professionalism as he did to anything that smacked of money. He was to become a great dress-designer. He knew who were the right people.

The rest of the house was attended to in due course, (except my room which, after brief words, was left to me to build). Our designer chose for us a bedroom straight from the depths of his own mind: a cross between the lair of a lion, and a bodega. One stood beside the bed knee deep in rugs like prairie grass. Skins were scattered everywhere. Against the purple walls were hung embroideries, sewn by Spaniards with too much time on their hands. Silk curtains hung from the windows, but he left the little one alone, saying that the gentle light from the courtyard would throw Dorothea into relief as she sat before the mirrors to paint her face. She said she adored the effect of simple grandeur. Max smiled and thanked her for her praise, with curled lip and glinting eye. She wanted him to think of something simply staggering for the drawing room, so parties could be held there, in his honour. I told him that parties were anathema to me.

The queen is not worthy of so long a look. Beautifully constructed cabinets stand in front of her, their contents labelled in fine lettering. Pale etchings lie in tattered sheaves against the panelling: they need immediate attention before they crumble away to nothing. On the other side of the panelling is my puzzle: the boy with the distorted head. It can only be seen correctly from the side, through a hole cut in the cabinet's wall. He is in profile, against a green field. A nimbus of unintelligible letters curves round his head on which he wears a jewelled cap, with a fat feather. Once again I bend to look at him through the circular hole. Standing thus I should be able to view him without distortion, but this isn't so. Whichever way I approach the head, it still remains distorted. The skull is always the same; a sideways elongation with the cap perching on the red hair like a wafer. A bulbous tip sits precariously on the end of the strange, colloidal nose. The single eye looks at nothing. The skin is luminous, the cheek flushed. There is no hair on the chin, nor much else to indicate manliness. But he is a sensuous boy with a supercilious air. Many times have I tried to un-distort him, but he defies me. I cannot fathom why he should when I have done as he directed, and put my eye to the circular window.

The wood of the window feels damp, despite the warmth of the room. I rub my fingers on my jacket and look down at him. James is standing beside my desk, below me. He has on his raincoat. Patches of water have soaked his shoulders and back. From the height at which I stand I can see the wet line of his collar curving round his red neck. His face is flushed. He looks up at me and grasps my leg. With a firm hand he shakes it. He shakes my leg gently, pressing his thumb into the muscle until the pain forces me to move as he directs.

'Get up higher. Get up on your toes. Put your fingers on the ledge again. Go on! Never mind the dust.'

There is no dust. The window is circular, and my fingers slide down the wooden ledge until they meet at the lowest point of the curve. The wood has a familiar feel. I push and strain as though there is too much effort involved, but the thumb on my calf doesn't slack. I pull upwards, stretching legs and toes taut. The pressure eases slightly and James' thumb slides round the curve of my leg. When I look at him he removes his hand, and nods encouragingly.

'Go on, go on,' he says. 'Look.'

It is raining outside. The window is streaked with wet where the slanting rain has penetrated. The glass is so cold it clouds with moisture as I lean forward. I feel its coldness on my face. Through the misty drops I see the gleaming courtyard where several plants grow greenly. Some lie on their sides but still grow upwards among the ruins of cast-iron stands intended once to hold them. They are red with rust. This was Dorothea's folly: she christened it herself and bought the plants and stands. They were to have formed part of a *trompe l'œil* which Max was supposed to paint. He never did.

A creeping vine with emaciated leaves cuts across my vision. No doubt it is only just alive, its roots in cement. Through the leaves I see the thin red lines of the cast-iron stands. The lines flow down the window pane, twisting as if they were alive like water snakes. The leaves of the pot plants are moving too, bending under the weight of water which pours on them from the guttering above. The gutter is almost overflowing, threatening to swamp the yard and soak the bricks, right up to the level of the window opposite. It looks grey in this moist light.

James shakes my leg again. 'Is he there? Is he there?' No lights are on in my room, but James' face shines. He looks up appealingly at me, his face alive with shadow and movement from the rain-spotted window. He puckers his forehead and the white spots shift across his face as though we are in a ballroom.

'I can't see. The yard looks afloat.'

'Not at the yard! Don't look at the yard!' He pushes his cap back on his head; it rests there like a wafer. He cannot stand still. His face works, the shoulders shift, in and out of his pockets go his hands. 'Look,' he says. I do as he directs.

It is raining so fast now that the window has been almost cleared by the wash of the downpour. Leaves and bowls and plant stands collapse in vertical lines down the glass. Spume is forming along the wall opposite. It is frothing underneath the sill. The room is grey: it lies on the shadowy side where, even on the sunniest days, the shadow of the house reduces the light. I can make out the colour of a wall, purple once, but fading now with age. There is movement in the room. Max comes to the window. He cannot see me because I am too high up. He stands for a moment looking straight ahead, looking at nothing; being short-sighted he can see very little without his glasses. He isn't wearing them. He isn't wearing anything at all. He stands, white and drooping, facing out to the withered leaves of the plant bound to die in a year or two.

A hand grips my ankle. 'Is he there? Is he there?'

Max has vanished from the window. The rain rattles in the yard. Looking at my face, James comes to a conclusion.

'He *is* there. I knew it!' He drags at my ankles to pull me down. His hands don't leave my body until he has first pulled me to a sitting position, then got me to the floor.

'What is he doing?'

'Standing by the window.' We have knocked over a jar of pens, giving me excuse enough to turn my back and pick them up.

'What did he look like?'

'Fairly normal, I should say.' The pens are taken from me and banged down on the table.

'Normal? What does *that* mean?'

'Er, natural. Natural is more the term.'

James begins to tremble. 'I know you. You're joking. That was one of your smaller jokes, wasn't it?' He has the intuitions of a woman. I should have known better than to joke. Both he and Dorothea sense things in a flash. It was a mistake to forget he is her brother. James is trembling still. He holds his arms tight against his body and bends over like a man with a stomach ache. He is trembling violently.

'Get up and look for yourself,' I say. He shakes his head and walks away from the desk to put his hands on the cool glass of my cabinets. Supporting himself on each piece of furniture against the wall, he goes from cabinets to file to bookshelf to photographic cupboards like a person in pain. He behaves like someone in a bad film who has been called upon to exhibit anguish. Finally he says, 'We must part them.'

He has said this to me innumerable times. It is his buttress against his inability to think of ways of parting them himself. Often he has come to me with long, long tales of injury. He has told me how Max has kept him waiting on scores of occasions, or never turned up at all. He has listed the excuses Max has made, and praised their ingenuity. He has come to me with tales of Dorothea's insults and what he answered back. He has made telephone calls to the house which haven't been answered. My sympathy has been sought for the hours he has spent skulking in the road outside, only to see them come out arm in arm. Such patience with no end result is hard to believe. When I saw them emerge engrossed in each other's company my action was positive: I went to my cupboard marked 'Photography', and took out my camera. To preserve human specimens is a difficult task, requiring promptitude. James has spent long hours with me trying to whip my feelings into as much fury as his own, oblivious of the radical difference in our natures.

He would burst in on me while I was engaged on some delicate piece of Spondylus cleaning and expect more than my murmured condolences. Ever since he found out about my window he has worried and worn me down with his questions: 'What had I seen?' 'Had I seen anything? Could he believe there was nothing to see?' I would shake him off with anecdotes about my work, and tell him how I was progressing. With patience I could woo him away from thoughts of hate by bringing out the best of my collection. With the Murex lobeckii in his hands he would think he held a priceless jewel, and fondle it. Some specimens I kept from him, mainly the ones whose beauty was brittle enough to break under the pressure of his great thumbs. Being a clumsy man, he would often upset me more by his carelessness than by tales of my wife's infidelities. One cannot explain to someone like James, with his constancy, that a certain freedom must be allowed by the owner to his choicest captive; that is, if he would retain her.

Afraid sometimes of his violent nature I would find other things to show him. He liked to be told how the work was done; I showed him catalogues and letters from distant parts of the world. The bargaining amused him. He wanted to know why I, with my wealth, should so much enjoy a good bargain. He couldn't equate such bargaining with my refusal to sell my forgeries. He enjoyed seeing the forgeries. He thought the Wentletraps I made were good enough to fool a Chinese. They fooled him, the rows and rows of tiny shells all made by me to look exactly as though they'd not long been picked from the ocean bed. When comparisons were made with the real specimen James could never tell true from false. He wanted me to sell but I said 'no'. He said I seemed to gain my satisfaction in vicarious ways.

My window figured largely in his conversation. To talk of it lessened his fear of what was happening beyond. It was a link between him and the horrible friendship he knew was growing beyond his control. But if he had cared to stand, as I had done, frequently up there, he would have relinquished all his hopes that Max could be regained. Dorothea's strong animosity towards her brother precluded social visits to the house. When he came to see Max, he was told that Max was out; Max was busy; Max was tired. Her whim decided when Max should be seen, so James visited me, spilling out all his fears to me in a welter of words, and histrionics.

'What is he doing now?' Once more James begins to push me against the desk. I resist because my papers are in danger. His cap falls off and lands among the pages of *Délices des Yeux et de l'Esprit,* knocking over a photograph. He picks up his cap and puts the photo back where I can see it. It is of himself and his sister standing up to their knees in the sea together, wearing bathing suits old-fashioned and identical. The sunlight is very strong and they bend their heads to squint towards the camera. They are seventeen years old but look much younger; the sun has washed away the shadows on their faces. The poses are identical: bent legs, bent heads, hands on hips, slight grins. After I had taken the photograph they rushed at me together, and pushed me into the soft sand.

James and I sit down, he at the table, I at my desk. His face is flushed. He is turning the cap in his large hands and bending the peak into an abnormal curve. Today his hair is more a washed yellow than pure red. The falling rain outside has made my room grey. He is sitting with me to wait, either for the rain to stop, or there to be some sound within the house. He waits for one, or the other, or both. The splashing of the water from the broken gutter drowns the sound of the tapping rain on the glass above. The loop of the window cord taps the wall. An unseasonal chill is in the air. James still has on his raincoat. Wet patches have spread across his shoulders and down his chest. His shirt is creased and everything about him looks worn and crumpled except the shining peak of the cap he is trying to destroy. I think his chin is quivering. It is a large and hairless chin with such a curve and lack of visible bone that in repose it can be said to quiver. He looks less tough than Dorothea; younger too. We sit and wait. We are both silent while he listens to the sounds outside.

I wait, as always, patiently, knowing that we are mutually bound and mutually suffering. At least, James has told me often enough that we are both suffering. He thinks it would be indecent if I weren't, but he suffers for two. I cannot contort my face sufficiently for his liking. He accepts that I am undemonstrative but says that I'm too calm. Have I given up hope? He asks me: 'Have you given up hope?' My thesis on the word and its lack of meaning for me are cut short by another question:

'How long has he been in there with her?'

'Since two o'clock.' We inspect our watches. It is four. The grey afternoon is already closing into greyer night.

'What are they doing?'

'You should have looked for yourself. I could see nothing. Why don't you climb up and look?'

He shakes his head. The jealousy can only be contained by not allowing himself to believe the worst. He mustn't give up hope, for without him as contender there would be no fight.

'What are they doing?' I don't know either. We sit and watch him play with his watch strap, and hear the rain. He will not be consoled today with his favourite story of my adventures with Strombus gigas. He huffs and sighs and clenches his fists while the room darkens and the loop of the window cord taps the wall. I fancy I hear the ticking of his watch. There is a distant laugh. A car passes. James raises his hand for silence.

Somewhere in the house a door has been opened. There is the laugh again coming from across the hall, then footsteps. James leaps to his feet and rushes over to the door. He stands for a second, listening to the steps, Dorothea's deep laugh, and the creak of the dining room door. Before the muffled voices have disappeared, James has pulled open my door and rushed into the hall. He leaps across the yellow boards shouting, 'Max! Max!' In the lull that follows I hear him stroll slowly towards the pair who are standing in the dining room waiting for him. His voice, descending from a high-pitched shout, comes to me where I sit beneath my window.

'Well, well, well,' he cries. 'Where *have* you been hiding?'

4

I sit on a bench in the centre of the gallery, and rest. Another portrait faces me but I refuse to look. This is a moment of peace before I move along the boards and into another room. Since all these rooms open one to the other it is possible for me, wherever I may be, to walk to an intersection and look along its length to this gallery. There is no reason why the system shouldn't work:

wherever I am I should not miss her if I wander. If, occasionally, I return to the cross-roads I should be able to make sure of her entry with no danger of her first seeing me. No harm can come from a brief saunter through these rooms. I shan't lose my way; I know them like my life. If I linger less long before each picture I stand less chance of becoming conspicuous. People will cease to sidle up to me with curiosity: attendants in grey who sit at stations round the rooms won't look at me with questioning eyes, wondering if I am up to mischief.

I do not know what time she will arrive, but I feel there is still a long time to wait. The static afternoon sets into timelessness. It will be an age before I see the red umbrella shining at the end of a gallery, and I shall see it, however far I am away: my distance vision is not bad for a man of my age and health. At forty-seven many men, far more resilient than I, have succumbed to sets of dentures, trusses, toupées, to aid them in the years of their insurance. Not I.

I only wish he had not snatched the photograph quite so quickly from my hands.

'A recent portrait,' he said, 'taken only last summer.' I didn't try to enlighten him, although, when we met, I had not expected to be handed such a thing. It was one I had always coveted, but in my naïveté I hadn't dared ask if I could keep it. Max forgot to tell me it had changed hands. All he told me was that the scene was set. He said he had played out his part with skill and panache. If it lacked the subtlety I had come to expect from Max when he dealt with unusual problems, my own part had hardly come up to expectations. The meeting should have been more occupied with details of her habits and her dress, and less with such insistence on her beauty. If she had really been a relative, he should have told me more about her. He should have been able (had I asked), to tell me whether she was slovenly and whether her word could be relied upon. Did she lie in nearly every detail, so that the truth was fairly easy to decipher? Did she look straight into your eyes when telling you a lie, defying contradiction? Was this a habit acquired through years of constant practice? Was she vain? Did she have strong, swimmer's hands which she tried to hide, and lithe back muscles that showed through the thin silk of her dresses as she sat before her mirror, massaging the lines from her forehead? She has two tiny creases on her brow which no unguents can eradicate. She spends much time attending to her flaws. The dressing table gleams with pots and jars and cut-glass canisters full of optimistic aids. Is she always over-made-up and over-dressed, preferring the patterned and the whorled to anything that will offset her natural, glorious redness? Does the absolute need for comfort and stability shine from her face at all times?

He may have noticed this look of hers, and translated it as greed. Having once seen the look, he was certain to draw up the contract with exceptional care, asking her over and over again if there was anything she felt should be included for her future security. He was sure to have had his own doubts about my liking her. It must have set him wondering why Max should have chosen this type of woman for me when he, left to the selection, could have done so much better. He may have wanted to offer me someone more to his liking, but Max had briefed him well. I wanted to ask to see the hidden photograph, underneath the one that slipped. I wanted to ask if he laid claim to kinship of the hidden girl. But the risk was too great. To have done so would have been to offend him deeply. Neither could I ask why he drew aside the blinds so often, to peer down across the empty courtyard; or why he cocked his head for sounds outside on the stairs. It was better to stay silent, suffering his words and prods: my retaliation took the form of giving dig for dig whenever he poked me too hard with his horny forefinger. It was late in our acquaintance when I discovered this method of counter-attack. The glass in his hand made no difference to his aim, nor to the amount he drank.

How much alcohol he poured for us I will never ascertain; in retrospect it seems like several rivers. Our link is a stream of alcohol. I can still see the action of his hand as he tips the bottle, the whisky gushing yellow into the glass. Then the hand, expertly angling the soda siphon, waits for my nod before sending down the jet of white to join it. 'Warms the hearty cockles,' he said. Through alcohol and a wad of notes of varying denominations I have laid my claim to him. I waited while he did his counting, watching the lamplight through my glass put patterns on my hand. It was our last meeting.

We had only two. I wanted more, but Max thought two would

settle the affair without disclosing double-dealing. He said there had been reluctance at first until a sum was named. Max had great belief in the powers of money to get what he wanted. He came home jubilant.

'I've made them,' he said. 'He's agreed to it. To everything. Now the pressure's really on. All that has to be done now is a little twisting of her arm... and a push to you.' He went to my desk and picked up the diary—the one I keep for visitors to see. It reassures them.

'Shall I write down Dentist, or Chiropodist perhaps? Or don't you care for anyone to see your feet?'

'Lies are what I care least about. I don't like lies.'

At this Max guffawed. He thought the joke enormous. He puckered his mouth and noisily blew out air, until I showed him my specimen of the Puffer fish. The resemblance was remarkable. He subsided, and wrote in my diary, on two blank Tuesdays, the word 'Confrontation' twice. He repeated the instructions for best bib and tucker (shades of the nicotine man) and told me to get there on time.

'There are absolutely no drawbacks to the whole thing, as far as I can see,' he said. He was very happy. 'Take some money with you when you go to him—but not too much, mind. Don't appear over-eager, or you'll muff it. On second thoughts I can't imagine *you* ever being over-eager.' Max pranced in front of me, giving instructions like a man handing over the office after giving in his notice. 'Tell him what you want. He'll expect to hear that. But don't tell him too much. No details mind, only what we've agreed. Then, lo and behold, he will provide! What a coincidence he should have the very thing!' His jubilation overflowed into a curious dance. 'What fun! I wish I could be there when you start the confab. But I'd be sure to give away everything.'

I had to promise Max again that I would do and say nothing to jeopardize his future. He became serious while he listed for me the reasons there should be success. He told me of the cruise, already booked, and produced from his pocket two liner tickets wrapped in sheaves of sunny brochures.

It occurred to me that it had been many years since he had done me a favour entirely unconnected with his own welfare. He has cherished himself to an extent unusually rare in a human being. Financially he can want little from me, although he demanded recently, and got, considerable sums to aid his work. He says he's in a cut-throat game where the unambitious fall like remnants. I am not the one to be parsimonious when I see my own dream coming true. I would rather he left my house happy than smarting at some hidden hurt he thinks I have done him, and for which, later, he might try to seek recompense. I shall see that Max leaves my house as satisfied as someone with his eternal discontent can be. For he is not a generous man, unless the circumstances are extreme: lack of finance has ever been his explanation for past actions. He used to say that poverty made of him a solitary. But when he said it he always grinned.

What Max fears most are relationships: he does his best to destroy them. He has a need for affection, but it must be one that's undemanding. Yet when it is his, he hates it. He needs abrasive love. Perhaps now that he has found it, he will keep hold. It will be difficult for him not to ask too much. He will have to learn to keep in check his greatest weakness; the necessity to be admired. He has gone to fantastic lengths to preserve his worth in other people's eyes. Dorothea once remarked, in a moment's irritated admiration, that Max was the only man she knew who could run with the hare, hunt with the hounds, while appearing to sit on the fence. Her remarks never bothered him because he knew he could rely on her devotion. She gave it to him from the very first, accepting that he could give her only limited devotion in return. She believed the war to be the cause of his withdrawal from her, and agreed that she took second place to the welfare of the troops. She called his brother officers 'Max's men'; when they told her he should be protected from women like herself, she concurred, treating such selfishness as a cherishable virtue. And Max let it be known that if she was to be his lifelong friend, she must protect him. Her protection went to great lengths. It drove her into marriage.

'You've got the money,' Max said. 'You're lucky. The man with the cash always catches the bride.' But he was unenvious. He came to the wedding without rancour, standing beside me gladly ridding himself of the responsibility of Dorothea.

He stood close in the half-empty church with its blacked-out windows, staring over my head at her. She didn't look at him; she behaved with decorum, her back rigidly straight, her shoulders squared, her lips set in a satisfied expression. The only organist we could find still in mufti played an enthusiastic version of 'Abide With Me' which subsided with a groan as the boy hired to pump the organ stopped his work prematurely. The ceremony was a hasty affair made memorable by the scent of Dorothea's flowers which she wore pinned to the dress that Max had made for the occasion. My bride looked palely beautiful and gave her responses as though she knew they were to be totally binding.

The reception was small and held in a nearby restaurant, the army having claimed our house. The food was spartan and our guests few; most of them were Max's noisy friends in khaki. Military songs of dubious taste were sung, much wine was consumed in our honour. Dorothea drank too much and talked to everyone in turn, impressing them with her knowledge of the life of an army officer. She was a great success. James didn't come, although I had sent him a letter requesting his presence. He was working in a factory from which, he wrote, he was not allowed the time for such frivolities as weddings. He wished us well, and asked that Max should remember him. At the wedding no one but myself mentioned James. I tried to speak of him to Dorothea when I could turn her attention from the festivities. I said he would have been glad to see his sister settled. She answered 'You bet', and went back to hostessing. She seemed happiest at Max's side, offering him admiration and comestibles until he pushed her back to me. With me she appeared nervous. On the steps outside the restaurant we posed for photographs. Dorothea complained of feeling cold, but when I tried to clasp her hand in mine she withdrew it abruptly, rubbing it on the crêpe of her dress as if I had marked it by my touch. The photographs were unsatisfactory. I keep them in a special folder labelled 'Wedding Day'. There is only one of me and my wife standing alone; for the rest we were joined by our gay group of guests who bobbed about and shouted ribaldries at the harassed man behind the camera. Over the years their blurred faces have been further marred by a slight discoloration. The photographs have turned brown, due to some fault or other in the processing. When I take them out now and look at the young, indistinct forms, knowing for sure that some of those men in the happy party no longer exist, I wish I could have kept the moment frozen perfectly. There is no other way to preserve them now. They came with us to the station, jostling a path for us among the crowds, pushing us aboard the train that took us to the country and my summer house. There was no confetti. We left them standing on the platform still whistling as the train drew out; waving and shouting warnings.

When we got to bed that night Dorothea turned her back on me. I asked her why she had thought fit to marry me and she answered, 'Because I've chosen to.' After accepting my embraces, she fell asleep.

She told me she always slept like that: on her side with her back to the person lying next to her. She said she didn't like the thought of someone constantly in contact. She wasn't telling the truth. I have seen her turn and face the man who lies beside her, his back to the window. The leaves of a plant that grows across the window pane cannot hide the way they lie. Nor what they did. I have seen her sleep in that position, facing him. Proof is in my file marked 'Sleepers'. Although the photographs are, almost all, rather dim (due to lack of light more than underdevelopment) they show clearly what I mean. Dorothea is a heavy sleeper. She lies so still that she seems nearly dead, for unless one bent an ear to hear her heart one could not ascertain her breathing. She doesn't move in sleep so that, on waking, only her eyes indicate the return from Morpheus. On rare occasions in her sleep her lids have flickered, their fretted veins stretching over the mauve and bulging eyelids. But in sleep she doesn't move, even when the lamp is turned off above her head. Dorothea is afraid of dark: she must have light to go to sleep by. She must be put to rest with affection and all the comforts she can appropriate, or else she hardly sleeps at all.

Left alone at night she finds it hard to go to bed. Hours are spent at her mirror with its rows of bottles. She plays with the stoppers like an organist. Sometimes, for an hour or more, she will leave the bedroom to go in search of comfort. I have heard her go upstairs to where Max lives. It has been many years since she was welcome. Never has she come to me. On returning to her room she will be carrying food, or pills, or books with which to avoid the night. In her solitary bed she fights the covers, pummels the pillows with her fists until they succumb to her tired head. She does all things injury. Books she has read lie on the floor in stacks; magazines are her coverlet, when she moves they slide to join the others on the floor. But always she leaves one pillow vacant, and always lies so there is room for another sleeper. I have seen her read until her head convulses and my eyes have stood out on stalks. During the past two years Dorothea, despite herself, has become well-read, using the library for its original purpose instead of a dance floor on which she and Max would try out tangos.

Each night her footsteps can be heard across the hall, entering the dining room and gradually becoming fainter as she makes her way to the books. There is the slam of the refrigerator door, as, en route, she stops for nourishment. Plates and cups tend to clatter from her hands for she is careless with objects. Things break, she says, whether she wants them to or not. It isn't her fault. She wants everything to be cast-iron.

The basin broke when she held it. The flimsy china lay in shell-shapes on her open hand. She was bleeding slightly. I told her the china was my father's prize Royal Doulton. She said she never cared for heirlooms. We stood in the dining room on either side of a careless breakfast hastily consumed. I was in a hurry to get to my shells; she finished as fast as I, not picking up the paper as was her custom, to spend the next hour studying the lighter side of post-war life. The wound was slight and she refused my offer of a bandage, saying it would look unsightly with the dress. It was unusual for her to dress so soon, or look quite so radiant on what promised to be a day, like all the others since our return, of putting our house in order. Her hair shone. Her face was smooth in the morning sunlight which gave her skin the same transparency as the china that she held. 'I'll get rid of it,' she said. 'You get dressed.' I helped her clear the table.

'Get dressed soon, won't you? And be a darling—put on a tie.'

'A tie? To go and sort Cowries?'

'He's coming today,' she called from the kitchen. She had already begun the washing-up. Water ran into a clean sink. The floor was spotless.

'Today?'

'Today for certain. But he couldn't say when. So it may be soon.'

'When was this arranged?'

'Oh, after he'd seen the rooms. He said the first floor would suit him well. He's very happy about it.' She whirled the dish cloth with unnecessary vigour. 'Don't you remember me telling you?'

'No.'

'Well I did. I remember your saying you were pleased that the rooms would be put to use.'

'I didn't know things had gone this far. Why didn't you tell me that everything had been arranged? Why didn't you ask me if he should come today?'

'I didn't like to disturb you.' Dorothea bends her head over the sink to hide the strong colour in her face. 'You leave all the other worries to me. Why not this one?' Composure regained she bustles about the kitchen, hanging up cloths and pushing the china higgledy-piggledy into cupboards. 'What difference does it make? The rooms are empty. They're never used. We hardly go up there. They're so empty they make the house seem like a prison. It echoes, you know.' As she leaves the kitchen and goes back to settle the dining room chairs she says, 'He noticed it.'

'How discerning.'

The window curtains are the next to be rearranged. She pulls them back roughly, revealing more of the ruin that used to be the garden. Wanting me to say something else about today, yet afraid to hear it, she puts her back to the window so that I can't see her face so clearly. The furniture divides us.

'He's unreliable, Dorothea.'

She says it doesn't matter. Why should it matter what he's like? He's only coming here to lodge. Dorothea already knows what he is like. She looks at me with set face, waiting to refute whatever else I have to say.

'He has his own friends.'

'Lucky man!'

'They're different from us. They're not the kind of friends we'd choose to have . . .'

'We'd be lucky if we had any at all. What's wrong with his friends anyway? They've always been jolly nice to us. I've always found them very amusing.'

'We can't belong in circles like that. They're closed to us.'

'Don't talk nonsense. I've met most of them, and they're charming. What you lack is an open mind.'

'Have you met his *friends,* or merely his acquaintances? In this case there's a difference.'

'Of course I have. So have you as well. But you forget. We've met all his friends.'

'His *intimate* friends?'

'Those too.' She whirls away from the curtains and goes back to rummage in the kitchen. 'If you can call them intimate . . .' she calls. 'Max doesn't seem to show much interest in any of them.'

'Not even James?'

In the kitchen there is a silence. Dorothea comes to the door, duster in hand, and looks at me. 'Not even Jamie.' She begins to dust the furniture vigorously. 'He hasn't seen Jamie for weeks and weeks.'

'I thought they were living together.'

'Then you thought wrong, didn't you? He's been on his own ever since he was demobbed.'

'He told you this?'

'I know it.'

'They've always been great friends.'

'Friendship has a habit of weakening.' She speaks with unusual refinement, intoning the words nasally to give them weight. I have heard Max use that self-same tone of voice.

'I would be glad if you could see your way clear to getting out of that dressing gown.' I have been dismissed to change into something suitable to receive our visitor.

We pass the next hour or so in polite discussion of future arrangements for the house. I suggest we have a daily lady to come and do the cleaning. Dorothea suggests a covey of gardeners hired to put the garden right. They will know best how to set out arbours and nooks and rockeries. She would like our garden to look like those she has seen in magazines, where acres of flowers wash over the lawns, and every alley reveals a folly. There will be cherry trees all abloom which she can gaze on from the windows of the dining room as she takes her breakfast in the morning sun. Rather, she would like a nice conservatory built outside the window, in which she can lie among her plants, sipping coffee while the birds sing. The house itself will be remodelled in exquisite taste. Won't Max come in very useful here? He has hundreds of lovely ideas on colour and form. We must ask his opinion. He would know what to do with the drawing room and how to disguise the horrors of the library. Couldn't it be converted? But I refuse to have my father's work debased into a drawing room. As for our bedroom—she thinks it needs colour. She thinks it needs warmth, to offset its present barren atmosphere. Don't I agree? Max can do as he pleases with the first floor, can't he? Genius shouldn't be restrained. I answer 'yes'. She asks me whether I would value Max's advice about my room. I answer 'no'.

'Why do you want such a huge room?'

'It won't be large by the time I'm finished. I plan to build benches along the walls. There'll be other cupboards and a sink, and files for my notes and things. Partitions too, so that I can get rid of the screens. I need the space.'

'It seems a waste to me,' she says, and leads the way from the dining room into the hall. Under the arch she stops. 'We could have parties in there. Like your father used to.'

'What's wrong with the drawing room?'

We cross the hall. The yellow boards gleam. She opens the door of my room. Our footsteps echo as we enter.

The room is huge and blue: dark blue. The smell of new paint fouls the air. Through the curtainless windows can be glimpsed the desolate garden with its long grass and unkempt trees, waving their tops in the breeze like fans. They send some of my room into shadow because of their height. They must be lopped, there is too much growing going on. The walls are still quite bare of furniture, except where cabinets brought from the country have been installed. My desk is in place, looking shabby against the brand new plaster.

'Are you sure the workmen have finished in here?' I assure her they have. 'It looks ghastly.' I explain once again that the plaster and brick must be allowed to dry before decorating can be finalised. She kicks the packing cases strewn on the floor. 'Aren't any hiding in there? I'd search that straw if I were you! You might find a labourer or two!' Straw catches on Dorothea's shoes. She sighs and looks out to the garden. 'What a mess. It's cold in here. And it smells.'

'Shall I open a window?'

'Yes,' she says. 'Open that one.' She points above my head to where a loop of rope hangs down. It is fixed to the pivot of a circular window, set high up in the bare wall. Nine pieces of glass, divided by wooden frames, make up its shape. The central glass is octagonal. The window should pivot from two bars embedded in the framework. I pull the rope, but the window stays shut.

'It's stuck. Must be the paint.'

'I'll get a chair,' Dorothea says. Before I can tell her I have a chair, hidden behind the desk drawer, she has crossed the room and gone out.

First on to the chair, then on to the desk I climb to pull at the rope again. But it's stuck. I reach up and put my fingers on the window's wooden ledge. My hands slip down until they meet at the bottom of the circle. With only slight exertion I can see over my fingers and through the glass. I can see a courtyard.

It is open to the sky, but badly lit since it is enclosed on all sides by the house. Although dust and paint obscure my view I can see the neglect out there. Broken and dirty bottles lie in heaps on the cement. Dust has covered them, and every jutting surface. Old scraps of paper lie withering in the corners. The leaves of a luxurious creeping plant grow wildly across my window; its roots, I know, are buried under the concrete. There is a door to the yard, but no one has used it since the war. Many times has Dorothea complained about the yard, and threatened to alter it. But she is waiting for Max's advice. The window of our bedroom looks out on this ruin. I can see the window now, reflecting brickwork. Behind the reflection Dorothea blooms. She walks past the window and stands beside the bed. She has picked up a chair, which she carries back the way she came. I hear a door.

With one sharp push the circular window pivots. I open it fractionally and test the cord for rottenness. Then I climb down.

When Dorothea enters with the bedroom chair, I am standing looking into the wilderness that is our front garden.

The question is whether to walk through the entire gallery fast, so as to arrive more quickly at the obvious points of focus, or to ignore them until I come upon them unawares. I have to ask myself whether there is anything to be gained by reaching my goal too quickly, having paid no attention to what I have passed, when all I must do at the end of the line is wait. Time must be killed, and the best way of doing it today is to pay attention to the excellent permanence of this place—to the form and plan, and design. Great satisfaction can be gained by noting such things as spatial relations between walls and intersecting arches. The model was an ancient one, based upon the Golden Section. A formal, mathematical approach to the art of living was one that the Greeks fully understood. They knew how best to suppress natural disorder, the kind that breeds corruption and decay. They built for permanence so precisely that today we build as they did then, and give our public buildings a show of strength.

From here I can see with great clarity along the total length of this long floor. Before me are three rooms, each open to the other. In the distance, confronting me, is the pale magenta tone of a blank wall, against which can be made out the curling line of a stair rail. In perspective the three arches are concentric, dividing not only the rooms, but seeming to govern the colour and texture of the floor. The boards at my feet give way to wood blocks where this room ends. No doubt a decision made for aesthetic reasons. I would like to know whether the weak light coming from the high windows was taken into consideration when the floor was built. I have a sort of shadow where I stand, but it is so slight that it merely accentuates the lines between the boards until they are stopped by the blocks of wood. The blocks themselves pick up the light in zig-zag patterns like a scratched fret on a single surface. With ruler and set-square I have worked out such a system of flooring for my own room (on a limited scale, of course), taking into account every aspect of light, taking into consideration the time of day at which light falls on certain areas. My task would have been easier had the sun stood still, but at least it could, and can, be relied upon to perform its movement with regularity.

The floor at the intersection of the second arch is broken by a triangle of light on which no patterning appears: this must be due to an inconspicuous window. Light from the corridor adjacent to these rooms may also be affecting it. It is possible to wander all these rooms and corridors without retracing one's footsteps.

Beyond the triangle the pattern of blocks becomes fainter, with only a slight unevenness apparent in the surface. My room's floor is exactly level. The tracks I make as I move about are erased from day to day so that the colour stays uniform. Here the colour of the floor fades from me, until, when it reaches the wall with the painted rail, it has lost entirely all its colour, absorbed by the light. I have never cared much for frivolous decoration, that harms the eyes and wears away. The walls in the next room are papered and patterned in such a way they detract from the room's purpose. I do not approve of the heavy mauve that backs the glittering portraits. The paper already shows signs of fading; its blemishes are such that they force the eye to find the wall with the white rail, seeking for signs of permanence. There is relief in looking upward at the glass squares of the ceiling lights which can be relied on never to alter their neon glow. They throw into shadow the ribbed lines of the curved roof where the plaster-work is deeply cut and intricately rendered. There is no visible dust up there. The motif of leaf between two roses has been carried out all along the edges of the ceiling. The roses have four petals each and a convex centre, after the style of a Tudor rose. What an excellent way in which to capture that flower's brief glory. I have seen it rendered more naturalistically in paint, held between the fingers of a ginger boy, but not so perfectly.

People and imperfections are synonymous. They wander across the wood blocks, marking them with squeaking rubber soles. They cross the triangle of light and pass the white rail at the end. The sound of their feet doesn't accurately indicate where they are. They must be seen. Several have sat down on the bench in the centre of the nearest room. While they are still they make a monolith there. I would like to have my camera with me now, to record the moment when they sat so still in their dark clothing on the dark bench. In the next room another bench is reflecting the ceiling lights like a mirror. I would like to fix forever these chosen objects and have them to myself. Anyone can see, by standing behind me and looking where I do, the table and chair in silhouette beyond the second bench. The blackness gives them a thinness of structure which I'm sure they don't really possess. They look incapable of supporting any weight at all, as if they too are exhibits around which ropes should be put. Presumably the table is for the convenience of an attendant; one of the many who stroll these rooms. But it takes a man like me to appreciate the symmetry of the table with its centrally placed label which I cannot read from here. The label is identical with those beneath the portraits: gold and shining. The chair is central too beneath the table, and pushed in square so that only its back shows.

From the table with its accompanying chair the eye automatically rises to the level of the farthest wall. There the eye rests, drawn to it as much by the thread-like rail as by the large portrait that hangs above it. Without effort of focus I can see that the portrait is clear, complicated and colourless. The subject has a large head which faces front. The face is pale, with a tendency to fade from yellow into the whiteness of what must be a collar. There is no way of telling (from here) what is below the whiteness, for the entire body is masked by the pale grey square of another portrait's reflection on which can be glimpsed the faintest gold of its frame. The man is entirely encased in gold which dims even further his dull, grey shape. His body is a box.

He lives in a block. He lives in a block of flats which are formed on the principle of the Cube. He lives in a series of cubes conjoined to form, with the floor above and its set of conjoined cubes, another, larger, perfect cube. He is lucky. I too live in a cube, but an imperfect one (if this can lightly be said of geometric shapes). Try as I have to improve it, my cube is only loosely so, while his has the perfection one associates, mistakenly, only with the work of Inigo Jones and his contemporaries. There is purity in the perfection of a cube, in which orderliness is second nature, not something striven for, but the essence and the ultimate. On sight I admired the purity of form apparent in the frontal view of the block he lives in. I had not imagined that builders in the Thirties had time to meddle with the Golden Section. Three-quarter view confirmed my hopes: here was indeed perfection. The courtyard was a peerless square, made of Macadam, and nicely firm to the tyres' tread. No trees or shrubs marred my sight of the place as I stepped from the taxi and paid off the driver. It was a revelation to stand alone surveying the superb way in which his block had been repeated to left and right, identically. Orange lamps set at regular intervals, and decorated sparingly with Acanthus, lit the three buildings equally, giving to them that drama of atmosphere one usually associates only with *Son et Lumière*. On closer examination the building had further signs of Hellenic affinities: narrow Ionic columns flanked the central door, over which was the merest hint of a pediment. As one advanced the building seemed to cry out that fitness of design was all that mattered in the modern world, lulling the senses into believing that anything could be achieved if only order was maintained.

I feel something close to envy of his living in that block. He is surrounded by so much that is pure in form, tracing a pedigree that goes back so long, that I have doubts about his fitness to inhabit such a place. The point is whether he should in any way be extraordinary in order to do justice to his surroundings, or whether justice is done by his throwing them into relief with the banality of his mien, conversations and habits. Being manifestly banal, he is therefore absolutely fitted to live in such a state of banality as the cube imposes. Only a man of great strength of purpose could overcome the domination of his box. Unfortunately my conjectures do not take into account the fact that he is totally unaware of his advantages, at least in the architectural direction. Although I formulate a latent theory, at the time of our first meeting I mentioned something that would have set a more perspicacious man thinking about his surroundings. 'This place is perfect,' is what I said.

'Good little hidey-hole,' was his reply. He said it had been a cold day. I told him that I hadn't noticed. I endeavour, as far as possible, to have nothing to do with weather or its changeabilities.

He said it sounded as though I had central heating. I told him my circulation was quite satisfactory.

'No, no, no. I meant your house. Central heating in your house. Expensive to instal, but worth it in the long run, eh?'

We stood inside the door, but he made no attempt to take my coat. Finally I took it off and handed it to him; he felt its weight and looked inside at the maker's label. I in my turn examined him, coming to the conclusion that he had been tailored by someone with an eye to excessively tight fit. This was true not only of his suit, but of the shirt that stretched across his chest. I was able to glimpse a few wiry hairs peeping through an opening unconcealed by the flamboyant tie. The room was full of the smell of cigarettes; smoke enveloped me, the air being so clouded that I was forced to close my eyes. I tried to follow him across the room, only to find my legs entangled in a chair which I knocked to the floor and fell upon. It was several seconds before I was helped to my feet, had my back brushed down and could bring myself to notice what it was that had tripped me. 'Devilish chair,' he said. It was of an unfamiliar pattern, being composed entirely of what looked like twists of golden rope, curving to form the legs and back. It looked too fragile for such a copious weight as his. 'I have never seen such delicacy in a chair before,' I said to him.

'Delightful, isn't it?'

'But does it bear weight?'

He laughed. 'Mine you mean? Wouldn't risk it! It's for a client. She's coming tomorrow.'

'Oh. I'm not the only one then?' My remark was received with iciness.

'Do I misunderstand what you're saying, sir? I hope you haven't got me wrong. "Client" to me means business. You understand? The antique furniture business is what gets me the bread and butter. Keeps me here from morning to night. People come here at all hours. Didn't Max tell you?' I begged his pardon. 'This flat is my showroom. And don't forget it, sir.' He waved his hand across the illuminated welter of *choses* which crowded the room. Dutifully I looked, waiting for the faint flush of subsiding anger to leave his face. He was pocketed and lined about the face like an ancient clown whose tiny, watching eyes were waiting for me to prove myself. I felt I didn't know the rules. But Max said my part of the bargain consisted of saying the minimum. He had told me to concentrate on trying to answer correctly any questions, however personal. When Max had said, 'Answer him with care, but every sign of openness', he was trying to school me in a line of behaviour he had made especially his own.

We walked over to the table on which were bottles, glasses and a smouldering cigarette wasting away in an ash tray. 'Whisky?'

'Please.'

'Soda?'

'A dash.' Nothing wrong with my answers here.

After handing me my drink he laid his fingers on my arm and whispered conspiratorially, 'It has been very cold today, hasn't it? Do you find your heating adequate?'

'Yes, I think so. Why?'

Ignoring my question he carried on. 'How about your car?'

'How about my car?'

'Was it inconvenient getting here so late? Or getting here at all?'

'It's quite early for me. I never sleep before two.'

His face began to flush again. 'Sir, are you deliberately trying to be difficult? Have you anything to hide? What I'm asking you is whether or no you have a *motor car*. I didn't hear you come. Nor is there one in the courtyard. Do you follow?'

I begged his pardon yet again and told him of the strain I felt at making his acquaintance under such strange circumstances.

He laughed and prodded me with a hard forefinger. 'That won't do at all,' he said. 'We've shaken hands, haven't we? Max has told me all about you, hasn't he? I know what to do for you if you'll only let me. Max can't be here to encourage you all the time, can he?' The prodding and patting continued while he spoke. 'We're grown men. Of similar age, I should say. Now all you have to do is trust me. And let me say right now that any confidences you care to divulge shall be as safe with me as if you'd told your own father.' I changed my laughter to a choking cough. 'Also sir, I wish to say this: if anything is to come from this relationship, there must be co-operation. I can see from the look of you that I'm dealing with an intelligent man, who knows that *teamwork* gets the best results.'

He went over to the window through which shone the orange glow of street lamps. Lifting a slat of the blind, he looked out. The curve of his back made me think he resembled somebody I had once met, a long time ago. But the face wouldn't come. He craned his neck to see below as far as the blind allowed. 'We business men must stick together, mustn't we?' he said as he released the blind and came back to me. The fat folds of skin and slight puffiness beneath the eyes precluded confidence in him. He looked at me with what might be called a 'searching look'. We stood looking hard at one another for several minutes, our drinks tilted precariously in our hands.

'The street appears empty,' he said. 'Where is your motor car?'

'I haven't one. Taxis are much more useful in the congestion of St. John's Wood. And there are always plenty to be had, even at this late hour.' The answer seemed to satisfy. I consulted my watch. He caught and held my out-flung arm in a tight grip.

'Gold?'

Not feeling capable of releasing my arm without an unseemly struggle, I let him hold me. He bent closer to examine the timepiece, turning it over to read the maker's name. At last we separated to raise our glasses to our lips and to allow him to smoke another cigarette.

The next question on his agenda was whether I was in good health. How was my eyesight? Could I see the second hand on my watch, or read the minute figures? He pressed me further to say whether my eyes were serviceable for reading, writing, golf et cetera, and whether recently I had had cause to visit an oculist. He thought it better to know of any aberrations, so that he could feel assured about my future health. I didn't tell him that my eyes could read the speeds and distances on a camera so accurately in any light that the subjects were always captured at the exact moment I wanted them. He wouldn't have appreciated the intricacies of focus involved in leaning from a window, keeping the camera steady in the hands, to watch two people coming down a path. Distances must be judged and time set before they have blossomed in the graticule. As they approach, holding hands and laughing, I squeeze the release before they have had time to unlock shadows and return to their polite, social ways. I have got them forever locked together, back from a secret somewhere with the memory still on their faces. I called it 'The Return'.

From eyes, we progressed to general health, during which he told me at length of how fit he was—considering his age and occupation. Here he winked at me. I was recommended to the same course of daily practice with the dumb-bells, and nightly yoghurt eaten by the pint. He said he could see I needed building up, and recommended oysters to boost my morale. I told him that I had long since given up the consumption of Molluscs and Crustacea, the temptation to save their shells being too great. Two samples, at the most, of any specimen were sufficient, especially of the common ones. 'Back to work,' he said.

Money was what he meant. Having been warned by Max that I should need to provide evidence of my solvency, I had with me enough paper proof to quieten even the smallest fear that my financial future was anything but sound. At his request I furnished details of holdings and securities, and offered them with all the contempt of a man of means for such paltry behaviour. Lists of figures changed hands; as did the addresses of reliable men in charge of all my larger assets. I told him that they would gladly furnish him with innumerable assurances that all was well in the wealth department. Only one small detail did I omit: I didn't tell him of my contributions to Max's business. Since this was a purely practical arrangement that didn't concern him in the least, I felt no harm could come from its exclusion. He produced a specimen copy of the contract which, he said, had given him great pains. If I would care to run my eye across it at my leisure, I would see that nothing had been omitted. I would see that, although stress lay on the financial side of the arrangement, the document had been phrased with delicacy so as not to give offence to any feminine feelings. He hoped that I would forgive the ultra-legality of the phrases, and appreciate their necessity in producing a contract of doubtful nature in the eyes of the Law. 'Ladies delight to be blinded by science,' he told me. 'Especially when they're getting the good end of the bargain.' The very thickness and feel of the pages with their crisp seals was enough to reassure the most reticent party-of-the-second-part. What a pity it couldn't be signed there and then was his moan. 'But who buys the goods without first seeing them!'

We did not sit down. We stood roughly in the centre of the room before a table on which lay the pertinent papers. With the exception of a passage to the door, we were hemmed in: we were trapped by furniture and silks and prints, cushions with fringes, rugs, curtains, candles, wrought iron and mirrors. Other people's bric-à-brac is so much more obtrusive than one's own. The room's intricate lighting only served to heighten the shadows and double them. The mirrors doubled the sight of everything, of furniture and fitments; making of the two of us a full committee. It was hard to tell where walls stopped and turned back in reflection. In an alcove, mirrored too, stood an aquarium in the shape of a double cube. Fish, and shadow fish swam in the water and the glass in constant circumscription. Everything in the room had a neat and polished look, more like a museum than a home, with only the labels missing. There were books on shelves in such regular rows I was suspicious of their contents. They could have been the doors to a cupboard in which he kept a secret supply of liquor. Certainly we consumed enough alcohol that night for him to need hidden reserves. Repeatedly he filled my glass, and his.

There were photographs everywhere, each set in a polished frame and standing in its own proportionate amount of space. Most of the subjects were women.

I walked over to him and looked at what he held. He smiled at me. 'She's a grand person,' he said. 'Not tall. Just right for you. I bet you like her straight away.' His larded truths caused me to smile myself. Since he didn't call me 'sir' again, I concluded that his wrath had gone. There were no further questions as to my resources, financial or otherwise, so I felt free to explain how I proposed to spend my time in the future. Never before had I realised what help alcohol can give to anyone with a wish to be mendacious. I told him about vacations to be spent idling by a distant sea within the sound of bouzouki music coming out over the waves from the distant shore where the distant natives wove their distant huts; of yachts to sail in, manned by crews so skilled that the ice would barely clink in our glasses as we cleft the Attic waters under the perpetual sun. I told him of the quest for beauty in any shape or form; of how we would go only to the prettiest places, eat only the most delightful of foods, wear only the most luxurious in clothes, and search for *objets d'art,* the like of which he would never clap eyes on. He was with me all the way, applauding when I reached the moment in my story when, in the studios of some poor artist, we found a painting worth five thousand pounds, which we exchanged for a salami. I excelled myself. The evening seemed distasteful and long only in retrospect.

When it was finally time to go he pushed me into my coat with enthusiasm. For one moment I was afraid he was going to button me up like a child out of school, but his hand went down to clasp mine while I breathed in his fumes of nicotine and spirits. No time was lost in showing me to the door. He stumbled once, then stood with his toes on the edge of his carpet as he shouted directions about controlling the lift. It had a will of its own, carrying me, in one smooth second, up to the top of the block of flats. In my dimly lit, claustrophobic box I admired the man. I pressed the button and descended the shaft in another swift second into the lower half of the perfect cube. I found myself emerging in the basement. As I searched for the stairs up to street level, I admired the man. It wasn't until standing in the road waiting for a noctambulant taxi that I realised the whisky was affecting my judgment, to the detriment of my usual sensibility. Next time I resolved to use the stairs.

'Your friend is unpleasant,' I told Max. 'He doesn't like me very much, and the feeling is mutual.'

He laughed. His feet were upon my desk, creasing the papers there. He was rocking his chair on the polished boards, no doubt deliberately. I showed no obvious signs of annoyance. His attitude seemed, more than usual, one of superiority, but being accustomed to his many moods, I wasn't unduly surprised. After several minutes while neither of us spoke, I realised that Max was showing signs of nervousness, or even fear. He let down both feet suddenly with a double bang.

'You're going, aren't you?' he said.

'Why should I?'

'But you agreed. It's your part of the bargain. You can't back out now. Look how long it's taken you to go to see him. You can't do anything else now.'

'Couldn't we think of some other way it could be done?'

'Certainly not! I've racked my brains enough already on your account. This is being done for *your* benefit. Or have you forgotten? If you give up now you'll ruin everything.'

'For you?'

'*I'll* be all right. Don't concern yourself with me.' I refrained from looking at Max's face while he was enduring such uncertitude.

'What if your friend refuses to deal any more with me?' I said. 'He may refuse to see me again.'

'He won't. Everyone has his price, you know.' Max put his elbows on my papers. 'What did you say to him to make you think he's changed his mind?'

'We didn't see eye to eye, that's all. He persisted in patronising me.'

'So what? I've done a lot of groundwork on your behalf and don't you forget it. I've given him all the spiel about what a well-set up chap you are, and how marvellous she'd be, if only given the chance. He's swallowed hook, line and sink plug all the stuff about me being embarrassed at introducing friends, and so on. It was only thanks to me that we managed to get over the dodgy part—about there being a contract. Contract! I ask you! Now there's nothing to stop us.'

'But on whose terms?'

'He's entirely in my hands. I've told you. Everyone has his price.'

Seeing Max's self-assurance I felt an urge to try him: 'What if I have changed my mind?'

He sat upright and stared at me through the glinting glasses. He was trying to assess how serious I was, but my face gave nothing away. I was relaxed and breathing easily. I managed a slight smile.

He did some thinking and decided on sincerity. 'Look here . . .' he said, '. . . at least see him again. Go through with it, old chap, for all our sakes. What have you got to lose? I mean, even if the worst comes to the worst and she turns you down—which for one minute I don't think she'll be crazy enough to do—well . . . er . . . at least you'll have done your best. I mean for all of us.'

'But by the time the meeting's been arranged, she'll have signed the contract, won't she? I was wondering whether to call the whole thing off before it can get that far.' I took pleasure in keeping him on tenterhooks. 'We merely call the whole thing off,' I said.

'But I've long since started working on Dorothea.' Max was right in assuming that once Dorothea had been coerced into the plan, there was no going back. Once she had been persuaded, it was a *fait accompli*. It was a day of great worry for him which I enjoyed prolonging. In my hand were several cards of great worth, not least of these was the card called 'Cash'. Apart from any other fears he might have had, Max was willing to act for me while I still held the purse. His very natural worry stemmed from whether, if I didn't carry out his plan, he would still benefit financially.

'Why not call the whole thing off now?' I asked, and watched him blench. 'Why don't you two risk it? Go away now without saying a word. Slip away to somewhere secret, where she won't be able to find you.'

Max nibbled the top of his long nail. 'What if she finds out?' he said.

'She has to know sooner or later. Isn't it fairly obvious anyway, that you two will be going together?'

'Oh no. That wouldn't wash. She thinks Jamie's leaving for the Bristol branch. At least, I think she does ... And she can see just how busy I am with the collection here in Town. I couldn't possibly be going to Bristol, could I? Why, she can see for herself by all the papers and contracts that I couldn't go there.' He brightened. 'Anyway, who in their right mind would think of opening a boutique in Bristol, for Heaven's sake?'

'Have you given her any reason at all why you're quitting the house?'

'The premises are too small. Anybody can see that. She knows there isn't room for me to do justice to myself. Said so herself. She said, "You need a better workshop", so naturally I was bound to tell her I was thinking of a move. Quite used to the idea, she is. Why, the stuff's already going out in cart loads.' He looked at me appealingly. 'So you can't mess it up for me now.'

'What if she finds out that you're together?'

'Why should she? No one will tell her. You wouldn't be stupid enough to tell her, would you?'

'No. I don't think so.'

'You don't think so! For Heaven's sake can't you see the next few weeks are going to be touch and go? She mustn't get excited about *anything*. You stay away from her, and I'll think of something to keep her occupied. Give her some filing to do perhaps...'

'Isn't that enough to make her suspicious straight away—your needing her for something?'

'I shall do my level best not to rouse the darker side of her nature.' Max smiled at the thought. 'She's always willing to believe the best of me.' It was true. He had been able to remove Dorothea's will and replace it with his own. Gradually she had come to accept most of what he told her with a certainty that it was for her own good. Ideas that were once anathema had been absorbed merely because they had been planted there by Max. Very soon he would attempt the final coup. The training for it had begun. 'I've told her Jamie's leaving soon,' he said.

'And what was her reaction?'

'As expected. Copybook case of dark suspicion, followed by relief.'

'I can see the scene. Say no more.'

'So you see, old chap, there's absolutely nothing to it—as long as you keep your side of the bargain.' Delicately Max began to spit out slivers of bitten nail.

'The money, you mean?'

'Money has nothing to do with it. I'm doing you a favour, dear chap.'

'Then why not take James away tomorrow? Why wait a month?' This time I had him worried.

'Don't be ridiculous! How *can* I? The flat isn't signed for yet, let alone decorated. The cruise is booked. And I'm in the middle of a collection. What are you saying?' He walked over to the window and began to play with the blind cord.

'Max,' I said.

'Hmmm?'

'Has it ever occurred to you that I would have been happier if you'd taken Dorothea away with you?' He let down the blind with a clatter. 'Long ago. Have you thought that in all these years you've been living here, I would rather you'd removed her from my sight?'

'You could have thrown us out,' he said. 'But you didn't. So something stopped you. I ask myself, "What held you back?"'

'Perhaps it was laziness.'

'You know it wasn't laziness. You work away like a bloody ant in here. Collections all over the place, and every one in order. Theses written; learned papers to this and that society; workshop, files, drawers, cabinets, all made by you . . . Oh no. There's another reason why we're still together. It's locked away in one of those cupboards.' He pointed to a section under lock and key.

'Are you trying to refer to my photographs?'

'Of course I'm bloody trying to refer. Who else but you would have taken them one by one with such thoughtfulness? Who else but you would have kept them tucked away in here with all your other treasures, and brought them out when it suited your purpose? You've been enjoying yourself at our expense, haven't you?'

'I have been doing you all a great and lasting service. It may be beyond your capacity to understand now what I've done for you, but the fact remains that I am the only one who has managed to preserve you. You will owe your place in posterity to me because my methods have saved you from decay. The process continues, you will continue to fade and droop, then finally you will decay. Nothing will be left but what I have managed to preserve.'

'Preserve, my eye! We gave you pleasure, didn't we? Admit it.'

He had it all wrong. He gave me no pleasure. Only Dorothea did that. To keep her I had to keep him, for he didn't want the responsibility of looking after her by himself. That's why he'd stayed—in case she became too much for him; in case he tired.

'Dorothea has always given me pleasure.'

'You've a funny way of showing it.'

'She is my wife.'

'Well you're getting her, aren't you?' He went across the room to fetch two chairs. One he offered, the other he sat on facing me. 'Look here,' he said. 'You want her, don't you?'

'She's my wife.'

'I don't care two hoots about that.' He sounded irritated.

'Then you should. You should have cared, Max. You should have been jealous. You should have hated me, and wanted to take her away. Most men would have done.'

Max laughed. 'Hark who's talking! What did you do? Took our bloody photos! And there's another side to things. My career. I work for a living. I had to work to get where I've got, make no mistake. There were other considerations beside your wife. She wasn't everything.'

'What if she was to me?'

Now he was relaxing. 'My nature is a bit like yours,' he said, 'without jealousy or rancour!'

'That's the first time you have paid me a compliment, Max. Watch out, you may be losing your grip. Old age may be creeping up on you. One day Dorothea may forget you ever existed.'

He flashed me a hopeful look and drew his chair closer. 'Let's get this sorted out, shall we? Are you going to see this man again?'

'Yes.'

'Good. Then I will finalise everything. Jamie's all prepared to leave—packed already! The flat's under control, the collection's under way and Dorothea's on edge. Now ... what about the money?' I decided there and then not to give him any more until I had her, secure.

'You'll get it when the deal is finalised. Not before.'

He had to believe me. There was no reason why he shouldn't. I have been generous to him in the past when he has come to me.

'Say nothing to Dorothea,' he said.

'Contact with my wife is rather limited.'

'Good. Don't see her at all if you can help it. It'll be easier when the time comes. Does she ever come in here these days?'

'Not often. She has never liked my room. But occasionally she has come. Not during these past few months, though. Strange, that. Have you noticed how she's been avoiding me?' As he lost interest, Max's eyes began to wander. 'She has been avoiding me and I find that significant. Dorothea has never avoided me before. Never.' He picked up a pencil lying on my desk and began to prod at my papers. 'She has always been a woman with the courage of her convictions, however misplaced. But suddenly she has changed character.'

'What do you mean?'

'She's afraid to face me now. Oh, I know we have only met in corridors, or briefly in this room and sometimes on the street, but she has never, up until now, tried to avoid me. She has always tended to flaunt her misdemeanours for my disapproval, almost (I might say) in order to enjoy them more herself. Now she has suddenly removed herself entirely from the area of my displeasure. I ask myself "Why?"'

'I don't follow you.' Max, not being interested any more in the subject of my wife, did not want to follow my reasoning. He began to doodle across the top sheet of paper on which were my notes on the Common Limpet. He outlined an eye, the tear duct and the curling lashes. As he drew, I tried to explain. It wasn't easy for a man like myself, long used to keeping what I thought to myself, to act towards him with something approaching unreserve. I have always tried to behave with careful politeness which put no strain on either. Now was the time to re-establish our roles.

'Dorothea has decided to hide herself from me,' I said. 'I find it strange. I also find it worrying.'

Max mumbled something as he started to thicken the lines of the nose he had drawn.

'It is my opinion that she has lost her self-sufficiency. She is suffering and afraid to face me with the sight of her defeat.'

'Defeat...?'

'This gives me hope that she will agree with your plan, but also makes me worried in case your behaviour has made her physically ill. Unless, that is, she is at the Change of Life.'

Max stopped drawing. '*What* did you say?'

'I said, "Is Dorothea at the Change of Life?"'

'What a disgusting question! How should I know?' He was startled at the irrelevance of my question. He didn't know the state of my wife's health, and what is more my wife had long been used to his indifference. He continued drawing, and frowning when the line displeased him or my notes intervened with his design.

'I have wanted to tell you, Max, for many years, of my thoughts on you. But I'm at a loss where to begin.' He had bent to his work and was now seriously trying to obliterate my words. 'It is my considered opinion that you have never loved Dorothea. In fact I will go so far as to say that you have frequently actively hated her. And shown it. For instance—what man would design such terrible clothes for a woman, unless he hated her? Come to think of it, all the clothes you design are horrible. She has suffered at your hands, Max, and I have allowed that suffering. I wanted to watch it . . . to record the changes it brought.'

He showed no sign of listening to me. The drawing had become an *œuvre*. He began to cross-hatch a section of the face between eye and cheek.

'Shall I tell you what I think, Max? I think that the point when you began to dislike her was the point when you took her from me...'

'What point where?'

'The point when you took her from me.'

Max looked bewildered. He hadn't been listening. I wanted to make him understand.

'The point when *you* took Dorothea from me was the point . . .'

'You let her go. You wanted her to go.' He finished the patch of shading and began to gaze at me. 'Don't sit there and tell me you didn't want me to take her. What a hypocrite you are about all that ancient history. Your brain's softening. You landed yourself with her and she was too much for you. She interfered too much with your precious collections, no doubt. So you pushed her off on to me.'

'She went freely. I couldn't stop her.'

'*Didn't* stop her, you mean. Found she took up too much of your time. Too much looking after. So you foisted her off on me. Only you were clever: you kept her in the same house, in case you changed your mind.'

It suddenly occurred to me to put a stop to the argument. If it descended to mere bickering about the past, then both our futures were in danger. So I agreed. 'You're right,' I said.

He bowed slightly. 'Thanks.'

'Therefore I am willing to go and see this horrible friend of yours again.'

'Not really a friend, more an acquaintance. Known him years though. I've redecorated him several times. Did him in '51, I remember.'

'How impecunious is he?'

'Oh, he's reliable. He needs the money. Like me in that respect.' Max had put down his pencil.

I looked at the drawing. The head flowed across the complete first page of my notes, obliterating most of the words. It was a man's head he'd drawn, but full-faced and feminine, with a thick mouth and hair that lay in tight curls over the ears.

There were footsteps on the hall. 'That's James,' I said.

He came into the room. 'Stinks in here,' he said. The friends smiled at each other, and James came over to squeeze Max's arm. He saw the drawing. 'What have you two been doing? Playing pictorial consequences?' In the ensuing silence he picked up the top sheet of my notes and, screwing it into a ball, threw it dramatically across the room where it lodged on top of the Venetian blind.

Max had turned pink. 'Calm down, Jamie,' he said. 'This is strictly business.'

James sat down on my desk, resting his feet on Max's chair. He was wearing his raincoat and holding a hat which sprouted a flamboyant feather. He looked at Max with disbelief. 'What business?'

'For heaven's sake, dearie, understand. I told you the other day.'

'Oh. Has he been?'

'Of course he's been. What do you think I'm doing in here? Chatting?'

'Why not? I wouldn't put it past you.'

I sat and listened to them discussing the situation, aware that my comments would not be needed.

'Your temper is marvellous, my dear, but learn to control it, will you?'

'What happened?'

'Everything was just fine. They got along like a house on fire. Didn't you?' My answer was ignored. Shifting his position on the desk, James further ruined my notes. 'Then what about the money?' he said.

'We'll have it soon.'

'What do you mean, soon?'

'When he's ready to part with it. And, quite understandably, he isn't ready yet.'

'When will he be ready?'

'After the second interview, I suppose.'

'Not like you to be so slipshod, Max.' He took a packet of chewing gum from his pocket, unwrapped it and offered some to Max who refused. He put all the gum into his mouth and began to chew. 'What do we do if he funks it?'

'He isn't likely to "funk it", as you so amusingly put it. The man's grown up. He won't back out now. Why should he anyway?'

'He might have second thoughts about the money. Mightn't you?' James directed his fierce stare at me.

'Why should I? Already you have enough evidence of my goodwill.'

'You wouldn't dare use those photographs in court. You'd be asked straight away why you waited so long...'

'I was referring to the money I have already contributed to Max's business.'

'You did that for Dee. She asked you for it.'

'I have said this before, and I'll say it again: I am willing to give you more on condition you both remove yourselves from this house. For good. Max will receive the money in due course. In fact, in one week's time.' I didn't tell him that subtracted from the sum would be Max's cut from the Shadchen.

'But he'll be in hospital then. Won't you, Max?' Max nodded and smiled.

'You must deal with the financial side of things for me, Jamie. Be my little business manager, hmm?'

I was beginning to find their mutual delight in each other's company irritating. James removed himself from my desk, giving me time to collect my crushed and crumpled papers and take them to the safety of a file. As I tried to reassemble them I could hear James' petulant voice childishly wheedling his friend into letting him visit him.

Max said he wouldn't be looking his best. He seemed to be enjoying his new avuncular role. 'I'll *make* them let you in,' he said. 'The nose was your idea, so I'll tell them you've got to come and see how it's progressing. I'll force them to let you in whenever you want to come. But Jamie . . .' and here Max raised a thin hand, '. . . no flowers please. If you bring flowers it will seem like a funeral instead of a birthday!' They laughed softly.

'Oh, you mean your *nose's* birthday!'

I began to roam my room in an unmethodical search for diversion while they continued the joke: how they should celebrate the first anniversary. By the time the discussion had reached the stage of agreeing as to the colour of the cake, I had decided that an inventory of all I possessed was a necessary precaution in view of future changes to my life. Through my thoughts on this new project came snatches of their conversation. James concentrated on talk of their new life together, while Max endeavoured to describe to his friend the effect he was aiming at with his new collection. It sounded like two simultaneous monologues. Their voices rang optimistic in my ears.

It was the silence that brought me back. Having been engaged for several minutes in examination of a dubious Cone, I became aware that they weren't speaking. When I looked up they were both staring at me. On his face James had a threatening look. Max, as usual, looked mildly disdainful.

'Well will you?' James shouted.

'Will I what?'

'What I said.'

'What did you say?'

James turned to Max and sighed. 'What did I say? You heard me, didn't you?' Max gently nodded. 'Then why didn't he? Is he getting deaf, or something?' He sprang towards me from the other side of the room to stand, arms akimbo, looking at me accusingly. Max strolled over and put a restraining hand on his arm. 'Shsh Jamie,' he said. 'He won't let you down. He'll hand it over. Won't you? While I'm in hospital, I mean.'

'The money? Oh yes. If you mean it about going into hospital.' James took a threatening step towards me. 'Of course I will. If everything goes all right between now and then . . .'

'See what I mean. He's trying to back out already,' James shouted. He lunged at my chair and kicked it across the floor. It lodged on its side against the door. He followed it. 'I'll go,' he said, 'before I do him an injury. Don't be long, Max.' With a thunderous bang the door was swung open, and closed. James was gone.

Max smiled at me. 'What a temper,' he said.

'Just like his sister's used to be. No difference. Red-heads both, don't forget . . .'

'Ah, but such a difference in their natures, don't you think?' Gently Max ambled across to the door where the chair still lay. Pushing it further to one side he opened the door quietly, smiled once again, gave a tiny wave, then went.

5

Although I find these galleries restful, there is a certain impatience in me that does not allow me to settle. I am unable to sit for long, looking at things. In me this is unusual. I who have spent my life in gazing at things feel a faint, persistent desire to continue indefinitely this somnambulistic walking which is curiously attractive. Its attraction may be because it involves only the slightest participation on my part, which can be terminated at any time, entirely by my own choice. I can sit, stand, face left or right, walk forward or back, look, see, or close my eyes. Nothing else is required of me except I wait. Nothing much interferes with the simple act of perambulation: there are few offending sounds, only the tread of visitors, the muffled rattling of the lifts, and the whine of the air-conditioning. I could wish for more air in here, but if there is any smell, it escapes my nose entirely. I am as secure as if I had never left my room.

There is the longing to have done with the waiting, but it is tempered by much uneasiness. The unexpected is foreign to my nature, and I am far from sure what the outcome of this affair will be. I am far from sure whether I shall like the outcome, whatever it is. Having trapped my specimen once, I failed to keep her. What if I fail again? Or can't do justice to my catch? I must be sure this time. The important thing to remember is that I have *acted*. There lies the cleverness: to have put into motion a chain of events which will lead me to the prize. Just as the capture of Solen siliqua depends on a well-laid plan of shifting sand and throwing salt, so does this depend on cleverness and patience. I have planned for a prey whose only difference is one of size. Or am I doubtful still of the behaviour pattern? I should really be quite sure that she will come.

He'll make sure she comes. He will come with her. I should have thought of it before. He would be a very foolish and unbusinesslike man who did not see his protegée kept her part of the bargain. It is up to him to see she fulfils every detail of the agreement. He must guide her while she signs; he must blot the paper dry. Having so much to lose by losing her, he won't dare risk a thing. I suppose then I shall see them both coming through the arch.

She may not come! If he has described me to her in too much detail, she may have guessed. Many words will have passed between them. He will have told her of my worth, and how much of a bargain she'll find me. He is sure to have stressed the security. He will surely stress her own diminishing powers of attraction. I hope he hasn't said, or implied, that there might be defects in my nature. Unless acquisitiveness be one, I have no faults. My nature is fairly simple, judged by others' standards. It is true I can be extremely cunning, but this was learned rather than inherent. I had great teachers who, with their lies and subtleties, showed me the ropes so to speak, and gave me my ideas.

Having been taught the Edwardian virtues of acquisition and retention, I grew up old-fashioned: a mild defect. I am forty-seven now but feel no different from those early years. I am aware of the passage of external time only by slight differences in my outward self: the speed with which the comb goes through my hair, slight changes in the texture of the skin and timbre of the voice, a slight alteration in the gait, and the need to sit upright when I swallow food. Who would not be aware of such alterations? I try to ignore them, giving myself more and more to perpetuating what I own. I have them still, the necklace of shells I rescued after Dorothea had thrown them all away.

'I didn't want your beastly old necklace,' she said, 'so I threw it away. What of it? You *gave* it to me, didn't you?' She was lying beside me in the sand, kicking great spouts of it into the air so that our backs were covered with fine, dry grains. 'You're miserly.' She rolled over to face the sun. 'Shall I tell you something? I saw you boring holes in them, and you didn't want to do it. You didn't even want to lose a single, tiny piece of each shell. You looked as though you were going to cry.' Leaping to her feet she ran from me, shouting, 'You're miserly,' until her voice faded and only the sound of the wind bounced off the baking rocks. She had gone to join James who was building bucket castles round a moat with great concentration. Heads bent, crouched together under the massive cliffs that sheltered them, they looked like two pink infants. James raised an arm to beckon me to join them, and I ran down the beach to splash my way through the foam and climb the breakwaters, taking the long way round, but glad to be included.

The tide had claimed yesterday's castle; we tried to build it up again, remoulding the moat's walls as the grimy water undermined them. James made a place for me beside him and we worked together in opposition to the tide and Dorothea's digging whose fury sent the flying particles in all directions. She dug like a dog, treating the sand as an enemy. Sand had clung to the fine hairs on her arms, and was on her cheeks. Like James she reddened in the sun which burned and devitalised her light hair. She swam so frequently and took so little care that the salt clung to her with the whiteness of snow. She never tired. I admired her strength and ability to battle with the sea. Neither James nor I could swim so far with such grand strokes, or when the sun went down race across the cooling rocks to be the first to the summer house. She trod the rocks like a mountain goat and laughed at us because we chose to stay on terra firma.

'She's stupid, you know,' James said. He said it quietly in my ear while Dorothea dug her way towards the incoming tide.

'Why is she stupid?' Her bathing suit was stretched across her sandy back, the shifting straps leaving lines of white whenever she moved.

'I don't know. Because she's stupid, that's all.' Dorothea had reached the water and was kneeling with her back to it, trying to defend the moat she'd dug by making a wall. Her bathing suit was beginning to sag and swell as the heavy wool got wet.

I felt James touch my arm. His hand was hot. 'She's not really stupid. I was only saying that to find out what you'd say. She's really jolly clever—for a girl.' I watched her turn and plunge into the next wave.

'Why don't you look at me when I'm talking?' James said. His temper was something to be wary of: I looked at him. 'Dorothea can see you looking at me,' he said. 'You'd better stop it. She'll be furious.'

'Why should she be furious?'

'Oh. Nothing.' I was glad when he turned over and let the gulls monopolise the afternoon. We lay on our towels and Dorothea swam. When the sea lapped at our toes we crept on our bellies towards the rocks, dragging the towels beneath us, to lie for a while on a dry patch of sand. Heat bounced from off the cliff face, as did small stones that the gulls dislodged when they landed on some precarious ledge. If I looked up I could see the bright clusters of mesembryanthemums clinging for dear life to seemingly soilless crannies. And far above the flowers, swept by the breezes, and sweeping itself across the static-seeming clouds, a patch of wiry grass, its roots exposed by the last rock fall. There was no hope of seeing Dorothea until our shadows cooled the rocks, and inland birds began to fly in noisy shoals towards the safety of the land. She had to be shouted at and threatened before she would return with a plunge and splash to the shore.

The sand soaked up the drops which fell from her as she stood over us shaking herself. Water splashed the rocks. James howled, rolling away from the shower. She dropped her towel on to my knees and said, 'Dry me.' I picked it up and began to smooth the ginger hairs, dark with water, into lines which followed the contours of her calves.

'Hurry up. It's late. Let's go back and eat.'

'Cook's day off.'

'I'm not cooking it,' James said. 'You're beastly unappreciative, both of you. Last time you left me with the washing-up. You ran down here without me.' He began to collect his things. Dorothea's legs were dry. I kissed her knee and tasted salt. She kicked me in the chest with a hard toe.

'Jamie will cook us eggs, won't you? *En cocotte?* We *love* them that way, don't we?

'Then why did you say last week they tasted dirty?' James dropped his bundle and stood up.

'It's only your *fried* eggs that taste dirty. He can't help being a dirty cook, can he? There are some famous chefs who won't allow anyone into their kitchens because of the stench.'

Dorothea had ducked. The flying sand from James' fist struck the side of my face. By the time she had leaped to the safety of a distant rock, he was ready with another handful. She watched him warily, keeping her distance, ready for a fight.

But James suddenly dropped his hand and let the sand trickle to the ground. 'I find you unutterably boring,' he said. 'So I will arise and go now and go to the house, where I will make an *omelette aux fines herbes,* for myself and my injured friend here.' He helped me elaborately to my feet, then collected his mirror, comb and towel.

'Jamie, you're beastly mean,' Dorothea called. She scrambled over the rocks, gaining the beach first, ignoring the shout behind her of 'You're the one who's mean'. She led the way up the beach to where the dunes began, while a brisk wind, which had started up, warned that the sun would be setting soon. There was only one path back: up to the knees in yellow sand, stubbing our toes on the strong grass sprouting like hair in hummocks and rising until we were at the level of the cliff tops where the rocks began again. This was our daily journey back to the summer house: off the dunes, on to the cliff top, down to the road and through the white gate to our own private path home.

Dorothea let us catch her up by the time the path was reached. There was just room enough for three of us to walk together.

'If you want to know who's really mean,' she said, 'it's him.' She jostled me with her elbow. 'Compare me with him and you'll see what I mean.'

The path was dry, due to the drought, but the grass was green enough. Butterflies were still on the flowers, and brambles grew in arcs across our way. There was a pleasant stillness in the lane which the sea wind didn't reach. Only the tops of the trees stirred lightly, bringing down to us the fragrance of lime bloom.

With her long strides Dorothea pushed our usual route turning her head to talk to us.

'I'll tell you why he's mean, Jamie, shall I?'

'Don't take any notice of her.'

'He *collects* things.'

'What things?'

'He keeps . . .' she stopped dramatically, '. . . funguses.'

'Fungi.'

'*Funguses.*' With a toss of the head she walked on. 'He has a drawer full of toadstools. And another one with *grass* in it.'

'You shouldn't have looked.'

'You told me to.'

'I didn't!'

'Oh yes you did. You told me to come up to your bedroom and look at your things. It was when your father was out on one of his strolls.' She waited for us to catch her up. James saw the squint she gave me. He smiled because he knew she was lying.

'What else does he have in his drawers?'

'You should know, Jamie. You helped me open them.' With a shout of 'Liar', James pushed her into the hedge among the nettles.

By the time she had extricated herself and removed the burrs that clung to her damp bathing suit, we were almost at the house.

'Why do you like collecting things?' James asked.

'Because the poor little dear's lonely.' Dorothea walked close to me now, rubbing her arm on mine in rhythm with her strides. The salt had made her skin abrasive. 'Why don't you try collecting girls?' she said. 'Be a terrible flirt. It's jolly good fun you know.'

'Not only is my sister stupid, but she's getting obscene.' James quickened his pace. When there was sufficient length between him and Dorothea he shouted, 'She'll be a whore by the time she's twenty!' She chased him right up to the front door where the punching, swearing, slapping and pushing caused my father to put his head out of his study window to ask for less noise.

There was a telegram waiting for James. He opened it with a show of boredom as though he was used to that sort of thing. After reading it so that we couldn't see the contents, he raced noisily upstairs to change, taking care to drop the telegram on the table in a prominent place. It lay in crumpled yellow folds, gently opening.

'He means us to read it,' Dorothea said.

'What if he should come down?'

'He won't. That's why he's making all that noise up there. He wants us to read it.'

'What about Father?'

'*He's* not likely to come down, is he? And even if he did, he wouldn't notice a thing. He hardly notices you, let alone a mingy old telegram.' With that she snatched up the yellow paper and spread it open. It said: RETURNED LONDON STOP PARIS BORING STOP COME BACK AT ONCE STOP NEED YOU STOP MAX.

'The beast. The beast, the beast!' She threw the offensive message down on the table and ran up the stairs to hide in her room.

It was I, the next morning, who helped James to pack. Dorothea stayed in her room and didn't come out to say goodbye to her brother. But I know she watched us from her window as we walked up the steep path that wound towards the road. Nothing could disguise the beacon of hair behind the lace curtain. At the top of the hill where the village road began, James asked me to lend him three pounds. He promised to let me have it back by Christmas. He was very cheerful. I heard his whistle long after he had disappeared behind the high hedges on his way to the station. The whistle of the wind accompanied me back down the long path to where the house, with its unruffled trees, lay sparkling in the summer sun.

All over the house I searched for Dorothea. No one knew where she had gone. Her bathing suit lay in sandy folds where she had left it in the bathroom. Towels were strewn on the floor. I peeped round the door of her chaotic room and trailed the upper corridors softly calling her name, so as not to disturb my father at his work. There was no sign that she had been in any of the downstairs rooms: the expected litter of books and cushions across the drawing room had been neatly cleared away: her breakfast still awaited her in a corner of the kitchen. Cook said she couldn't wait all day for people's pleasure; if I found her I was to send her back to eat like a civilised person should. It was Cook's opinion that Dorothea was sulking somewhere by the sea. So there was nothing for it but to quit the house and take myself the long lane down towards the water.

I found Dorothea beyond the sand dunes where the cliffs begin, hidden from sight by the blowing tufts of long grass. Her scarf, streaming upward at every gust of wind, signalled she was there. When she saw me she rolled over on her back, put her arms behind her head, and closed her eyes.

'Go away,' she said.

'Cook says if you want any breakfast you're to go now and have it.'

'Damn Cook.'

I sat down beside her. Below us the cliff face fell away in a ragged curve to the rock-strewn beach beneath, where the drying sand was blowing in tiny gusts, covering yesterday's flotsam. Small cloud shadows raced across the bay, losing themselves in the sparkling, white-capped water. Above us glided the gulls, lifting and dipping out of sight in the constantly changing air currents. The entire cliff face was alive with them, perching, preening and sheltering on the ledges and boulders too barren for the wild flowers. Taking care not to dislodge the unstable soil, I could sit close to the edge and see the gulls without disturbing them.

'Go away,' Dorothea said.

'No. I want to watch the black-caps down there.'

'Go and watch them somewhere else.'

'I don't want to.'

'Go and pry on someone else.'

'Cook says you're sulking.'

'What does *she* know about it? What does anyone know about it?' As she sat up the scarf ends whipped across my face, entangling me in their softness. She wrenched the scarf away, dragging my head round with it. 'I want to be alone to think.'

'Think about what?'

'You wouldn't know.'

'Oh yes I would. You didn't want Jamie to go, did you? You're sulking because he's gone and he didn't ask you to go with him.'

'He can go where he beastly wants. Don't think I'm the one to worry.' Swivelling round, she pushed me with her foot. '*You're* the one who didn't want him to go.'

'Me! I helped him pack.'

'Yes. And I've seen you before "helping him". Always together.' Her face came near to me. 'He tried to hold your hand.'

'You're lying!'

She laughed, raising her arms to pull at the errant scarf that sailed like a cloud round her head. 'Holding hands! Very sweet! I wonder what your dear father would say if he knew.'

'You're a wicked liar. It's Max he likes. He's gone to Max. That's why you're angry—because he's gone to Max.'

'Shut up!' Glaring at me she clenched her fists. 'Shut up or I'll tell him about Jamie. *And* what you tried to do to me.'

'You let me. You let me. You told me to come back when it was quiet. I had to promise. You wouldn't let me go.'

'Poor little frightened cowardy custard, wasn't he? Terrified of his father's shadow. And terrified of a girl!' The mockery was swallowed up in another sudden gust of wind.

'You're not a girl, you're a . . . a . . . Loch Ness Monster!'

She slapped me across the face with the flat of her hard hand. As my head jerked back I put out an arm to balance, and hit her on the shoulder.

'You little beast!' She dived at me and we rolled on the resilient grass, dragging at each other's clothes. With screams the gulls rose from the cliff face and spiralled away with the wind. There was nothing to do against her wiriness and weight but kick and wriggle and struggle to keep her hands from my hair and face. Then onto my knees with my shirt throttling and her hands slipping as I dived to escape her tightening hold. The sharp nails tore down my leg. Off came my shoe. She gripped my foot, twisting me over and over. Our panting drowned the sound of the gale, but not the noises coming from her throat. Once more she turned me until I was pivoted on my palms. I felt the loose soil falling away under my fingers and saw her face among the white folds of her scarf which whipped and fanned across her shoulders. 'Got you!' she said. As I flexed myself to push her off, the scarf sprang out and veiled my face, blinding me. My foot was released; I was thrown away onto the crumbling earth that yielded with a sudden rush of upward air as I fell. I rolled with the rocks in a deafening boom from ledge to disintegrating ledge down to the beach below, where I lay with the scree still scattering about me. The rocks had pinned me down. Both my legs were broken. All Dorothea did was stand and cry, 'It wasn't my fault!'

Room number six; higher and lighter than the other rooms with a box-like glass roof illuminating the whole area of floor. The diagonal pattern of the wood blocks shines in uneven patches because of the surface's irregularities. As I walk across it to the bench its yellow, almost orange, colour fades into brilliance. The walls in this room are papered an unfriendly violet, totally without gloss that appears to recede behind the paintings. A faint, stencilled fleur-de-lys is visible on the paper, but in certain shadowy parts of the room the motif disintegrates into gloom. I sit on the shining bench, feeling the curve of wood under my fingers. I am surrounded by a sea of light which sparkles and reflects off every surface in view. The floor shines yellow; picture frames give off gold glitterings in their carving. The frames are whorled and flowered; crisply three dimensional, their inner edges lined in black like so many ancient funeral cards. Beside it each picture has its own dark shadow. The paintings in this room give off their own individual light—they are Georgian men and women exposing their love of finery in a welter of chiaroscuro. They shimmer in their clothes, roundly they stretch the satins and lace in healthy amplitude, their well-fed faces expanded by their curling wigs. They stand, not against flat masses of plain paint on which are inscribed their names, but against fine country scenes of trees and cultivated lands in which stand their houses. Here they have absolute control, forming a closed society into which no intrusion is allowed. The very similarity of their faces precludes familiarity. Each has a name, identically inscribed on a gold plate beneath his frame, which has to be approached and read with care before the anonymity explodes in a resounding title.

A Fourth Earl this one, securely wrapped in his coat of velvet and braid; a flat blue ribbon across his chest. He looks at me through the safety of a haze of varnish and glass, his decorations diminishing as I pass on. Another pair of eyes takes up the gaze, those of a woman who, judging by the magnificence of the canvas, must surely have been royal. She is gigantic, towering over me like a great green bell out of which the tiny head rises like a handle. Her face has a clouded look, powdered over like the wig she wears: all traces of her character have been lightly dusted over leaving the satin dress as foremost evidence of her glory. I cannot look up at her face for long; she is too high; it is to the winking, gleaming facets of the skirt that the eye is drawn, to the sumptuous carelessness of gems scattered about her like childish toys. Through the pearly green folds my face peeps out until I side-step, sending my small reflection into the next pair of staring eyes. Strange how, in Room Six, not one of the sitters is looking to right or left. They seem to be defiant looks with no gentleness in them, and they stare straight ahead with the aloofness one expects from the illiberal. All these eyes are weather eyes permanently on the look-out for the anticipated deception. On all sides I am hemmed in by these people; I bump into them if I cross the floor. Decapitated heads of marble and of clay squat under glass, the hollowed mineral eyes as distrustful as the painted ones. The man in the clay cap grins with split mouth and wrinkled lids. The skin is pitted, lined and veined, as though, if I could put out my hand to touch the realistic surface, it would pulsate. There is the chance that he is made of wax, which would melt under the heat of my hand. Such perfection would surely not be made of anything as transitory as wax whose use, for me, is limited to covering spires and spurs before immersion in the nitric acid. I hate to think what would be revealed underneath his epidermis.

It is hot in here. Once again I smooth my hair and press my finger to my ears to rid myself of the rushing noises. In the distance doors bang, footsteps and voices mingle in the hall. There is an air of excitement in here that makes me rise to search for room, and air. The people close in, pushing together, packing me into a space so small that I cannot see the floor. I have lost the ability to judge the distance between me and the crowds coming in under the arch. Against the dark wall rises James' head, shining pale and ginger. His pose is formal; between his fingers he holds a Tudor rose, delicately.

It is too hot in here. There are too many people for the size of the drawing room. I should have been at the door to welcome them, but with each new batch I was pressed further and further into the centre towards the supper table, to be buffeted and by-passed by the seekers after food and drink. Whether or not music is still playing is doubtful; laughter and conversations drown any lesser sounds. I hear no apologies for prodding elbows and stabbing toes, nor for the contents of glasses spilled on my suit. It is easier to let myself be manipulated by the crowd; to smile at the passing mouth, shake the high-held hand, clink mine to the outstretched convivial glass, and shout an answer to the questioner already out of ear shot. Grey smoke hangs above our heads, faintly whirling as it sucks upwards into the light shade then across the ceiling, to flow down again in whiter wisps over our heads. The jostling which keeps me on the move precludes the possibility of suffocation from smoke and overwhelming mixtures of cosmetics. There is no danger even of being set on fire by a clumsy cigarette, since it would surely be doused by such frequent splashes of alcohol. I am beached by the shoal among the weaker members, or those replete enough to want a general view. By holding close to the wall, some movement round the room is possible. I creep past the bare backs of startled ladies, climb over the knees of resting gentlemen, tread glass into the carpet and help too vigorous a dancer to her feet, all the while keeping my eyes on the head of Max between the revellers. He is at his amusing best—the centre of a group forced to keep their distance by the cigarette which he holds between finger and thumb and rotates widely as he speaks. I hear Dorothea's strident laugh and see her satin redness and Max's hand descend on to her shoulder. I am blocked from sight of them as someone lifts her billowing dress and the heads close in. There is another burst of laughter. Applause breaks out as the women spin round, raising their arms above their heads. It is difficult to decide whether they are dancing. Behind the moving heads I see Dorothea bounce, coming and going in red fragments between the black shoulders. Her unmistakeable laugh—something like a throaty cough—sunders immediate conversations. Only by constant shifting can I make out whether she and Max are in close contact. She wears his dress, to celebrate his first success.

A path is possible between the furniture if it is treated like an obstacle course. Collisions with extended legs are unavoidable, the wrinkled carpet traps my feet in its folds, several ladies wish suddenly to have me on their laps. I must choose a spot to stand where the crockery isn't ankle high, and *canapés* are less profusely scattered on the floor. The greedy are still eating; spearing the last of the silverskins, stuffing olives, scraping the last of the cheesecake from their lapels while their eyes rove the cluttered tables for undetected titbits. Some find time to talk to me about the pleasures of the night. They mutter with smiles that it's been a long time since such a beanfeast as this was theirs. I am told where to look for talent. A voice in my ear asks me whether I design too. I shake my head. Then maybe I'm a cutter. Or do I buy? At the last shake he says, 'Oh. Just another friend of Max's, eh?'

'Just another one.'

Passing guests make the task of shaking hands more hazardous. We manage by pressing so close that our glasses imprint their shapes on our shirt fronts.

'Can't recollect meeting you before. Quite a party, this, eh? Trust Max to see the liquor flows. Ten to one he gets it wholesale!' The remark is breathed into my face with a sweet gin smell. From his veined eyes I would guess he has drunk too much. Whichever way I turn my head I cannot escape his glassy eye. He doesn't want to lose me yet.

'Lovely place this. Lovely furniture ... really lovely. Taking some knocks though. Long time to get over a do like this.' A scuffle going on beside us underlined his statement: there was a brief battle for possession of a settee cushion before the collapse of both parties on to the floor.

'Must have cost a pretty penny.' He seems not to have noticed that the couple beneath our feet are seriously engaged in removing each other's clothes.

'Somebody's got the wherewithal. Wouldn't mind betting Max didn't pay for this. Not that I hold anything against him, mind ... Great fellow. Done me some favours.'

I hear Dorothea's laugh. The couple have gone from our feet to seclusion behind the settee. Their place has been taken by a lurching lady in velvet.

'Know what he did?'

'No.' The lady in velvet has put her arm through mine. She is leaning on me and digging her chin into my shoulder. Her grip is quite tight.

'Had my eye on his receptionist. Lovely piece. Had what it takes, if you get my meaning ...' The lady has decided to enfold me. With one hand she ruffles my hair without releasing her steely hold. She is nibbling at my ear lobe, making it difficult for me to follow the course of the receptionist's fate.

'... so it was settled. Just like that! For free!'

I am being told what a little darling I am. Fingers thread my hair and poke between my collar. The velvet lady cannot be shaken off: after an experimental push I find she is too pneumatic to be further handled. She breathes warmly along my cheek.

'Get off you bitch! I'm talking to my friend here.' He pushes her away from me, and she staggers with a clatter of pearls into the arms of a group of welcoming gentlemen.

'As I was saying ...' From his pocket he removes a bottle from which he fills his glass. This time it is whisky. 'Ah! Well of course, I had my suspicions. Wouldn't be surprised if she was giving him trouble. Would you? A great one for keeping his nose clean.' Faint trombone notes can be heard above the general din. A tray of tinkling glasses is handed precariously above the heads of the swaying dancers.

'Great man though—Max.' He stares over my shoulder. 'Can't mistake him. Like a bean pole. Wouldn't look at him twice myself, but he stirs them you know. Oh yes, he stirs them.' He chuckles into his glass. 'They tell me he's able. Good designer too. Cuts his own patterns. I've seen him at it at twelve o'clock, still working.' He leaned forward confidentially. 'Burning the midnight oil.'

We are forced closer by a press of people pushing past to join their friends. Coarse hair brushes my face. Now we stand shoulder to shoulder, looking across the room.

The crowd under the light has broken up. Many are still dancing, while others have sunk to the floor or spread themselves on the furniture. I am reminded of Gaulli. Max and Dorothea are going to stand by the fireplace. They have their backs to us, looking up at a picture on the wall.

'He's got a muscular one, hasn't he? Think she was a boy from the back, wouldn't you? Tastes certainly differ, don't they? Don't suppose she's as much trouble as his other . . .'

'What other?'

Suddenly he has turned his head and is staring at me hard. The nearness of his face makes nonsense of the focus: one eye is in the middle of his forehead, the other, against his nose, is losing itself. As I force myself backward I see his hand waving above my head, trying to indicate that there is someone standing behind me.

I back into James whose voice pipes in my ear. He holds me by the elbow. My drunken friend has faded away.

'Hello, hello! A lot of shits here tonight, aren't there?' He too is holding a glass. 'What made you get this crowd?'

'Dorothea.' I ascertain whether she and Max are still in view. They aren't.

'What's the uniform for, James?'

'I have yet to find one of your jokes funny. This is a dinner jacket. Didn't want to disgrace anyone. At work I wear tails.'

'Am I to gather that you've been promoted?'

'I'm no longer a waiter, if that's what you mean, you sarcastic bastard.'

'Does Max know you've given up servility?'

'Not unless you told him.' We both look round the room. There is still no sign of them. '*She* wouldn't tell him. Got it in for me, she has.' He empties his glass at a gulp and lurches to where a bottle shows signs of liquid. I help him to unstopper it.

'*Why* has she got it in for me?' Systematically he begins to look round the room again. Someone has turned off the central light. I watch his white lashes flicker as he tries to penetrate the gloomier corners where conversation has ceased. Along each wall he searches, studying every person he can make out, especially the more occupied ones. 'Nice place this, now you've done it up. Clever, the colour scheme. I like the furniture too. There's some really lousy stuff in the shops. You wouldn't think the war'd been over five years, would you?'

He doesn't expect an answer. He is still searching the room, chin up, bulbous nose shining in the heat. He smells faintly of perfume, strongly of drink. There is Dorothea's shout, and the high laugh of Max. James swings round and stands on tip toe. From the back he resembles his sister.

He cannot see them. Although the crowd has thinned, the few that are still dancing intervene between him and the back of the room. There has been a general sinking to the floor, probably in search of air as much as privacy, since the ceiling is no longer visible through the fumes. The crowd has thinned. People have vanished through to the dining room and kitchens. Some have gone to try their luck upstairs, others under the arch. They must have tried the doors and found them locked. Max and Dorothea have disappeared completely.

'Let's go and sit down,' James says. 'I'll get a bottle, then we'll go and sit down.' He ploughs across the room ignoring curses and clutching hands, sorting through the bottles he finds, in search of a full one. When he has found it he raises it on high for me to see, nods towards the hall door, and beckons me to make my way towards it.

We meet in the dark hall and go under the arch together. Earlier tonight I locked the doors of rooms where guests would be unwelcome. The keys are in my pocket. While I fumble for the keyhole James keeps his hand on my shoulder, waiting for me to guide him into the dark room. Once inside the door is re-locked and we stand in the peaceful, empty room in which the only light is that of the pale moon faintly illuminating the floor and walls, and lightly touching our faces. In here it is comparatively cool.

'Must sit down,' James mumbles. I fetch two chairs and help him into one of them, clutching his glass and bottle. He pours himself another drink. 'Got to help,' he says.

'What is it you want me to say to you? You have always expected too much of me, James. I'm not your answer.'

'Control her. Con-trol . . . her. You can do it. Done it before. You married her.' Our voices sound loud against the faint cries and footsteps that come and go outside the door.

'She needed security. You know your sister as well as I do. With her and me it's only the money.'

'If you believed that you wouldn't be in this house now. You're like a man with a death wish. Wish for it long enough and it'll happen. Control her, I say. Control her.'

There is a banging on the door and muffled shouting, then whoever it was goes away.

'You're right, of course. The money hardly comes into it. She stays because she needs me. Forgive the banality of the expression, but she requires protection.'

'And what do *you* need, hmm? Her. Right?' He has swallowed his drink and is pouring himself another. He draws his chair closer. 'Well, I'll tell you this.' I watch his throat as he raises his head to pour the liquid down. 'It's Max that needs protection. Can't you see he doesn't really want her? He hates her. I know.' James taps his head. 'I know. Makes her dress like a tart in stupid clothes his clients won't buy. You buy 'em, don't you?' Although his glass isn't empty, he refills it and takes another gulp. 'You buy 'em.' He taps me playfully on the shoulder with his glass. A stain of alcohol spreads rapidly on the floor.

The glass is raised again, and with a wave of his arms he slops its contents in bright moonlit beads over my head. His blink rate has increased.

'This place is too big for you.' Now he scans the cupboards and walls, stopping short at the sight of the window cord looped against the wall above my desk. 'Get kids. Get kids to fill it. Fill all these rooms with little kids. Give me one room upstairs, and fill all the rest with . . .' He swallows the residue of his drink, sets the glass down carefully, and carefully gets to his feet. 'What's this window for?'

'To let light in.'

'Get funny and I'll thump you.'

He measures the distance between himself and the window before attempting the short walk. Two steps bring him beneath it. He climbs warily on to my desk and stands up. It is easy for him to lift his arms to grasp the circular window ledge. With a grunt he raises himself until his chin is on the level of the ledge. His shirt cuffs gleam white like beacons. Another grunt as he lowers himself to the desk again.

'Little courtyard. Moonlight on a little courtyard.' His face becomes cunning. 'Bet you didn't know about the room, though.' I catch him as he flops off the desk and sinks to the floor, still clutching his glass. 'Room with people out there.' He closes his eyes and rolls the glass across his forehead. 'Somebody in a room out there,' he mumbles. 'Somebody in dark room . . .' He lets me lean him gently against the table leg and place his hands on either side of him in case he falls. His head has flopped on to his chest.

As carefully as I can I remove my keys from my pocket and select the one that fits the largest cabinet. The moonlight is strong enough for me to find what I want and to check that the camera is set. Distance will have to be guessed at, so will the exposure. My guess is that five seconds will suffice if my subjects are where I imagine them. James shifts at the noise of the cupboard closing, but when I creep across the room and open the hall door, he makes no further sound. As a precaution I lock him in.

Both Dorothea and I possess a key to our bedroom. Tonight I saw her put it into her handbag. 'I may want to powder my nose,' she said. Our door is locked, as I guessed it would be. From the lounge come the faint sounds of laughter and music, enough to drown the scrape of the key being slowly inserted in the lock. It makes no sound as it turns. The handle gives easily under slight pressure, and I open the door half an inch. Now the only risk is a sudden burst of festivity that would startle them or, worse still, someone coming suddenly upon me in the hall with my ear to the black crack of my own bedroom door. I wait and listen, a small pulse beating in my ears.

I hear a moaning like the sea in flood; a whining like a seal; a sucking, sighing, groaning, and in between, the thin music of the distant party forming the accompaniment. Fabric is being moved, being crushed, and rustling, being pulled, and dropping. There are sighs and murmurs so low that they become the antiphon to the remote psalm. As I put my shoulder to the door jamb I hear them louder, the groans and snorts, the growls and moans. Dorothea is a noisy lover. All I have to do is move fractionally to the right and edge my way inside. A certain amount of moon shines mildly into the centre of the room, hardly lighting my subjects adequately, but now they barely move. Distance has to be guessed, and the camera held against my cheek steadily for five long seconds. Only the whine of a far off trombone deadens the click as I squeeze the release. There is the sibilance of a whisper. Max has turned his head. He cannot see me in such shadows, for without his glasses he is blind.

The same caution must be employed in removing myself from the room. Backwards I sidle out, gently dropping the handle so that the door closes without a sound. Then the key into the lock once more, softly turned to shut them safely in.

James is still where I left him, slumped against the table leg, but his eyes are open. He watches me go over to the cabinet and lock away the camera. He sees the bunch of keys that I pocket.

'Where have you been?'

'Doing my duty as a host. How do you feel?'

'Keys. You had keys in your hand.' With the help of a chair he drags himself to his feet. The once-neat suit is crumpled, the cuffs hang down over his huge hands with their ridiculous rings. In the moonlight his face is colourless. Suddenly he staggers towards me and puts a heavy arm around my shoulders. His bulk is stifling.

'You took a key,' he says.

'The key to this door.'

We stagger together as he shakes his head. 'No, no, no. Another key. Key to another room.' Together we roll across the room towards the door before he regains his balance sufficiently to grab at my pocket. I am out and into the hall with James behind me, shouting:

'Give it here. The key. Give it here.'

The lounge is like a battlefield: bodies lie stretched on every available piece of furniture; some are on the floor, swathed in the gathered carpet. Smoke still hangs heavy in the room, encircling the fallen chairs, floating in wisps above the heads of a couple still clinging close and rocking in time to nonexistent music. The gramophone needle scrapes a monotonous rhythm on the centre of a forgotten record. There is a whispering stillness broken by James' entry. Cursing, he climbs across the barrier of legs, trying to reach me. Someone tells him to shut his face. 'And the door...' another calls. With my back to the wall I watch him go through the guests like an obstacle racer to the safety of the mantlepiece. The clinging dancers ignore him as he pushes past to the marble anchorage. He scans the room. As I edge my way along the wall to reach the kitchen door, he sees me.

His face is very red. 'I wanted it,' he says. There are tears in his eyes not copious enough to spill over. 'You wouldn't give it to me.' He has his arms along the length of the mantelpiece and he watches me move slowly towards the door. When my hand is on the knob he says, 'You wouldn't let me see them.' From his pocket he drags a handkerchief to wipe his face.

'I'll kill her. I'll kill her. You know that, don't you?' His nods answer his own question. 'You stopped me doing it.' Briefly one or two interested heads are raised, but his remarks are only audible at close quarters. The party has better things to do than try to listen to the ramblings of a drunken man. He talks from bravado, to relieve his sufferings, not believing his own words.

'She's a whore. Told you a long time ago ... Wouldn't believe me then. Won't now. Now it's too late. You stopped me getting her, didn't you? Are you happy?' Several people answer 'yes'. He drops his arms and stands alone, feet straddling the rug. He manages a step in my direction.

'Give it to me!' As he lunges at me a faint cheer echoes round the room. I jump to catch him before he strikes his head on a table where glasses lie broken. He thumps my shoulder with a slow moving fist and lets me pull him to a chair. The rest of the room subsides.

I manage the unpleasant task of feeling his forehead and find his temperature is high. His hair lies in sticky curls along his forehead. 'I want water,' he says. But before I can rise to go into the kitchen he has found his own. 'This'll do.' Beside him on the table is a vase where a bunch of flowers have managed to hold their own. He removes the bunch and drinks the greenish water. The flowers drop from his hand one by one, until he is left holding a single flower delicately by its stalk.

It was hot in there. Dorothea said so earlier this evening. 'Will it be too hot in the drawing room?' she said. 'There may be quite a crush. I hope so anyway.' Already she has spent the best part of an hour putting on her make-up. Seated at her dressing table she was busily disguising her neck under a bright layer of pink powder. The colour extended down her neck and on to her chest. The straps of her dress were covered in powder. It was Max's dress, designed especially to celebrate his first big collection. Dorothea was very proud to wear the swathed and ruched monstrosity that swirled about her like a lampshade. She had painted her nails to match it, so that when she waved her hands, it looked as though dismembered fractions of her dress were flying in the air.

'I do hope everybody comes,' she said. 'Parties can be ghastly if the rooms are half empty, can't they?'

I told her I didn't know, since this was my first experience of this kind of thing.

'Come, come,' she said. 'Surely you can remember before the war, when your father held so many here.'

'But they were formal affairs, full of etiquette and gallantry. From what you've told me of Max's do's, this one is liable to be more of a bun fight.'

She turned on me coldly. 'How on earth did you form *that* opinion? You make it sound as though Max is always having fearful free-for-alls. When did he last have a party?'

'Never, as far as I know.'

'There you are then!'

'He has always managed to see that other people throw them for him. Like this one.'

She continued to apply powder, shaking it over her freckled arms as though she were fish and chips. Her mood was optimistic. She laughed at me.

'Well, it's the first time we've given a party for him, isn't it? It's the first time we've given a party for anyone!'

'It will probably be the last.'

She ignored me. Having completed her face to her satisfaction, she attended to her hair; then to her stockings, roughly pulling the fragile material over her muscular legs. I watched her progress standing up, having been warned not to destroy the illusion of middle-class urbanity before the first guests arrived. Dorothea herself tied my tie and straightened my lapels. She told me I looked fine. When I put my hands round her waist she twisted free, leaving the sensation of something rigid, shiny, under my palms. It was a red silk dress.

The ability to reproduce exactly the quality of fabrics is one that few artists possess. Strolling past these paintings, in all of which there has been some attempt to describe what the sitters wear, I have the distinct impression that they have failed. While the faces look out with such a degree of realism that one can believe they continue to breathe and grow, there is no such conviction that the clothes have anything more than two dimensions. Few can adequately suggest the depth and darkness of velvet, or point the constellations in a mass of corrugated silk. Many have tried: as I pass each painting I score off the attempts to fool the viewer that here is truly the genuine thing. But if I put my sleeve against the glass, the painted one behind it becomes ridiculous. How can these dabs of paint and streaks of varnish piled pell-mell be anything but forgeries? I would never think of copying something in paint if I wanted the truth of it. All I would have to do is make sure my camera was loaded. It is easy to stand on a desk, on a pile of books, resting easily on a window ledge with the camera at my elbow. One can stand for hours in that position without undue strain, given practice.

Max went into the room first. I heard his footsteps as he descended the stairs and crossed the hall. I listened for the movement that indicated his arrival at the front door. But the steps had stopped at the door of the bedroom. I heard him enter.

The asset of being an organised man came home to me that day as I unlocked my photographic cupboard. It occurred to me that my continual state of readiness could account for much of my success as a collector. My equipment was always to hand in tip top working order; so were my books—several volumes of A *Voyage to Madeira*—carefully selected to give me maximum security of balance when standing on the heights of my somewhat fragile desk. They never let me down. An astute observer may have seen traces of dust on the upper one and the vague imprint of my shoe; nothing more. If one had looked closely at the wall there might have been a few hand prints discernible directly underneath the window frame; but nothing else. There was nothing to show how I could climb so high without risk to wind and limb, and stay there happily, (almost in a state of trance) whiling away the hours at my favourite pastime.

Max was searching for something. He had already opened several drawers and peered into the wardrobe by the time I recovered him. The wardrobe mirror flashed as he opened it, sending his back reflection to me almost as clearly as if I was standing in the room. I could almost disbelieve the existence of two layers of glass between us. The recent snow had cleared the bedroom window panes, giving me an image crystal clear. Snow still lined the courtyard in a smooth sweep of white. Some had fallen off the roof to deepen that already there and hide the skeletal remains of an erstwhile folly. Ice had weighed down what was left of the dead tree with its roots in cement so that I could see the window clearly with its ledge of undulating white.

Garments were flung in all directions as Max searched the wardrobe. He didn't seem to care what happened to Dorothea's clothes. He trod on them as he crossed the room to try his luck at her dressing table. There was no careful putting back of what he disturbed: in turn he opened each drawer, raking out stockings, scarves, gloves like a conjuror in a frenzy. He left them where they fell. He scratched his head, carefully smoothing the patch he'd disturbed. Where to try next? Ah, the bed! But the flourish of the counterpane revealed only Dorothea's nightdress. He searched the bed thoroughly, tossing off the pillows, putting his head inside the blankets to burrow further for the mysterious something. Then underneath the bed with a dive that lost him from my sight. What he wanted wasn't to be found below; all that he emerged with were his spectacles which he replaced on his nose. He spent several seconds adjusting them. Both of us ducked as the doorbell rang.

Max let James in by the front door. I heard the boisterous conversation as they walked along the hall. Their mouths were still moving as they entered the bedroom together, Max brushing snow from James' shoulders. Then they embraced and parted. One of them closed the door. Lucky that without the second source of light I could still see so clearly. Snow is a wonderful reflector. The state of the bedroom was discussed with many elaborate gestures from Max: a closer look at his face showed he didn't care. James was amused by the arm-waving; he laughed with abandon, throwing himself on the bed to curl up with mirth. This seemed to excite Max to furious demonstration. He whirled about the room picking up the trampled clothes and tossing them into the air. I felt, rather than heard, the high-pitched laughter and hilarity. They were too occupied to notice me. James had his back to the window, stilling the fear that he might have remembered the outlook from my room, and turned to investigate. Max was keeping him totally entertained; surpassing himself with an exhibition of skittish glee at odds with his usual superior ennui. Not that he was often to be seen in that room. His trips downstairs to Dorothea had become so infrequent that I had almost given up hopes of capturing him there again. His non-appearances had been the cause of many fruitless hours at my post: they had been the start of Dorothea's sleeplessness.

Now he was at the wardrobe, diving further into its recesses to pull out armloads of clothes with which he staggered in an exaggerated roll towards his friend. James sprang up to help him with the pile; to spread the haul where they could examine it. They held up garments which hadn't seen the light for many years. I thought I glimpsed the dress she wore the day she said she'd marry me. I recognised her wedding gown. Snatching it from Max's hand, James tossed it into a corner with assistance from his foot. One by one they sorted through Dorothea's things, laughing over each discovery. James held against his chest a dress of shining red and gold, its sequined scales shimmering with the same intensity as on the day Max had made it for her. Out came each horror of his drawing board, each beautifully retaining its terrible splendour. The garment was inspected, laughed over, and thrown down upon the crowded floor. Their jackets joined the pile. Max was taking off his tie and shirt. With great speed they were both undressing.

I raised the lens to my eye in time to see Max struggling into a purple dress whose train ensnared his ankles. James helped him with the fastenings and stood back in admiration to see the preening and the pirouettes. The dress hung limply on Max's tall form, giving him the sad dignity of a flamingo lost in a Northern climate. He tossed his head and pulled at the long skirt, apeing the careful self-consciousness of one of his own models. There was a moment's consideration before the wardrobe mirror, then the decision that an improvement would be made by the removal of his vest. James thought so too. As an afterthought he removed Max's glasses and threw round his shoulders a feather boa. They applauded the effect. It was difficult to keep them both in view while they searched about on the floor for something suitable for James. At last he rose from the debris holding up Dorothea's party dress, shaking the ruched skirt in delighted repugnance. Off came his vest too before he raised the great lampshade up over his head and belly-danced into it. There was a laughing struggle with the zip, and a disappointed abandoning of the idea that they could fasten it. James was too broad for the stretching silk. I saw the fibres straining across his freckled chest, threatening to split under his bare armpits. Eleven years is too long for there not to be deterioration. James was pleased with the dress's effect, not seeming to mind the cutting shoulder straps and sagging bosom. He experimented with a waltz, in which Max joined to the best of his ability, hampered as he was by the clinging skirt. Progress was small, since at every turn they had to kick their ankles free of the strewn floor. Neither noticed the incongruity of thick socks and laced shoes protruding from the delicate gowns. The dance had claimed them. With brawny arms flexed, James somehow achieved the swoop and sway of an ecstatic girl with music in her soul. They spun and twirled in their restricted circles with a perfection of rhythm that made me suppose they must be singing. I caught them like that in an action shot of splendid vitality. Max has his eyes closed, his head thrown back in a smile of sheer pleasure. His high-bridged nose curves over the fluttering feathers; he is a very gay bird indeed, caught at the height of his dance of courtship. I consider I did justice to their performance, catching the atmosphere of gaiety without a trace of blur; not erring on the side of graininess for the sake of extra detail. As it is the photograph pleases by its unaffected rendering of a scene with all the magic of a Degas, yet with all the accuracy that's lacking in a painting. Movement is the hardest to retain.

They tired eventually of spinning round, and clung together momentarily, heads bent, to catch their breath. They relaxed with happy smiles to gaze with satisfaction at the ruins of the room. A sudden fall of snow from off the roof tumbled down into the courtyard, causing me to duck. The snow had settled by the time I dared to rise again, but Max and James had hardly moved. A sort of torpor settled over them. They looked about to disappear under the mountains of their own making. Max went over to the dressing table to rummage there, half obliterated by the garments which he tossed like tissue paper over his shoulder. James stood watching, hand on hip, looking in repose far too like his sister. What Max was looking for he found underneath a pile of Dorothea's underwear. With red face and ruffled hair he emerged holding up a pair of dim pink corsets in his hand. James ducked as he whirled them over his head by the strings, then made a dive to grab them. A tug of war began in which Max, with a sudden sharp pull, became the victor, sending James staggering back to fall on the bed. Neither heard the sharp bang of the front door closing: certainly their mouths were open wide as if they were roaring with laughter. Max had the corsets held against his front when he heard the footsteps coming down the hall.

As the bedroom door opened I got them in my sights—two rigidly defined figures, exotic fritillary pinned forever at the moment of their trapping. Dorothea stands just inside the door, her hand raised clear of the handle. It was a pity I couldn't have waited another second to record the full expression of shock on her face. There was no time to prepare the shot; no time at all to get my subjects nicely placed within my frame. All I could do was squeeze the release and slowly lower my head from sight. My last brief look disclosed nothing beyond the pale ornamented figure of James, bleakly staring out into the ice-bound courtyard.

6

There is a roaring in this room. It sounds like generators. It makes me think I have faulty hearing. I press my ears with both fingers, but the noise continues. It is best, when beset by noise, to ignore it, concentrating on the other faculties. Sight is my best bet: mine is well-developed and in good working order, despite the fact that there is continual deterioration of the eyes from the age of twenty-five. I am good at looking: I can always discover the truth of things after others have rejected what they saw as useless. Perhaps they see the truth as good for nothing. Am I the only one who cherishes it? Am I the only one who kills for it? When grappling with the living shell I feel only elation at the thought that I'm about to end the life of its inhabitant. I perform the ritual lovingly, singing the words 'chloride of sulphate of magnesia' as others would their prayers; stirring the crystals into the salt water like a thaumaturgist. Slowly the animals expand and stupefy, and with a shout of jubilation I plunge them into alcohol to kill them. It is so pleasant and so easy to give permanence to something greatly valued.

If I turn I can see, under the arch behind me, the rooms through which I have come. And still no one waits for me in the room marked Seven. I feel no warning surge of excitement to tell me she may be coming through this maze. How long I have waited now I don't know: it is impossible to tell what time it is by the filtering light. My watch has stopped, as it often does when I deliberately forget to wind it. The ticking on my wrist is far too persistent a reminder of how much further I have to go in the eternal battle. I know it is still afternoon: there are no signs of the extra activity that happens with the ringing of the closing bell, when agitated attendants spring from nowhere to herd visitors towards the exits.

People are still walking unmolested in and out of these rooms as though the afternoon is only half-way gone. They wander past me sitting here, not knowing that I see them in the picture that serves me for my present mirror. The post is not completely satisfactory.

I cannot catch a perfect image of what goes on behind: by a trick of light the glass is giving me a double view of things. To check my facts I would have to turn; yet if I turned would I be sure that what I saw was any less or more truthful than what is in front of me now? There is an arch at about thirty yards' distance, with lines of seeming movement at its edges. Do I see one arch, or hundreds? And which is the real one? The picture frames repeat themselves in one continuous pattern right along the wall. Everything is affected by my view of it in this black mirror: everything is doubled, tripled, blurred at the edges, so that such solid things as chairs and tables have the disturbing quality of paintings by the Vorticists. This shadowy twinning confuses me. When I hear steps behind me I think I hear an army on the move. I watch it coming down the boards waving duplicated arms, legs precisely following their neighbours'. Once out of range of my pale reflector the army becomes two people who wander down the room in casual irregularity, heading for the ornamental stair.

The shadowy figure in front of me shifts. I raise my hand. He raises his. I rise and so does he. We're walking towards each other, and towards the people in the painting. There are three of them there, sitting round a table and I am standing between them, making my presence felt. I cut through the folds of the tablecloth, a giant among pygmies. They look down at the cloth, on the pieces of paper mathematically arranged. I want them to know that this shadowy me, so vaguely glimpsed in triplicate, is coming to join them. There must be a way in which I can cut through the deceptive lines that separate us, and get to the truth.

She raises her head when she hears me cross the floor. James looks up and grins. Dorothea looks at Max, but he is watching me come, carrying the parcel. For an instant I see his eyes as the light goes from his lenses. They crease and grow small: he smiles and raises his brows.

'Well, well, well! Look who's here. Do you come bearing gifts? Or has there been a fire?'

The others laugh.

'Must have been a fire,' James says, 'to get him out into foreign parts!'

The ribaldry was to be expected. Ignoring it I go to Dorothea whose back is turned to me.

'Had an accident with a Bunsen burner, then? Is the precious room in flames?' Max is mildly amused. 'He's carrying all he could save from the priceless collection in a tiny paper parcel!'

Dorothea half turns and smiles. James bangs the table with his palm, bouncing the breakfast crumbs. There is nothing else left on the cloth. I place the parcel in front of Dorothea. Her cold hand touches mine. She has old hands with swollen veins. I have come to give her her birthday present.

'How old are you today, Dee?' James asks.

She looks at Max quickly but his face is serious. James is grinning at him across the table. They watch her grapple with the knotted string and exchange glances.

'She's got a lovely birthday gift!' Dorothea doesn't notice the way in which James is turning his wrist to look at the bracelet round it. The silver plate attached to the huge links reflects the morning light. It has been engraved, but from where I stand it is impossible to read the words. He is displaying the bracelet for Max's benefit, but Max shakes his head and looks away.

Dorothea has removed the layer of brown paper. Now she is unfolding the sheets of tissue and throwing them in balls on to the floor. The card marked 'Happy Birthday' joins them on the floor. It doesn't interest me: many years have passed since I made the mistake of writing anything on it but the greeting. She mutters 'Well, well' and 'He never forgets' as she progresses.

'How old are we today, Dee?' Max is grinning.

'Ask James,' she says. 'He'll be able to tell you.' She has arrived at the box. The lid is removed. As the first wad of notes is taken from its wrapping she says, 'Well, you *have* done me proud this year.' Her fingers find the second wad. She raises it, feels its weight then tosses it on to the tablecloth. 'This isn't one of your jokes, is it?'

I wait while she probes deeper into the box, bringing out the fat wads of notes, each bound by a paper ribbon. I walk round the table to watch her face. She doesn't know whether to smile or frown.

'It's not a joke, Dorothea. It's real enough. I had it made up in bundles of twenty-five, so there's no need to count it. There are thirty bundles in all.'

With whistles and gasps Max and James each take a wad and riffle it. Then they begin to count in earnest, while Dorothea stares at me. James is excited by the sight of so much money. He piles the wads like children's bricks, laughing boisterously. It pleased him to run his hands across their sharp corners and feel with his thumb each note he counts.

'You can take my word for it—there are seven hundred and fifty in all.'

For Max the game has already ceased. He looks at me warily, his usual expression of disdain softened into one of worry.

'What the hell are you playing at?'

'Playing at? I've brought Dorothea the usual birthday gift, that's all.'

'Some gift!' James is still fingering the money, re-arranging it in front of himself in balanced rows, one wad on top of another like a pierced wall. Dorothea is waiting for Max to say what he thinks.

'What's it for?'

'For her to have some money of her own.'

'But why so bloody much? Why didn't you buy her the fur, or whatever it is she wants? This is childish. Bloody bad taste.'

Dorothea's pale eyes are still on Max. The strong light flooding in from the garden renders her face heavy and colourless, increasing the lines of age, revealing the sheath of fine hair with which her skin is covered.

'Is it bad taste to give someone a present on their birthday?' she asks, sliding her fingers across the cloth to touch his arm.

He shifts it away before she can get at him. 'For God's sake! You're over twenty-one, my dear,' James giggles. 'Or did you ask him for it?'

'I have never asked him for anything. Ever.'

He ignores her. 'What's wrong with the usual cheque? This sort of thing is pure histrionics.'

'It's just money—but real money, that you can touch and feel. I wanted her to get the feel of real money. Her bank account is something over which she seems to have lost control.'

'Guesswork! Pure guesswork. You shouldn't have given one to her in the first place. You knew she'd squander it.'

'And now I'm giving her another chance.'

Max flicks the piles of notes with his hand, causing them to topple. James carefully retrieves his bricks and begins to build his wall again. 'Pity there aren't more of them,' he says. 'Damn good for playing with. Wasn't it a bit mean not to make it the round thousand?' Always he looks to Max for applause.

'At least someone remembered my birthday.' Dorothea has a mournful dignity in her reproach.

'Meaning me, of course.' Max sighs. 'Some people have other things to think about. If you feel *that* badly I'll give you a cheque tomorrow. How about that, hmm?'

The morning sun now fully floods the room with a yellow brilliance that surely cannot last. It sends sharp shadows across the table and bounces off the metal links around James' wrist. His wall is almost completed now.

'Why didn't you give her the round thousand?' he asks. 'After all she is your wife.'

'Shut up, James.' Dorothea blinks quickly at him. She sees the brilliant bracelet. 'Did you get a present today?'

'Of course. I do have a few friends, you know. Want to see the hallmark? It's silver.' As he puts out his arm, exposing the thick links round his hairless wrist, Max intercepts, pushing it away from Dorothea.

'Now don't be childish, Jamie.'

The wrist is withdrawn. James smiles down at the bracelet and hugs himself.

'Who gave it to you?'

He grins at Dorothea. He looks younger than his sister, but less vulnerable. 'A friend. A very dear friend gave it to me.' He wears his hair in oily ginger curls which he would toss if he could. 'Ask me who that friend was, and I'll tell you, dear.'

There is silence except for the slight rustle of unfolding paper on the floor. Max sits very still. There are no birds singing in the garden, and the distant traffic sounds like far-off thunder. Like a grand, discarded game the money lies, wrinkling the tablecloth. James still plays with it, peering through the gaps he's made in his wall to look at Max.

'Be your age!' The notes jump under Dorothea's fist. James sits up, irate.

'But I don't feel old. I don't feel old at all. To tell you the truth...' he leans forward with the secret, '... I did once, like you, but I've suddenly got younger. I feel quite sprightly. Wonder why?'

'Monkey glands? Your own?'

Ignoring the rudeness, James continued. 'You were born first, weren't you, Dee? Makes a difference you know. Even a couple of minutes makes a deal of difference. You age faster. And it shows. Tell me... have you looked at the base of your throat lately?'

Her hand twitches on the cloth, but she manages to keep it there, clenching her fist.

James makes a great affair of removing his tie and undoing studs. Chin up he twists his head from side to side, like a mating bird. 'See,' he says. 'Not a wrinkle.'

There is no glance from Max, warning him that he has overstepped the prescribed bounds of decency.

James pats his face with both hands, running the fingers under his lower lids. 'Here is where it shows too, Dee. Under the eyes. At the age of forty you get either puffy, or wrinkled. Looking at you I would say you tended towards the wrinkled.'

She turns on him. 'And you towards the puff! Watch it. You're the type to get heart disease. Suddenly. Layers of fat collect round the heart, then the valves stop working.'

'Life begins at forty!' He fastens his collar and begins tying his tie. 'But watch the throat lines, Dee. Don't let your gorge rise!'

Max joins in his laughter. Dorothea sits hunched, her swollen hands resting among the money. She listens closely while I tell her to put away the notes safely. I tell her not to spend it unless it is absolutely necessary.

'And what do you call necessary?'

'You will know soon enough when you need it. Invest it, if you don't think the time has come for using it on anything else.'

'There's nothing I can think of that I need right now.'

'It will give you more independence.'

'What are you trying to say to her?' Max has caught the thread of our words. 'Are you trying, in the nicest possible way, to suggest she needs help?'

'I'm telling her that an investment would give her independence.'

'What if I want to invest the money in a business? Someone else's business.' Max has relaxed again.

'The money is for you. You only. It's for no one else. Not even Max.'

'Then I can't accept it.'

'I'm giving you a chance. Can't you see I'm giving you a last chance?'

'If I take it I shall put it into Max's business. Surely you knew that?'

Max pushes a wad of notes towards her. 'Take it,' he says. Rapidly he piles them on top of each other, covering her hands. 'Take it. Take the bloody money. Lock it up. Hide it, do what he says with it. I don't want it.'

'Neither do I.' The pile falls as she withdraws her hands.

James joins in the game, pushing the notes back across the table, forcing his sister to hold out her arms. 'Take it,' he says. 'Take it. Feel free!' The cloth begins to slide. Both Max and James are shoving the wads with both hands against her resistance. 'Take it. Take it.' It has become a vicious little battle.

'I shall only take it to put into your business. *Our* business, Max.'

'He's right. You might need it some day,' Max says.

'Yes. You might need it. Some day.' James' smile is broadening.

'Take it, do.' Max puts out his hand to touch Dorothea but she backs away from him.

'Get away from me.' She stands and shouts down the table. 'I won't touch your bloody money. What are you trying to do? Break me up?' James is guffawing and banging the table. 'Shut up, James, you hyena.' She picks up a wad of notes and throws it at him, aiming badly. He ducks, still laughing as a second wad comes flying in his direction. As her aim gets better he slips from his chair and slides beneath the table. Laughter comes up from the folds of the cloth.

Max is still sitting in his chair, neat and upright. 'Take the bloody money and stop behaving like an ass, Dee.'

'Do you know what you're saying to me, Max?'

'Of course. I'm saying that if he's good enough to give you a present, then you should be grateful enough to accept it, that's all.'

'To keep for myself?'

Max nods his head regally.

'How can you!' She stamps her foot. The sideboard rattles. She crosses the room and noisily goes through the garden door, leaving behind her its reverberation. With a rattle of glass the conservatory door is open and shut.

James' laughter subsides into a snigger. He comes from under the table clutching wads of banknotes. 'Here you are, my dear. Your gift has been refused, I think.'

Together we collect and pack the rest of the scattered money, wrapping it again in crumpled tissue paper. James neatly folded the box back in its brown paper: Max carefully tied the string. By the time we've finished, the sun has gone from our part of the house, leaving the table in partial shade. This means that the morning is further advanced than I would have supposed, yet neither of them show any signs of haste. Surely James is due soon at the restaurant, to serve the midday lunches.

'Oh no. Not today. I'm not going in. Got the day off for moving.'

'Where are you moving to?'

'Why, here.' He looks distrustfully at Max. 'Didn't you know? Hasn't Max told you?'

Max shrugs. 'No, I didn't tell him. Should I have done?' He looks unconcerned, despite the surprise on James' face.

James thumps the table under Max's nose. 'Of course you should have done. Tell him now. For God's sake tell him. This *is* his house, you know.'

Max takes his time arranging his legs comfortably. He settles himself with great slowness before drawling out the words: 'Jamie's coming to live with me here. That all right with you, hmm?'

Colour has crept to the roots of James' hair. With much distress he wrinkles the cloth under his hands, plucking at it and resmoothing the disturbance. 'Why didn't you tell him? Why?'

'He's never around.' Max accentuates his slow drawl.

'You can go and see him, can't you? He *lives* here, doesn't he? All you had to do was come down the stairs.'

'Don't bust a blood vessel, Jamie. I was too busy to get around to it. Anyway, it's not as though we're going to encroach, is it? We'll make ourselves as quiet as mice, so no one will even suspect we're there.'

'Sometimes you forget whose bloody house this is, Max.'

'Ah, don't you underestimate him, Jamie boy. He's well aware of the way things are. He doesn't miss much.'

I point out that I would like to be consulted about new arrivals, in case I wake up one morning to find an hotel has sprung up without my knowledge.

'I mean to pay my way.' James is still embarrassed.

'Of course you do, Jamie. Haven't I paid my way here too? Haven't I also paid for his *wife* as well? What does he want—people to clock in and out?' Max is getting angry. For once he isn't fully in control of the situation: the abuse, usually mild, and done as a matter of form, takes on a nastier tone. 'James is coming to live with me. He'll pay his way. He won't interfere with your precious privacy. In fact, if you like, he'll try not to let you see him at all. And he'll sign out at the door when he goes to work each day. Would you like his cheque for any food he consumes on the premises?'

'I'll be having my meals at the restaurant anyway.'

'Don't explain, Jamie. For God's sake don't explain. I couldn't bear it. He'll only store up what you say and keep it for future reference. He has that sort of mind. If you tell him you'll be eating out, he'll go round examining crumbs for your fingerprints. He's like that.'

I ask James if Dorothea has been consulted. He says that Max has told her.

'And does she approve of the plan?'

'Don't answer him, Jamie.'

James tells Max to answer me himself. Again I ask if she approves. Max is on the defensive.

'She agrees, if that's what you mean.'

'What did she say when you told her? What were her exact words?'

'Do you want the look on her face when she said them, too?'

'Yes. If you can remember that much about my wife's face.'

Max sits up, ready to do battle on familiar ground. 'Have you noticed that whenever he's defending Dorothea he always refers to her as his wife? Interesting, eh? What a pity he's so small, otherwise I might feel like knocking him down. But it's no fun knocking down a midget.'

James gives me an apologetic look. 'Shut up, Max. Don't exaggerate. This is his house, and I want to live here with you. Don't mess it up for me. Please.'

'You worry too much, Jamie. Of course he'll let you live here. He has no option. You see, he knows that if I leave, then Dorothea leaves too. And he couldn't stand that. Could you?'

'What did Dorothea say when you told her he was coming to live here?'

'Tell him, Max. Tell him. Please.' James is almost wringing his hands.

We wait for Max to make up his mind. He scratches his nose, raises his eyebrows, pushes up his spectacles, and speaks. 'She wanted to know why he had to live here.'

'And you told her the truth?'

'I told her the lease was up on his flat, and there was plenty of room here for all of us. *That's* true, hmm?'

'What did she say?'

'She said she wasn't overfond of her brother.'

'Beautifully understated. How did you get her to agree?'

'I used no crude methods. No threats or anything like that.' He explains how Dorothea sees eye to eye with him about the need for expansion in business. He says she is enthusiastic about his ideas for setting up a restaurant run by James. He is to be responsible for the décor. Plans are already under way.

'So she has lost her money already. Just as I expected.'

'She hasn't complained.'

'She has no choice. How many shares has she bought?'

'Shares! What are shares to a *woman*—mere pieces of paper. No, no. She trusts me, you see. I've had long enough to prove I can feed and clothe her in the manner she shouldn't have been allowed to become accustomed to. She can be bloody expensive. I think I'm entitled to a little rebate after all these years.'

James has heard enough. White-faced, he gets to his feet. 'Why don't you return the bloody product and get your bloody money back, then?' He punches Max's arm with a hard fist, and immediately regrets it. I cannot wait at such proximity to see the reconciliation. It is better for them to be left alone.

It took me half an hour to find Dorothea. She was in the garden, standing behind the rockery, looking at nothing. Hearing my steps on the path she folded her arms across her chest, defensively. I saw her figure rising from the masses of tall flowers of which she seemed a part. Several times I lost her in my efforts to cross the crowded borders, having to push my way through clusters of shrubs and plants whose healthy profusion concealed the fact of their eventual decay. Her head looked like a flower itself, a sad hybrid growing in temporary splendour. It seemed that Dorothea was waiting for me and had, in her usual perverse fashion, hidden herself, so that the task of finding her was made more difficult.

When only the rockery divided us she said. 'I've been looking at the insects. There's a bee trapped in a foxglove. Look, the whole plant's weighed down with him.' The foxglove swayed as the bee swung into another bloom. Dorothea made no effort to help me across the dangerous rocks, and as I came towards her, she backed away behind an alpine outcrop.

'Look out,' she said, 'you're treading on the Thyme.' Its smell rose acrid in my nostrils. 'Be careful. It takes a lot of growing. Mind the Lobelia! And *please,* take your foot off that Charieis.'

'Only an annual, I believe.'

As I reached her side she said, 'Well you're wrong. It's a perennial. Comes from the Aster family. I should know. I grew it.'

'Growth is not something I wish to discuss.'

'Oh please don't start about metamorphosis and how you hate it. All I said was that I grew the bloody thing.'

'It doesn't matter to me whether you did or not.'

'It matters to me though.'

'I haven't come to speak about your gardening prowess.'

'Why don't you learn to talk like a human being? It would be marvellous if, just for once, I felt as though you were human.'

'Don't be insulting, Dorothea. I've come to ask you a few questions, and I want you to have the courtesy to reply. They concern you.'

She put herself beyond the rocks again, where the humming insects gathered above the plants that spread like matting. Traffic sounds filtered from afar, but I kept my voice low to avoid attracting unwelcome attention from the house.

'Max has told me about the move,' I said.

'What move?' She shouted the question so loudly that a blackbird flew off from the trees behind, emitting warning cries.

'About the lease being up on the flat.'

'What flat?'

'I thought you knew....'

Arms still folded she stared at me, the protruding eyes blinking quickly in immediate disbelief. 'Look, try to speak clearly, will you? My hearing isn't what it was. You see, today I'm a year older.' The light was unkind to the lines on her face and neck. Leafy shadows gave her hair a curious, crinkled look.

'Max told me you knew. Today is the day for it.'

'The day for what?'

'For James to move. He's coming to live here.'

Did her face turn pale? I cannot remember any other reaction. It was difficult to see beyond the shadow of leaves undulating over the freckles, accentuating the hollows of her cheeks and neck. She had so many lines of age and anxiety.

'Max said he'd told you.'

'The bastard.'

'They're bringing James' things over this afternoon.'

'What time?'

'I don't know. But they're still indoors. They haven't gone yet.' I watched her closely. 'Didn't Max ask you whether you minded James living here?'

'He may have mentioned it,' she said, half turning so I couldn't see her face. 'I don't remember.' She plucked at a pluming plant. When I could see her expression again, it was one of distrust. 'Are you telling me the truth? You wouldn't be lying, would you? For some strange reason of your own?'

I told her briefly how the conversation had gone in the house. I told her that Max had said she knew.

'Max can't have said that. He knows I would never agree. He wouldn't dream of doing anything to upset me.' Hurriedly she stepped over the rocks towards the house. 'You're lying,' she called. 'I'm going to ask him what went on in there.'

Across the lawn she went. When she reached the sundial she turned to shout back at me, 'Who told you all this? Wasn't Max, I know. It was Jamie, wasn't it? Wouldn't put anything past *him*.' I could see the faint shadow of Time across her hand on the clock. But she didn't continue across the lawn towards the house, instead she wheeled about, and came back to me, her heels sinking into the turf and earth as she grappled with the garden.

She came in a hurry to stand at my side, panting from her rock climb. 'You're not telling me the truth,' she said. Although the sun's heat had lessened she looked hot. The thin material of her dress was stretched and stained about her arms. She touched my arm, pressing it with her strong thumbs. Her habit of touching the person to whom she spoke was something I had forgotten. The sudden proximity was unpleasant. 'You're not telling me the truth. Say you're not.'

The light, so strong a moment ago, had faded, fading too the shadows into a pale haze of grey. Traffic sounded louder as the insects deserted us in search of a sunnier section of the garden.

'I don't believe you anyway.' She let me back away from her. 'There's nothing I don't know about Jamie. You want to hurt me, don't you?'

Again the explanation of James' intention to come and live with Max. Again the reasons for the move: how the lease is up on the flat, and how they mean to go into business together. 'They say they need to be near each other to work on the plans.'

'If Max says so, then it's true. Yes, I do remember him saying something about asking Jamie over. But not to live. You've made a big mistake. He's only visiting. You'll see.'

I suggested that she go and ask for herself about future arrangements. It seemed a good time to ask, when she would find them both together.

'No,' she said emphatically. 'You only want me to degrade myself in front of Max. You heard him say he hates jealous women. That's why you've cooked this up, while my back was turned. All that nonsense about the money was only to make me look small. Why don't you leave me alone? You watch me all the time—everything I do, everything I say, all I eat even. God, it's like having a shadow when there's no sun.'

I was giving her a last chance. 'Max doesn't want you any more. He wants James.'

She didn't attack me as I had half expected. 'You bloody liar,' she said. 'You nasty, bloody liar.' She ran from me, hurting her ankles on the stones, trampling through the Salvia, Bergamot and Sage, divotting the lawn. I heard the glass shake as she went into the conservatory, then the second thump as the kitchen door was slammed. A mosquito whined about my head as I stood with my feet in the Thyme bed, having achieved nothing.

Then it was necessary to walk slowly through the garden regaining equilibrium before attempting the return indoors. The light was definitely going. Sharp flower colours were lessening: now there was little to choose between the pinks and reds that, in normal morning light, were so far apart on the spectrum. Distance was intensified, making the paths, already lengthy, into straight avenues fading back to a misty nothingness. The paths themselves felt insecure with a hint of slime on their surfaces not apparent to the downward gaze. A certain dampness was in the air, of thunder perhaps, which had not yet broken. All bushes, shrubs, plants, trees were immobile, fading into each other with a strange flatness at odds with the paths' perspective. I walked away from the house first, in the direction of the rose garden, turning right to the land given over to the lettuce. Between the rows of vegetables were tiny heaps of bran to poison slugs: insecticide whitened the runner beans. Birds were alighting on the cherry trees to tear the flesh from the overripe cherries; their whistling blanketed by the first distant thunder. Nasty places gardens, with so much change going on. No rain was falling, but as the sky turned purple the air began to moisten, making breathing difficult. I was forced to stop and gasp for breath like a drowning man, mouth open before the next quick exhalation. Moisture slid down my throat before I was aware of it on my lips. I made a slow circuit of the vegetables, breathing quickly, fighting the atmosphere.

Under the cherry trees there was some relief; there the air was clearer, with a slight breeze—usually so annoying—coming over the surrounding wall. The trees were less unpleasant than most, having smooth bark that didn't flake or fall incessantly. I inspected them and found them inadequate as shelter, should it rain. Thunder was rolling in the direction of the house, breaking through the birds' calling, and subsiding in rapid claps. The rain didn't come. I waited fearfully for several minutes, looking up at the dreadful purple mask. To get wet is a terrible thing. It was foolish to stay out so long in such an alien place.

I made my way back as quickly as the treacherous-looking paths would allow, circumnavigating the lawn with its unwholesome, marshy look. I caught my coat on several thorn bushes disguised by roses: an optimistic spider tried to catch me with its thread. But no rain had fallen by the time I reached the safety of the path that led to the house. I left the damp prints of my tread on the flags as I crossed them on my way to the conservatory. My feet made no noise, or if they did, the complaining birds were louder. Not until my hand was on the latch of the outer door did I hear the greater sounds within, coming from the dining-room.

I stayed outside, pressing my face against the glass in an attempt to see what was going on beyond the second window. The double thicknesses of glass muffled the voices, causing them to be transmitted as echoes from the depths of some well. The echoes overlapped, bursting in sudden furies that coincided, I could see, with the widely open mouths of Max and Dorothea. There was rage and chagrin on their faces: necks twisted, arms waved; they circled each other with open mouths, shouting dumb shouts, hardly pausing to listen to the other's invective. One or two of Dorothea's deep screams of abuse came clearly to my ears. I was glad to be denied the full effect of her anger. She jerked her arms and shook her fists at Max, who kept his distance, answering her with fierce barings of the teeth, rapidly spitting out the words I couldn't hear. Suddenly James came into view, throwing out his arms in circular thrusts and looking at his feet. His ankles were trapped in the tablecloth. His mouth too was moving as he circled and swung, trying to clear himself from the heavy folds. He straightened once and crossed his arms, working his mouth rapidly. I couldn't see who he was addressing but Dorothea interrupted him, answering with the same rapid mouth movements, making little flurries with her fingers, stabbing the air. There was hatred on his face. As Max began to speak again, Dorothea went over to the table and leaned on it, hiding James' face from view. Her whole body was shaking with the vehemence of what she said. Out shot her finger to point at Max, and down came James' hand on the table to thump it so hard that I felt the glass shake under my cheek. There was a roar and James was banging the table again and again with his fist, while Max stood rigidly, spectacles flashing, mouth saying the same words over and over again until the banging ceased. I took advantage of the momentary lull to wipe my breath from the glass. Now all three were standing by the table. Their mouths began to move more slowly as though some crisis had been passed. I couldn't see James' face, only the icy coldness of Max and Dorothea's outrage. Something between them was being settled.

Rain began to fall: small drops of water touched my forehead. I felt them on the back of my neck. When I looked for him, James had disappeared from view. My soles squeaked on the wet concrete. Raindrops were blurring Dorothea's body, liquidising her moving arms. Her mouth became a gaping streak of black. Through the lines of water starting down the glass I saw James on the other side of the room. He stood with one hand against the door, the other circling the air in a rainy undulation. He turned to leave, entering a large raindrop that magnified his head for an instant, changing him into an angry dwarf. The bang of the door as he went out reverberated through the conservatory, echoing the travelling thunder.

There was a change of movement when James had gone: Dorothea put her back to the window and spread her shredded arms: Max came towards her through the distorting water like a plant in an aquarium. His head rose above hers and clarified as rain poured down the glass, taking with it any lingering drops. He raised his arm. I couldn't see her face as he struck her. All I saw was the arm descending in an undulation to his side again. They both stood very still, facing one another. Moisture penetrated the back of my jacket and ran inside my collar. I felt the water drops through my thinning hair. It is a terrible thing to get wet.

Neither Max nor Dorothea looked surprised to see me enter the dining-room; neither remarked on my condition. It wasn't until I had gone over to the sideboard and helped myself from the decanter that anyone spoke to me.

'Wipe your feet,' Dorothea said. 'You've dirtied the floor.'

I did as she asked, having to put down my drink on the table to avoid spillage. Max picked it up and drank half the whisky. 'Must be your nightcap, surely,' he said. The tone was heavily sarcastic.

'Nightcap?'

'Leave him alone, Max.'

'Yes. The day's over for you now, isn't it? It's been so full of event up till now, you surely can't keep up the pace much longer. You'll drop dead from exhaustion if you don't look out. Other people's affairs can be really taxing on the system.'

'Leave him alone, please, Max.'

Max contented himself with whistling the first line of 'Little Man You've Had A Busy Day.' 'Well,' he said, 'Jamie's not going to forget today, is he?'

'Damn Jamie,' Dorothea said. Her mood had changed from mistrust to affectionate belief in Max's intentions. She had won the battle over where James was to live, and now she was happy to make concessions to the loser. Yes, she agreed that Jamie would make an excellent business partner; had she ever argued to the contrary? All she required from now on was his absence from the house.

'I have to see my partner,' Max said. Briefly he eyed me.

'But only in business hours.' Dorothea's smile didn't extend to her eyes; they were too busy watching for his answer with avid attention.

'Anything you say, Dee.' He managed a brief brush of her arm with his fingertips. 'I must say Jamie'll make a wonderful partner though. So full of good ideas. You wait and see, he's bound to come up with something quite unique to launch us. And did you know he's an author? Yes he is. He's written a book of recipes. Think of that! I've got a copy. Beautiful they are.'

'Like you,' Dorothea said.

'What?'

'Beautiful like you, I said.'

'What's that got to do with recipes?'

'I can tell you you're beautiful, can't I, Max? Or would you call that bad taste as well?'

'Trust you to change the subject out of all recognition.' Max looked at me. 'She tries to pick girlish fights, doesn't she? You'd think she'd have grown out of them by now.'

I told him I had forgotten how she used to be.

'Do *you* think it's bad taste to tell him he's beautiful? I can say that without being accused of bad taste, can't I?' She pushed my arm encouragingly.

Max looked exasperated. 'The point in argument here, Dee, is whether you should say it in front of *him*.'

'I can't say it in front of him! I can't say it in front of Jamie! You don't want to hear it when we're alone! So when can I say it?'

'Shut up, Dee.' Max was beginning to fidget with annoyance.

'I have always said you were beautiful, haven't I? Didn't I say that Max had a Rathbone profile? I did. Remember? When Jamie first introduced us I said, "Your friend has a Rathbone profile. He has a glorious nose."'

I was curious as to James' answer, but Dorothea had forgotten it. Max told her to shut up about his nose. He rose to his feet, looking at his watch, and the streaming windows. 'I must get to work,' he said.

'Please don't leave me today. Max. At least stay and have lunch with me.'

He ignored her pleadings. He said that duty called. As he went out of the door he shouted, 'Don't wait up for me. Bye.' Then he shut the door very quietly behind him. The rain outside, splashing down the gutters, sounded very like his footsteps on the stairs.

I followed in Max's tracks, pausing by the door as he had done to say goodbye to Dorothea. She was sitting rigidly at the table, wearing a red dress. 'I won,' she said. I bowed to the victor and departed for my room.

7

The roof overhead is dry: no rain has fallen for several weeks, and none is forecast for today. Therefore I cannot blame the inclemency of the weather if they do not come. And I cannot have missed them: from any part of this gallery I can keep sight of the room through which they must pass, and reach it by a swift walk along the yellow boards.

She will not come alone. She will not be able, having caught sight of me, to turn and run because she will be hemmed in by her two supporters. They will bring her to me, walking close, hands under her elbows—carrying her if necessary—continually whispering words of encouragement in her ears, telling her that they bring her to a happy future, to the security of a new face, a new bed, new money, new freedom. She will never believe me when I tell her that nothing is new for more than the most lightning flash of a split second, be it just-born baby, unfurled leaf, upthrown rock, or splitting atom. Whether she can see it or not, there is always corrosion, decay, attack, melting, putrefaction; of which she is as much a victim as any growing thing. I shall tell her this. Already, since this morning, she has come an irrevocable way: her skin has lost a few hours more of its elasticity, her legs a fractional proficiency, the very marrow in her bones has hardened slightly. Yet I shall be able to tell her I have her before she came that short, irremediable way, caught at the moment of waking in the friendless bed. She will rejoice with me that I have saved one moment of her morning, and thank me for it. She lies in my camera now safely locked away, waiting for me to perform the miracle of delivery. It is so easy: process, develop, rinse. Fix, rinse and wash. Up comes the perfect negative.

Before I left the house today I made sure that the cupboard was locked, in case an inquisitive mind should wonder where I had gone, and take the opportunity to inquire into my work. It was not a worrying thing, to leave them in the house without me: today they will have other things to occupy their minds. There were no sounds of excessive movement as though there was packing going on. For fear of Dorothea seeing me I didn't venture up the stairs to ask Max if everything was ready. He could have told me whether he intended coming himself today. It is my guess that he will come: both of them must come with her, leaving nothing to chance. There is sure to be a meeting at the house. Max will use the plea of ill-health to make sure that the three of them start out together. There is the greatest possibility that the party will leave the house something like two hours after the forgathering. It will be some time after lunch, at which James will not be present. The question of dress will be attended to, and Dorothea will be kept under close surveillance. If persuasions have to be used at the last minute, then there might be some delay. But Max was optimistic; he said she had no choice. If this is so it means that I should end the waiting soon, perhaps within the hour. If the arrival is by taxi, which no doubt it will be, owing to Max's laziness, then we are all in the hands of the man who drives it. Now is not the time to give much thought to this unknown's capabilities, or the conditions of the vehicle, to the state of his tyres and the unseen rust creeping over his bodywork.

I told the man myself that great care should be taken with the details. He hold me he was thorough, and never let a job be skimped.

He stood by the window, parting the Venetian blinds. The whisky in his glass he swirled about with a circular motion of his other hand. 'I never leave anything alone until it's finished,' he said. 'I'm like a dog with a bone,' is what he said. 'I'm a stickler for accuracy. Aren't you?'

I joined him at the window to see what he was searching for in the courtyard below. But he lowered the slats before I had a chance to see, and proceeded to poke me in the ribs.

'We business men must stick together, mustn't we? Wouldn't do for there not to be closed shop, eh? If Max is a friend of yours, then you're a friend of mine. Get it?'

He kept an open box of cigarettes from which he helped himself. The box looked always full; how this was so escaped me. My estimation of his rate of smoking was something in the region of six per hour, at least in my company. He puts us in a devilish haze of smoke.

My words to him were simple: they put everything about the situation in a nutshell: 'I am not in a position to give you guarantees,' I said.

'But I am. Full guarantee, or money back.' I laughed, but didn't feel the humour. Once more he sunk his yellow nose deep into the glass, as if he were about to blow bubbles there, but the danger passed and he raised the glass to pour some liquid down his open throat.

'Know many of Max's friends?'

'Not many. We don't move in the same circles. I've met many of them though. He once had a party at my home and I saw them then. But I can't remember their names. It was a long time ago. Would it be possible that you were there too? Your face seems familiar.'

'Depends on the kind of party, doesn't it? If you get my meaning.'

'There were many women there. I remember the women. They were all over the place.'

'The type is more interesting than the species to a connoisseur.' His laugh was unpleasing; it had the quality of a Mynah bird. 'I have parties here,' he said. 'On home ground, so to speak. Very interesting some of them are too. I can recommend them to you—speaking as one connoisseur to another. Have them roughly once a month, I do. Strictly invitation, of course. Let me know where the interest lies and you'll get an invitation. Dinner jacket plus personal paraphernalia, but no friends. Here you'll find all the friendship you can get.'

'No thank you. My interest lies in a more permanent direction. I thought Max had made it clear to you.'

'So he had. So he had. But a man still has a weakness or two. Yours might lie in the direction of parties, mightn't it? Esoteric parties might be in your line, mightn't they?'

The light from the street lamp was casting its orange glow on the slats of the blind. He walked over to a lamp and switched it on, diffusing his face with colour. He smiled at me through the light with a sinister wrinkling of the muscles. His eyes looked black and sharp. Looking round the room for somewhere to sit I noticed the agglomeration of cushions. They were everywhere. The sofa seemed to throw up cushions as the sea throws up wrack: it would require an effort to plunge into their softness and submit to the disease of so much luxury. To sit on the sofa was to lie; to give up oneself to this gross piece of the upholsterer's art and be held immobile, a prey to the man who owned it. The light shone round his head like an unholy nimbus.

'I don't like parties of any kind,' I told him. 'Hasn't Max made clear my needs?'

'Yes, yes. Your specific needs are well known to me. But I'm not used to working through the agency of another person. Usually I prefer to do the initial selecting and questioning myself. Understand that?'

'I don't wish to waste too much time on this side of things. Time is precious. Hasn't Max told you that?'

'My dear sir, I know full well in what direction your tastes lie. And I'm a very astute observer. I'm not saying that I could have told by looking at you ... but over the years one gets a pretty good idea of people's weaknesses ...'

'My requirements are not extraordinary. Except to the colour of the hair, I cannot see anything unusual in my demands. Can you?'

'My dear sir, you misunderstand me. The aim is to please. *Please*. What I'm saying is that a gentleman with your esoteric tastes would be more than welcome to my little coterie. My little parties here would give you a new ... window as it were ... on life.' I swayed with the punch. There was no use in pointing out how much I detested close contact, hating his horny finger.

'Hasn't Max told you that the liaison will be one of a permanent nature? My days of vicarious pleasure are almost over. There comes a time when the collecting must begin in earnest.'

'Max tells me you're a great collector.'

'I've done my share.'

He brayed with laughter. 'So have I! So have I! In a manner of speaking we enjoy the same pursuits.'

'I don't collect furniture.'

'Ah, no. I'm referring to another kind of hobby—to the greatest collection of them all. To the collection in which my own interests lie. To Life's great collection.' The stripes on his shirt dazzled.

He refilled my glass. 'We're beginning to see eye to eye,' he said. 'I don't think there'll be many difficulties sorting out this one. Rely on me. All we have to do is find someone suitable, and then come to an equally happy arrangement concerning your investment.'

'What investment?'

'In antique furniture ... that you intend purchasing. My dear sir, you are, if I may be a trifle outspoken, a bit slow. We business men must keep our wits about us at all costs, mustn't we?' He went on to say how like furniture women were, with their pretty surfaces and basic fraudulence. He always classed them together—as merchandise. And he had acquired the happy knack of striking good bargains for them. 'My taste is excellent,' he said. 'You'll see. I have in mind for you a product which has been highly recommended. What a pity that the reproduction isn't to hand now. Tell Max to remind me on that score.'

I asked him if I was committed at this stage. I wanted to see the photograph before any pact was agreed upon.

'You're not committed, sir. But remember, satisfaction is guaranteed. Pay your money like a man, sir. After all, there can't be business where there's no mutual trust, can there?'

'What if I refuse right now?'

'There, I'm afraid, you've got me. No one has ever refused me yet. It's human nature and natural curiosity. They want to go on with the transaction; go a little further along the fascinating road. I find my clients aren't men who give up easily. They have a curiosity to satisfy, and they're willing to pay for it. They're right, don't you think?'

'I do not follow you.'

'I am saying, sir, that the choice is yours: either you wish to enter the antique furniture field, or you do not. If you do, certain guarantees are required from you to prove your good faith. They must take the form of cash. I in my turn will provide you with what you desire, when you desire it, and for this you must allow me a little more time—your taste being a bit out of the ordinary. Take advantage of my help, sir. Offers like this are difficult to come by, especially for a man like you.'

'Like me?'

'Of unusual tastes, I mean. You have to be *catered* for.'

'Max has put to you my tastes. I have nothing else to add.'

'Ah, I think we've said enough for tonight, haven't we? There's a hint of tiredness in your voice. Me, I can go on for days, even years. It doesn't pay to tire, especially when one's clients arrive so late. Ah! What's that?'

A car passed, being driven down the empty road at speed. I managed to drink the last of my whisky as he dived for my coat.

★

The temptation to leave this section of the gallery is strong. Having made a vague estimate as to the time of their arrival, I feel the urge to venture beyond the line where I can be sure of seeing their entry.

There's no doubt as to the direction I shall take: I have always known where I should walk, if the choice was mine. Now to go is a pleasure, because I cross the yellow boards and turn away from the splendid sight of public benefaction to walk along a narrow corridor that leads to a more attractive site. Few shuffling visitors come this far into the deepest parts of the gallery, where the walls are all inner ones, and the light is only electric. Not that the light is very different from that in the other rooms: diffused daylight filtering through double glass has little chance of keeping its identity. But in this corridor there is the feeling that I am deep *inside,* protected from the world by layers of sealing stone and steel. My footsteps echo in a different way, the sound bouncing off the walls, or fading suddenly into silence as I pass a small room, like a cell, full of coloured prints. There are several of these tiny rooms tucked away along the length of the corridor. I know them all. Into each one I poke my head to check that everything is as I last saw it. Positions of pictures are noted, so are the white patches on the walls where something has been removed for cleaning. Everything is kept in perfect order: nothing is allowed to deteriorate. The sameness is reassuring. I can be certain as I pass that the same eyes of the same sitters in the same portraits will follow me for a while until I pass the door jamb. I know that by the time I have reached the daylight again, the eyes will have lost me. As I progress, the light on the floorboards whitens. It is daylight whitening the floors and doors, and the uniform of the sleeping attendant. I welcome it because it means I am in my favourite part of the building, where everything is so familiar that I feel as though it is mine.

First I look at the right hand wall to make sure that nothing has changed. No one has been up to their tricks in here, moving things around when my back was turned. All the pictures are in their usual places.

The room is an octagon, its shape repeated in the glass ceiling which is divided into octagonal shapes by thin lines of wood. As I stand under the arch, the windows are on my left and right. They are large and, unlike those in the other parts of the gallery, a view can be seen from them. A Venetian blind masks one of them, but through the slats I can see a sloping roof made of dull, reeded glass. I have my back to the sleeping attendant who has never been known to wake, except when roused by the going-home bell. The picture opposite, taking up the entire wall, is absolutely photographic: its subject has entirely disappeared behind the glass, leaving a mirror for the outside scene. For the first time I see blue sky above the grey brick of old buildings, from which the flagpoles rise. There are chimney pots on the roof line, yellow against the sky; but as I move, their edges blur and I lose them. Then the portrait behind the glass hoves into view—still the same old man holding the skull in his right hand. He doesn't bother me. I know the painting well; there are no secrets left. I have no need to go closer, looking for fine brushwork: varnish destroyed it years ago. I am no longer interested in the jaundiced man with the myriad wrinkles, who follows me with his accusing gaze. I sit down on a bench and turn my back on him, so that the windows are on either hand.

The window on my left looks out on a variety of roofs of buildings, all grey brick and all constructed differently. Each building has its own collections of windows, set at varying levels, and all of different size. These windows have to be counted. It is easier, when counting them, to start from the right and work diagonally across to the left, then down to the right again. They are positioned roughly in this way, and since they aren't all alike, or on the same levels, some simple system is necessary if they're to be counted at all. I favour the right-to-left-diagonal system as my usual method, but if I want extra diversion I count them in a much more complex way; that is from left to right, keeping the counting horizontal. Since this way is almost impossible, results are always wrong. By careful calculation, spread over a period of ten years, I have come to the conclusion that there are twenty windows to be counted from this bench. But mistakes are easily made.

If I stare too long at the outer air my eyes take time to accustom themselves to the dark pictures on the walls. I must wait until the shapes reappear, then the faces. Not that I enjoy them when I can see them, for at certain times of the day in here there appears to be something badly wrong with each of the canvases on the wall beneath the window. Not only do they seem to be warped and undulating, but the very surfaces themselves seem to have been attacked by a dreadful fungus, which has spread a greying film across the paint. The sitters are about to meet unhappy deaths which I can only stop by moving my position on the bench. If I approach any one of these pictures, then everything is back to normal, yet when I regain my seat in the centre of the room, and turn to look at them, the terrible disease is once more rife.

Perfection is what I require in here, so I do not often look under the window. In shape the room is perfect; being an octagon it satisfies the need to feel enclosed without giving rise to thoughts of claustrophobia. It is a room in which to breathe, to look on pure, symmetric shapes and clean lines; to sit considering its innate harmony. It is a room in which to indulge in counting: it absolutely cries out to be counted, whether one starts from the windows outside, taking in the patterns of the grey glass roof, or considers first the four octagons that close above my head like an open box. There are the lines of the floor, the same in number as those that cross the ceiling where, for immediate diversion, the octagonal lamp may be considered. In it sits another octagon, directly above my head like a geometric nimbus. When the light is switched on, it shines on my head in correct, saintly fashion. The switches themselves are worth considering since they lie in a pleasing pattern close to the floor by the sleeping attendant's feet. There are seven switches on the bronze plate, and underneath it lies a mat made of black rubber. The mat presents a problem since it cannot fully be observed: the feet of the seated man partially cover it. Nevertheless one can ascertain that its construction is hexagonal, and reach the number three hundred before giving up. The floorboards afforded me the same problem at first, being partially covered by the bench on which I sit. A certain amount of mental measuring is necessary to decide how many lines are hidden beneath me. This is not altogether easy, since the boards themselves diminish as they reach the centre of the room. In fact, taking a complete view of all the lines in this octagon, it is true to say that my position here is totally central: I am at the centre of everything in the entire room. At the hub of things I can sit here and see—by means of numbers, lines, shapes, light—everything with any meaning for me. I sit upright, slowly and quietly, listening to the peace of the place. I can hear no generators in here, only pigeons cooing on a distant building, or in the cherry trees. Counting in here has a double pleasure: it lets me know, categorically, that everything is in order, nothing has changed; and it enables me to take my time before the pleasure of looking at the picture on the wall which faces me. I am at peace before I look; at ease when I do so.

My position is such that my own reflection does not intrude on the man before me. I can look at him without interruption, fully absorbed by him.

He sits in a large room, in a comfortable chair at his desk, writing. At his feet rests a dog with an intelligent face and lively eye, with an alertness that gives the lie to the fact that he's stuffed. He was stuffed many years ago. So was the cat, a charming creature curled peacefully beside her master's chair. No longer do the animals cause havoc as they cavort beneath their master's legs. He can sit busily checking and cross-checking, making sure that all the data is correct, without their interference. He has quite forgotten his surroundings—the cushions flung everywhere, the heavy curtains looped back from the windows, the rugs ruckled at his feet. Lamps, pictures, mirrors, books, crowd the room and make an island of the space in which he works. Although it is daytime and the lamps aren't lit, they shine with a metallic glow, and tiny reflections glance off their fringes. The walls glow blue until they recede into the darkness of an alcove where a secret mirror hangs. It reflects every glint of light, and repeats the shadowy shape of the man at his desk. He does not look up to the window where the garden grows in great profusion of trees and shrubs that bend and sway with the noon breeze. Everything out there is shimmering in a green light filtering through the abundant leaves. There are glimpses of lawns and paths, cut and swept attentively. The windows are shut against the threat of summer dust that might sweep in and settle on the glass-fronted cabinets, or spoil the purity of high glass domes that cover certain specimens. A lot of time is spent in keeping down the dust; of devising ways in which things can be protected from corrupting grime. In drawers with locks are kept the rare and fragile shells like Murex lobeckii, whose pale pink fins would come to harm unless they rested on soft felt which hides them from the light. There is nothing to compare with the rare felicity of opening a drawer where the great Conus gloria-maris lies, and to gaze down on its splendid red smoothness which nothing can change. It lies there more beautiful than any flower, its flecks and dappling not products of a few month's growth, likely to collapse and fade before the week is out. No fish will ever have such scales as the handsome Clytospira, nor be so difficult a catch; the subject of years of correspondence, searches covering half the world, and a small fortune. Who can resist the enamelled polish of its surface and the perfection of its patterning? One could gaze forever on its precise convolutions in whose colours there are ever fascinating depths and variations.

This man knows the secret of looking at things; able to draw sustenance from the mere lowering of his eyes to look at the eternity of immobility.

'Tell me honestly, what do you think about all day?'

'On what level do you wish me to answer your question?'

'Tell me what goes on in your head when I'm not around.'

'When you're not here it's mostly work that I concentrate on. I suppose you could say that I think about my work.'

'Not about me? When do you think about me?'

'All the time, of course.'

'Saying "of course" has spoiled it. Don't give the right answers just because you know I want to hear them.'

'What is it you want to hear?'

'Tell me, honestly, what you think about.'

'About you, or about anything at all?'

'It doesn't matter. Tell me what you think about all day. When I'm not with you.'

'I've told you, I think about work. And about you.'

'Yes. But what about me? Do you think things like "She's got a lovely face", or "I love the way she puts her hands when she's thinking"?'

'To tell you the truth I hadn't noticed you putting your hands anywhere unusual when you thought. See if you can manage to think again, and I'll try to notice where you put your hands.'

'Very funny. I was using a figure of speech. I think.'

'I'm glad to hear it.'

'Why won't you tell me what you think about? Is it because you've got something to hide? Or don't you think about me at all?'

'Of course I do.'

'Then tell me what you think. Go on. Tell me what you think of me, and I'll tell you what I think of you....'

'I merely think that you're my wife. That's all.'

'Don't you ever wonder why I married you?'

'I know why you married me: it was your duty, and you had no choice.'

'Ha! Duty! What a fine word that is. You sound like your father when you say it. He used to use the word quite frequently. He was a great one for doing one's duty.'

'And you agreed with him.'

'I suppose I did. Once. I suppose I felt responsible for what I'd done to you. Heaven knows why. He was a terrible man.'

'Not terrible, only clear-thinking. He saw that I was your responsibility, as much as you were mine. You didn't disagree with him.'

'Disagree! With his authority? Did any of us ever dare to thwart him? Did you ever try?'

'He used to lock me in cupboards. But that is beside the point. He made me what I am, and for that I'm grateful.'

'And are you grateful for his making me marry you?'

'He had nothing to do with that. I decided myself to marry you. So I did.'

'He threatened to disinherit you if you didn't. Guess what he threatened me with ... Murder!'

'Time has distorted the truth in your mind, Dorothea. I was never coerced into marriage. My father saw that I wanted you, so he did his best to see that it came about. There was no reluctance on your part. I thought you were glad of having the responsibility of looking after yourself removed. You were never able to decide anything at all. You had no money, no real home, no training for any kind of work. No capabilities.'

'Poor little lost girl! Is that what you think of me now?'

'I merely think that you're my wife.'

'How very nice for you. Having staked your claim, you hang

on to it, like grim death. I should love to know what's going on in that brain of yours, which, if I may say so, is covered by very little hair. You're going quite bald. Is that usual at thirty?'

'There's no need to get upset, Dorothea. You're doing it to yourself. Why do you insist on talking about such things? There's no remedy for them. You always end up quite furious, and not able to talk to me all day. Use a little control.'

'Like you? Sometimes you're so controlled I think a motor runs inside you. I don't want to be controlled. I want to tear my hair and shout. I want to be what I want, and become what I want. I want to know what I am. Now, look at me and tell me exactly what *you* think I am. Look at me....'

'Please don't be dramatic. When I look at you I see you as my wife—which you are—and there is absolutely nothing else you can be. You have many good points.'

'There you go again, qualifying things. I suppose you have a list of my virtues in that thinly covered head of yours.'

'I don't require you to be anything other than what you are.'

'Aren't good cooking, neatness, tidiness about the house, nature-loving, on your list? What about an ability to make guests feel at home? I could, you know, if we ever had any.'

'Please don't get angry.'

'Have you ever bothered to find out what I require of you? Have you ever considered your duties as a husband?'

'Let us keep this conversation friendly, Dorothea. In answer to your question, I can safely say that I have considered my duties to you, and I try to fulfil them as best I can.'

'My God! *Have* you! You sound like a hen-pecked seventy year old.'

'That remark was in very bad taste. Don't speak about the years so lightly. If you must have an answer, I consider myself very fortunate in having married you, and I try to live up to it.'

'Well, why on earth didn't you say so in the first place? All I wanted you to say was that you felt lost when I go out of the room, and that you always wait for me to come back again.'

'Now, that isn't altogether true. I like to watch you. I like to watch you cross the garden, or stand at the window, or sit at your mirror. You look ... peaceful ... there's no other way to describe it. It may have something to do with the fact that no noise is involved.'

'You hate my noises, don't you?'

'I'd rather not talk about them.'

'Why? Do you think it not quite nice for me to make noises? Come on, be honest. Tell me that I disgust you.'

'I cannot answer that. I can only say that they surprise me.'

'After three years?'

'Yes, even after three years.'

'What about before we were married? Surely you haven't forgotten we used to sleep together before that.'

'No, nor how insistent you were that we did. But the noises came later. Nowadays you seem more like an animal than a woman. It's the change in you I can't tolerate.'

'There's been no change. Perhaps you are getting more sensitive. You always were. Almost as if you're frightened of contact. Are you?'

'When you're violent it frightens me. It frightens me that you find it amusing. You know that I dislike being mauled, yet you find it amusing. You're very strong, Dorothea. You tend to forget that. You are tough as any man, and sometimes you hurt. Sometimes it seems to me that you want to hurt me.'

'What if I do? Can't you stand passion? You should be glad I'm passionate, instead of cringing away on your side of the bed as if I'm going to eat you. You should welcome me. The genuine article is hard to find, or so you've often told me.'

'I have never told you that.'

'If I were one of those twice a year women, you'd soon come over to my side of the bed. Or would you? I do believe you'd be relieved.'

'Don't be vulgar, Dorothea. It doesn't become you. There is no need to discuss these gymnastics.'

'Well, I think there is. I want to discuss things, whether it's vulgar or not. What about my appetites? They're fairly normal, wouldn't you say? You talk as though you're married to a nympho.'

'Please don't be vulgar. It doesn't suit you.'

'Can't you bear to hear real words? Do they bother you? Is it reality you can't stand? I'm beginning to think it is. You'd rather read about love than make it; it's too messy for you, the real thing. That's it, isn't it? You can't stand the noise, the sweat, the wrestling.'

'Stop it, Dorothea. Stop before you say what you don't intend. I will not quarrel with you on this point.'

'So you call this a "point". You prove mine. You'd rather watch me than make love to me, wouldn't you?'

'There's no law to stop a man watching his own wife.'

'Well watch away little man, and one day the wife may surprise you.'

'What are you saying now, Dorothea? Control the words. They come too easily.'

'At least I feel the words I'm speaking. I *feel*. I shout, I breathe, I sweat. I feel pain.'

'Do you, Dorothea? Do you feel pain when you do wrong? When you lie, do you feel pain?'

'I never tell lies. I'm talking physically. I have a body and it is *living*. Not like those ghastly things of yours, kept under glass or preserved in Eau de Vie Camphrée. It seems to me you're getting more like those things every day. You're getting like a stuffed thing—one of those with the big, glassy eyes that follow you about the room wherever you walk. You're rapidly losing grip with reality, you are. One day you'll stop wanting food, and that's when the calcification will start. Or has it started already? Even now you can't digest things properly, can you, unless you sit upright. Maybe the process has started already. Then one day you'll stop breathing, and all your energies will go into your eyes. You'll develop huge eyes that stare night and day. They'll be luminous. Nothing will move but your eyes, swivelling round like a lighthouse, permanently switched on. You'll love it. Then you can watch everyone doing things, without having to do them yourself.'

'Are you afraid, Dorothea?'

'Afraid of what? Of you? That's hardly possible, is it, since you said yourself just now that I was more like a man than a woman. Besides, you're not large enough to be frightening.'

'I mean afraid of what I know.'

'Oh! The mighty brain, you mean. I must admit, it disturbs me a little.'

'Afraid of what I know about you and Max.'

'What about us? Who told you? Jamie?'

'No. Max told me himself.'

'When did he tell you? What did he say?'

'On holiday. I think he felt rather pleased with himself.'

'He would. But he's lying of course. You realize he's lying, don't you? You can't believe a word Max says. He's really the most terrible liar. We may have got together a couple of times in the dim, distant past, but it didn't amount to anything. You should know Max by now. You should know what he's like.'

'I appreciate your attempts to save my feelings, but it isn't necessary. I presume that Max is more satisfactory than me. I hope he does an adequate job for you.'

'Who's being vulgar now? So you would take his word against mine. And I'm your wife, you know. You're fond of pointing it out at other times, but now you seem to have forgotten it.'

'I will never forget it, Dorothea. Never. But please don't make pretences. You've done enough. I'm tired of having to protect myself from your violence and your subterfuge. Let it stop. Let me have some peace, please.'

'I shan't let you hurt me. I shan't let you drag my name in the mud. I shall not go from here. You can't force me. I'm still capable of a fight. I shan't let you take anything away from me.'

'As I have already said, Dorothea, let us have some peace. There is no need for histrionics. There is no need for anything but peace. I have no intention of taking anything away from you, or fighting. And I don't intend to drag your name anywhere.'

'Are you saying that you don't mind? Is that what you mean? Are you saying it doesn't matter to you? And that it's all right?'

'I have had long enough to get used to the idea. It isn't new to me. Max has been living here for a year now.'

'But it's new to *me*. I never thought you were quite so unfeeling. My God, you *are* slowly dying. Your feelings *have* calcified, haven't they? You wouldn't care if I left today, would you?'

'You aren't leaving, Dorothea. You are never going to leave. You are my wife, and you're staying here. What you do here is something that I can no longer find the strength to fight. I need a rest from you. There are other, more important things to occupy my mind. There is too much to do for me to engage in these wordy battles. They are alien to my nature. Now I am telling you that any talk of leaving must stop. This is your house, and mine. Nothing can alter that fact. And you will continue to behave as though you belong here.'

'I suppose it would be too much to expect you to feel anything as strong as hatred, wouldn't it? You don't hate me, do you?'

'Our levels of thinking are different. You wouldn't understand if I told you that, in my own way, I love you.'

'You are a liar.'

'I have told you the truth, Dorothea. But since you cannot understand my ways of thought, I cannot attempt to explain them.'

'I understand well enough, you'll see.'

'All I wish to make clear to you is that I intend to do nothing.'

'Well, if you don't, I might.'

'I doubt it. You would never act on your own. You are incapable.'

'That isn't true.'

'And if you think that Max might help, then you're mistaken. He can't be relied upon. Knowing his nature as you do, you know that Max can't tolerate responsibility. He requires absolute freedom. Max is a mean man, Dorothea.'

'I know what he's like. I know more about him than you.'

'Then you will be all the more prepared. You will be able to guard against the disappointments.'

'Why should he be any more disappointing than you?'

'Because you have always taken for granted what I have given you, and looked for little else. You have always considered what I have done as your right and my duty.'

'You married me, so you should look after me.'

'I shall always look after you, Dorothea.'

'I don't want you to look after me. Max will do that very well.'

'He is a mean man, don't expect too much from him. Unlike me he has not the power to give without return. Always he would rather take than give.'

'He'll look after me, I know he will. I won't need to take your money any more. Max will look after me. You'll see.'

'Be careful, Dorothea. Don't ask too much of him. He is incapable of many things, and sacrifice is one of them. He has no capacity for it.'

'He'll take me away from here. If I ask him to, he will. All I have to do is ask him. It's his fault anyway. He was the one who told you, wasn't he, not me, so he *must* take me away.'

'Don't be childish. For once in your life try to think clearly for yourself, as I have done. I made a decision. I made a choice.'

'What choice?'

'Between action, and inaction. I chose inaction. It will enable me to do what I want, and go forward with my work a free man.'

'And I shall be free. Max will take me away from here. I shall be glad to go. Even if you asked me to stay, I wouldn't.'

'But I'm not asking you to stay because it isn't necessary. I know, and you know that you are staying anyway. This situation existed long before we talked about it. Talking has done nothing for it but release a few heady words. And Max hasn't changed because we have talked. If he had meant to take you he would have, long ago—when he first told me how things were. That was when I made my choice. It's too late for you now, Dorothea.'

'I shall change things. I'll make up Max's mind for him. He listens to me. And I understand him. And he loves me. He does.'

'To put it in words that you can understand: he knows on which side his bread is buttered. Now, please say no more. I find it distasteful.'

'It is all your fault.'

'Please keep your temper, and I shall keep mine. I cannot see any point in continuing a conversation that merely underlines a fact known to me for quite a time. You are trying to air something that needs no airing. It is relatively unimportant. Max sees it as unimportant, so will you please do likewise.'

'You think you're in control, don't you? Well it's a lie. All you are is a tiny stuffed owl, with eyes like searchlights.'

'How many times have I told you that the loser of his temper is the loser of the argument?'

'I've won this time. I'll prove it to you. You'll see in a minute. You'll see.'

Dorothea leaves the room, banging doors as she passes through the hall to our bedroom. My reserves have been seriously depleted by events, and I have not the energy to climb upon the desk to see what she is doing. I am feeling no better by the time she returns, her arms full of blankets and pyjamas.

'Will you keep these in here, or shall I locate a room for you to sleep in somewhere else? Where do you want to be? Upstairs, or down?'

'Downstairs, I think. Where do you suggest?'

'You can sleep where you like, as long as it's not where I've just come from. Take these, please, they're making my arms ache.'

'Put them down there. I'll arrange them later, thank you.'

'Let me know which room you've chosen, won't you. Then I can have a single bed arranged. You'll need extra blankets, too, from the upstairs' chest. Would you like to choose your own? You can go and choose a room too, hmm?'

'Please don't make it sound like a birthday treat, Dorothea. I am merely changing my sleeping accommodation after all. This is not some great event, even if you wish to make it so. Please go away, and I will try to settle tonight's problem as best I can without you.'

'It's more than tonight's problem for you. You realize that, don't you?'

'Of course. Merely a figure of speech. Don't get alarmed. I fully understand. Please leave it at that, and leave me now. I have decided already where I shall sleep. I shall sleep in here.'

'Here?'

'There's plenty of room. The screens will shelter my bed, until I have time to construct something more permanent.'

'But the smell! How can you stand to sleep in the smell? All those acids and things. . . .'

'Only other people notice it. Now, please go.'

'I thought you might appreciate the opportunity I'm giving you to discuss things.'

'You have just put an end to discussion. Now take your worries away with you and leave me alone. There is a great deal of work for me to do, and you're hindering it. Go away.'

The door bangs, and she is gone.

He isn't a weak man, but he knows strength lies in giving way. Only by this method will he succeed in holding on to her. Because she is the unattainable prize he will wait until he can have her absolutely. He never tires of waiting; it is the answer to his problems. It is a pleasure to him, indeed a way of life, unexplainable to others who miss so much by their headlong plunge into action. Therefore he doesn't try to explain. He is working out how he can save her, and how he can arrive at a state of permanence himself. Nothing marks the passage of Time but action, and even this can be stabilised if it is set down, fixed forever by some means. In this way there will be one person who, when others have forgotten what they were and what they did, will have the truth of them locked away for perpetuity. If one waits for long enough in a seeming state of inertia, then the longed-for goal will be reached. On occasions there will have to be choices made, choices forced by others, but these will be aimed at one thing, the time when all action can cease, and he can be left alone to gaze forever on the crystallization of his endeavours, as unaware of what goes on outside as a Trigonia.

But the man who sits in this room is a virtual beginner, still full of the fears that grip a man when he has been forced out of his usual passive role. He is still afraid that Time can never be entirely conquered, that he himself will be its prey. Everything, so far, that has come into his possession has come there almost by accident: he has sent away for, and received, this or that specimen, but he has never been absolutely sure that what he has collected has been a pure and perfect choice. To have gone himself in search of specimens would have meant long journeys half across the world, facing the hazards of ships and the sea, spending days and weeks on nightmare boats, pulling up the lines, soaking himself with salt, feeling the ocean's slime, being buffeted by winds and storms, having to communicate with strangers; or wading the coral reefs among the lurking horrors of a rainbow world that savagely attack even the most wary. His father told him of journeys to the Great Barrier Reef in search of Tridacna gigas. He dreamed of the sunlight bright on the shallow water through which could be glimpsed the waving polyps and the blazing corals among which the spotted crabs lurk in search of prey. He saw the starfish and the spiny worms, the squids and stonefish seeking their sustenance beneath the curtain of numberless fish whose days were numbered. He knew that if one set foot in that aquamarine battlefield then the chances of coming out alive were almost non-existent. He sent for a specimen of Conus geographus, marvelling that its splendid brown and white striations should have covered the cause of his father's death. He would rather the cone that he held in his hand had been the actual one which his father had held when it jabbed him; how was he to be sure that death had been caused by its poisoned proboscis and not by some other lethal inhabitant of that liquid hell? Yet he could never do what his father had done, and risk himself for the sake of his collection. Risks had to be taken, but they were always taken after days of consideration, and usually consisting of nothing more than a letter written or a sortie made into the house, the garden or the street beyond. And if his mind should tire sometimes of the waiting, there was the revival of spirits that came with a visit to this place, where someone else's attempts to collect humanity could be seen.

How I thank heaven I wasn't here before the invention of the photograph: my task would have been impossible. Had I been a painter I would have been forced to stand, brush in hand, surveying my subject in the very throes of decay, powerless to stop the process in an instant; having to dash on the layers of paint at speed before my subject crumbled into senility. Somewhere in all these portraits is a line, a dot, the point at which the artist started to capture his sitter on canvas. But this young line is overlayed with others of a later date, and these in turn have been plastered by the paint he has steadily applied for weeks and months, until the present likeness is to his taste. By this time, when the portrait is complete, both artist and model have forgotten the purpose of the picture: that of holding fast to the instant when it was begun. Now it is only an amalgam of instances, each one giving the lie to the ones that follow, and we are left with countless faces blended into one dissembling whole. And so I walk along these rows of faces, trying to pick out in each one the imperfections and disharmonies, drawing strength from the knowledge that my truth is not distorted, for I can have, in a flash of a shutter, what has been denied to every one of these names printed so proudly on the little gold plates beneath the frames.

I tried to tell Max of my gift when he came to see me to tell me of his plans. When he told me that he and James were leaving, I tried to explain what the going would entail: I told him that if he removed himself from my surveillance, then he, and James, would lose the chance to be immortalized. I tried to treat the matter lightly, because he has a streak of flippancy in him that responds to the same tone in others. 'Although,' I said, 'my main attentions have always been concentrated on Dorothea, nevertheless you, and James, have sometimes come into the picture. I have managed to save a tidy portion of your lives which now, you say, will be spent somewhere I cannot reach you.'

He asked me if I had been drinking. 'I wouldn't be surprised if you had,' he added. 'It must have been awful in here all these years. I would have gone bats.'

I asked him not to change the subject when so serious a matter was under discussion. Never before had I tried to impart to anyone what my task had been. If he was so intent on leaving, then he must appreciate the sacrifice he was making, and be given the chance to change his mind.

'I'm offering you the chance of staying, Max,' I said. 'For while I can appreciate that you and James must be rid of the annoyance of Dorothea, it is much more important that you stay behind, like her, so that I can go on with my task of saving you.'

'But that's the trouble, old chap. We don't know what to do about Dorothea.'

A sudden alarm filled me. The idea that she might go as well hadn't occurred to me until then.

Max explained that when he had suggested leaving she had threatened to go with him, even to following him every hour of the day in case he decided on a sudden flight.

'Does she know that James is included in your future plans?'

'Have a heart. It was bad enough when I told her I was leaving, let alone including poor old Jamie in it. She went through the whole gamut, she did—tears, tempers, pleading me not to leave her destitute, threatening me with the law—as if that would get her anywhere—until I promised to take her with me....'

'But you can't. You can't.'

'Steady, old chap. I know I can't. Jamie would throw a fit. No, the idea is to play along with her. Let her get packed and so on, and let her know all the details about where we're moving to. It'd better be somewhere remote like, er, Scotland, and we'll have to do some homework to get our facts straight. I know a fellow who will send me phoney brochures of desirable residences and things like that. If needs be I could even rent a property up there.... Anyway, when we're all set to leave, farewells and things said, we trot off to the station together ... and that is where I leave her! Boom! I vanish into the blue, and poor old Dorothea is homeless.'

'Max, do you know what you're saying?'

'It should be fairly easy to dump her, don't you think?'

'Dump her! You can't know what you're saying! Are you suggesting that Dorothea is to *leave* this house? And that you'd be a party to it?'

'Hey, hey. Keep the old hair on! I thought you'd be glad to see the going of her.'

'How can you think that when all my life has been dedicated to...'

'She'd have gone years ago if it wasn't for me. And if it hadn't been me, it would have been someone else. So what's the great flurry for now? Are you suddenly missing her!'

'Dorothea is *not leaving,* Max. She isn't going anywhere.'

'I say, you *have* been drinking, haven't you? Just my luck when I wanted to get some sense out of you. As a matter of fact the subject's a trifle delicate....'

Again I told him that he was totally mistaken in thinking that Dorothea would leave the house. While I kept insisting vehemently, he kept shaking my arm, as though I needed to be brought back from a state of inebriation. He asked me how bad I was; kept repeating it, until I shook him off, and said, over and over again, that Dorothea was not leaving.

'I came to see you on a matter of finance, old chap,' he said. 'Now I can see there's not much sense to be got out of you today. Can't make head or tail of you. Pity if you've started to hit the bottle just when things are going well for you—just when you can look forward to a bit of peace.'

'Max, I am asking you to try to understand what I am saying. If you wish to leave this house, and all the opportunities I have offered, then it's up to you. But you are not taking Dorothea.'

'I say, you're serious, aren't you? Whoever would have thought you cared! We certainly live and learn. Still, there's nothing I can do about it if she decides to leave. I'm washing my hands of her.'

'You are not.'

'You must have been hitting the bottle! Never heard that tone before. Now, where are you hiding the stuff? I need one myself. I can see the going's tough.'

'And you are going to help me keep her here, Max.'

'I am not! I have other things to do than play nursemaid to your sudden fancies.'

It was then that I came to the decision to show him my work. Only by revealing what I had done in the past for him, and James, as well as Dorothea, could I hope to get his help. I had to show him evidence to prove that, whatever else he did, he couldn't take her away from me.

He watched with curiosity while I went over to the steel-bound cabinet and unlocked the doors. His face wore an indulgent look as I removed the first folder and brought it to where he stood.

'Sit down, Max,' I said. 'This will take some time to show you. There are quite a few.' And with trembling fingers I undid the cover, peeled back the tissue, and exposed to someone else, for the very first time, one of my precious photographs. Max's reaction wasn't what I had expected. I had thought he would reverently take hold of the corner of the pristine card and examine the detail, as I had done for the twenty years it had been in my possession. I had no time to tell him that its title was inscribed on the back, along with relevant data as to lens and focus: he flicked the photograph with his thumb and hastily looked at the one beneath. Then he shuffled them like a card player, muttering 'I see' under his breath.

But he didn't see. He couldn't possibly have seen in the time he took to look at them. I had to remove the set gently from his limp hands and hold them, each one in turn, under his nose.

'This one's called "The Marriage",' I said. 'Don't you think she becomes the dress you made her? I know your hand somewhat spoils the view of it, but it's her face that's all important. Can you see its impeccable smoothness? Not a line. Not a wrinkle.' Max said nothing, so I continued with the next photograph, while explaining that as cameras and methods improved, so did I. I showed him the poor quality of the printing that had to be endured during the war, before I printed them myself, and when materials were not the best. I have never had much faith in seaside chemists when it comes to getting good work done. But he seemed most interested in the print—quite insignificant to me—of himself and Dorothea standing close together in the sunlight, on a deserted beach. Since he stared at it with such concentration, I felt duty bound to tell him of its faults: how bad the printing was, how at the time I had been beset by sand fleas so that, at the very moment when I should have shot them, I had to scratch my calf. It was strange, I remarked, how they seemed not to notice the fleas. So this photograph was what might be called a 'second best', taken minutes later when there was less exposure of the skin, and therefore less obvious proclamation of their ages. I asked him if he thought I had captured them as they really were at twenty-seven and twenty-eight years old respectively. But he didn't answer. Although his mouth was loosely open, he didn't say a word: grabbing the photograph from my hand, he turned it over to read the back.

'As long ago as that?' he asked. 'As long ago as that.'

Gently I removed the picture from his hands and showed him the coiling lines of barbed wire that made a spiky background to the coupling. And if he wanted further proof, there was always my diary to refer to: in it he could find the time of day, the temperature, and how successful I thought the shot had been. He wasn't interested in my diary. He wanted to see more photographs. So I showed him the sequence of shots of Dorothea, taken by the sea during the long days of our wartime sojourn there, when she was willing, sometimes, to pose for me. He seemed not a bit interested in the little changes in her that I had photographed with such loving care. Even though I bothered to point out to him how Time's passage could be traced by the growth of hair and nails, and a coarsening of the epidermic layer, he gave the set a cursory look. I told him how I had done my best to give a running commentary on Dorothea, in her many moods as well as in her stages of deterioration. His interest only revived when he himself came on the scene: he looked hard at one shot of them saying goodbye on the station platform. I thought it perfect in its way—her with her sad, distracted face and twining hands, him in his handsome uniform, smiling down and clasping her. They looked like two halves of an open Mollusc. I asked him not to be surprised at the lack of photographs of himself in uniform, but he was to blame: whenever Dorothea was around he always seemed to wear only light attire, often preferring the Altogether. He could see by the pictures in his hand that this was true.

'Ha!' he said. 'You can't pin anything on me. Not with this little lot. You'll need more evidence than this.' The last photograph in the file was dated 1945. He held it out to me. 'Get tired of peekaboo, did you? Haven't got any more recent than these? These are what you might call "Old Hat".' He laughed, and relaxed.

But when he saw me go over to the cupboard again and extract another file, his face began to pale. He sat up suddenly and tensed himself. He barely gave me time to open the file and fold away the tissue before he had snatched it from me, fumbling for the edges of the card marked 'One' as if his life depended on it. This time he looked with greater care, often nodding when I explained the technicalities of this or that shot, or how it came to be taken. Now he seemed to find my studies more a cause for amusement than for stress: still he paid them more attention, once murmuring 'Good for you', when I told him of what patience I had mustered to obtain some of the shots he saw. He said 'Ha!' again when I told him of the troublesome day on which I had been forced to smuggle my camera into the gallery under my coat. His face showed he was vaguely pleased I should have thought him worth the effort of a whole afternoon spent stalking them through the rooms. I watched them play the old, familiar games, joke about the same faces, harass the same gallery attendants; all the time waiting for the moment when I could catch them still. Strange he never commented on the place at which they finally stopped: I expected him to notice the picture of the queen immediately; it shows behind them clear enough in the photograph. They were comparing her to Dorothea. Their heads were close together, but their raucous whispers could be heard as I pressed myself against the arch, ready for the long-shot. My camera then was a Kodak. What a pity I wasn't using colour. I could have done justice to Dorothea's red hair against the queen's silk dress as she bent forward to listen to Max. I could have brought out the beautiful whiteness of his hand hovering over the painted ones. I asked him whether he was comparing her rings to the ones he was wearing, but he'd forgotten. It had been too long ago.

One by one he shuffled through the second set of shots of Dorothea, not noticing the way she had fattened, and her taste in clothes grown coarse. I asked him whether he remembered how she'd looked on the day he'd come to live upstairs. Of course he didn't. She wasn't all that fascinating. So I showed him. I showed him the two of them together by the bedroom door indulging in a hasty hug before coming to face me with the news of his arrival. He wasn't so much interested in the pose, he'd seen it before, he said, as in the place that I had stood to take the photograph. 'Where were you?' he said. It seemed to puzzle him. Rather than answer such a question I showed him Dorothea at work in her gardening clothes: I thought the quaint costumes of the Forties might interest him. There was one of Dorothea eating; another of her puzzling over a magazine; a beauty of her when asleep, her face disguised by cream, making of her a sleeping clown. I told Max that novelties were not my usual taste, but one or two I had felt were worth preserving, especially when, like this specimen, they proved that Dorothea herself was trying to defeat the years.

'What on earth's this?' he asked, when he came upon a particularly dark example of my work. He held it up for me to see, although this wasn't necessary. I know that collection better than my own hand: I can go to it in the middle of the night and select, without error, the specimen I want without bothering to switch on the light.

'That one's called "Party Games",' I said. 'It's written on the back. I agree it's not one of my best, but that is due to lack of light. It came up rather grained, I fear, due to overexposure.'

Max almost laughed. 'You can say that again,' he remarked. 'Looks rather romantic doesn't it, with the moonlight?'

'Yes. The moon enabled me to place you in the graticule, so the composition is quite good. But I was never happy about your rigid back. While Dorothea is as relaxed as any cameraman could wish, you seem to be straining round, as though something had disturbed you. You said "Shsh," if I remember rightly.'

Max closed file number Two and looked at me. He was enjoying himself. His lips twitched in a sort of smile. 'I suppose it would be too much to suppose there isn't another one of these?' He held it up, and I nodded. 'I was afraid so,' he said. 'Well come on. Roll it out. I can see there's got to be the full parade today.'

File number Two went back into the cupboard along with number One. Then I brought out Three.

'You may have gathered, Max,' I said, 'that these go in files of ten years each. Not that there are the same number of photographs in each section; but I wanted there to be some system to the whole. I think this way has clarity, don't you?'

'Not more of Dorothea gardening?' he said as he saw the first one.

'Yes. But can you see the way she's changed?'

He tossed it to one side, but showed more interest in the next example of her progress: he had come out quite clearly in the shot, holding out his arms to adjust her dress. Taken from the vantage point of a high window, as were so many of my photographs, it showed to perfection her muscular strength, and how she was slowly fattening.

'What a ghastly dress,' Max said.

'You made her another—just as awful.'

'Fat, wasn't she?'

'She was contented then.'

'What's this?' Max said. 'Not Jamie too?'

'Why not? He was always hanging round for a sight of you.'

'Poor darling. I've a lot to make up to him.'

'The one you're holding is a classic of its kind. See the way he crouches as he walks; afraid to be seen slinking across the garden on his way down to the cherry trees. See the mathematical ways of working out what time of year it was by the length and lie of the shadows. But you can tell that by looking on the back. No? Never mind. The next picture will show very well how the trees weren't yet in bloom. The branches hardly hide you, do they?'

Max began to breathe more loudly. His smile had disappeared. There were three photos of himself with James; two taken out of doors and one inside. He didn't like the one called 'Evening Assignation', and said that 'Stairway to Paradise' was disgusting. I told him that I regretted the title afterwards, but ten years ago romantic titles had more appeal for me than they do today. Today I favour something more accurately clinical. It was hard to see why he found the staircase shot so unattractive: I had often looked at it with pleasure, rather proud of the effect of light and shade caused by the two close figures behind the banisters. It could have been called 'tricky', but there were compensations: he with his artist's eye should have appreciated the pattern of the interlocking arms, out of which the two heads rose as the focal point of the composition.

'Perhaps this is more to your taste,' I said. 'I call it "Venus Rising".'

'Was nothing sacred?'

'The slight haze you may perceive comes from the steam across my lens. As she rose from the bath Dorothea caused the steam to rise. Lucky it did, in a way: I was quite hidden from view. See the way she's so unconcerned as she raises her arms for the towel.'

'Serves her right. She'd never lock the bathroom door.'

'I believe there are signs of sagging of the breasts. The stomach muscles aren't so taut. Interesting how the skin is slowly giving way. . . .'

Without looking at the rest of the photographs in the folder, Max handed them to me. 'No more,' he said. 'I want to see no more.'

'But it's too late, Max. You must see them all. You've come too far to stop now. My pictures get better as we proceed. I can see that you're not so interested as myself in the simpler specimens, but in the next collection I'm sure there are one or two with great novelty value—if that's what you want.' He still seemed dubious until I mentioned that he and James were on several of the prints.

At least he was now treating my collection as seriously as I would have wished. There was no sign of his earlier levity as he turned over the cover of the folder and looked down on my first shots of a changed and desolate Dorothea. These pictures of her eating her solitary meals, or trailing the dark corridors at night, or sitting before her mirror massaging out the newly-discovered lines, were ones he thumbed through hastily before I had time to explain their sequence. He bent more closely to a shot of himself and James upstairs in the workroom having fun with new fabrics.

He frowned at the close-up of James' head wreathed in a daisy chain. I asked him how he liked the lyrical effect of his own dismembered hands holding the flowers like a crown. He said 'Ha!' but very gravely, and turned pale. Lying uppermost in his hand was the shot of the two of them trying on Dorothea's clothes. I took the opportunity to admire once more how precisely I had captured the details of the dress, yet not losing the contrast of skin and hair. Even the tiny fluttering fronds of the feather boa could be seen minutely, without a trace of blur, despite their movements as they danced, Max and James, completely immersed in each other's company. Max spent so long looking at the photograph—his hands shaking—that I felt obliged to reciprocate his interest.

'I'll show you my camera,' I said. 'Such a lovely one: Single Lens Eye Level Reflex'—words to conjure with. Gently I removed it from its resting place and held it out to him. He was the first person to clap eyes on it since it came to me. It was an honour he should not have taken so lightly. Ignoring it he flung the set of photographs in the air with a great shout of rage, and then he covered his face with his hands, cowering in his chair. My anger at seeing my precious work so badly treated stopped the amusement I would otherwise have felt at seeing so civilised a man behave like the most ignorant savage who fears the camera will steal his soul. Max sat cowering in the same attitude while I put away the camera and collected my photographs from the floor where they lay like confetti. Not until I had pocketed the cupboard key did he raise his head.

'How much?' he said.

I did not, at first, understand the question. 'How much what?'

'How much for the photos? I'll buy them from you.'

'Buy them! My photographs?'

'Including negatives. You know the ones I mean. Name what you want for them, and you can have it. I'm not a rich man but I'll pay your price. Just name it.'

'My work has no *price*. I can't sell it. I'm a collector. It's my job to *retain*. Not like you who design for obsolescence. Those photographs are a lifetime's work. They're priceless.'

Max stared at me for a moment with a cold expression. 'What do you intend to do with them?' he said.

Good question. My thoughts had been running along the lines of framing them, as an added precaution against deterioration. 'I'm considering the possibilities of *passe-partout*,' I told him. 'Or perhaps plastic would be more durable.'

'And then... What then?'

'Then, possibly, I shall put them in a special cabinet—the kind with a sloping front of glass, and a green baize cover. Cork might be a kind material on which to fasten them....'

Max leaped to his feet and rushed across the room. I couldn't understand his agitation. He paced the floor, not in his usual exhibitionist way, but as though I had offended him.

'Put them on show!' he shouted. 'On show? Exhibit them?'

'They'll be under glass. They won't come to harm.'

'And you'll let anyone who comes in here have a look at them?' He walked up to me and breathed hard on my head.

'I'll certainly show them to anyone interested. Anyone who takes an interest in the only possible permanence shall surely see them. They must have proof of stability.'

He raised his arms and shook his fists. I was afraid that he was going to drum them on my crown. Then he continued pacing the floor, saying, 'You can't. You can't,' over and over.

When he came back to his chair again, his tone had changed to one that I knew better: now it had a wheedling note. 'Sell them to me. For friendship's sake, sell them to me.'

'I can't do that, Max. What would I be left with? All of you gone, and nothing left for perpetuity. Don't you understand?'

'My dear chap, I'm not asking that you part with all of them—only certain ones. You know what I mean... certain ones.'

'I'm sorry, the line can't be broken.'

'Come on. What's a few mouldy photos between friends?'

'These sudden claims to friendship are rather novel, Max. When I compare its transitory nature to what I have in that cupboard over there, I'm bound to admit you come off worst.'

'Am I to gather from these ramblings that my offer has been refused?'

'Your offer...?'

'Of *money*. I suppose I should have known you wouldn't need anything as banal as that.'

'I don't need money it's true.'

Max sprang from his chair. 'What do you want from me?'

'Dorothea,' I answered truthfully.

He seemed surprised. He paced the room in silence while I waited. Halting by the window he faced me saying, 'And you want me to get her for you . . . ?'

'Not *get* her, *leave* her—here. She *must* stay behind. I want you to make sure she doesn't think of leaving. She is not to go with you.'

'God knows, I'd rather she didn't.' Max thought again. 'It could be done, I suppose. If I worked on her, she wouldn't want to come. It's touch and go between us most of the time now. Oh! I suppose you know that.'

'Yes. But would she stay here? She has what she calls "her pride". Lately it's taken the form of presenting me with household trivia such as bills and things. She suddenly wants not to be a burden.'

'An overworked word in her vocabulary. She might stay if you came to an agreement with her.'

'What kind of agreement?'

'I don't quite know. Something legal-like. What Dee wants is security above all else. She has to be looked after. A piece of printed paper might reassure her. If we turned it into a sort of business contract, she might find it more attractive.'

'And if she didn't . . . ?'

'There you have me. Now let's look at the situation objectively: she wants a home, and she wants a protector. Right? Right now she's pretty desperate. I don't want her. You don't want her . . . Please don't interrupt. So we have on our side her need for security. Against us we have the obvious fact that she's unwelcome here.'

'But I must have her. . . .'

'Quite so. Just be quiet while I give the matter undivided thought.' He eased himself into the chair and crossed his long legs. Putting his elbows among my papers on the desk, he leaned towards me. 'Leave it to Uncle Max,' he said. 'A solution is slowly dawning.' He stretched himself and closed his eyes, smiling a secret smile. When he opened them he said, 'I have a gorgeous plan, so beautiful I'm proud of it. But before I tell you, you must promise me to burn both photographs and negatives, here and now.'

It took me all of half an hour to assure him I meant to keep my work. Neither his little rages nor his threatening gestures could influence me. Only when I agreed to lock away the offending works and never show them to anyone again, did he calm down. Since he was the first person to whom they had been shown, he was partly reassured of my honesty. But being essentially dishonest himself, he wanted further guarantees himself. He wanted money. I could see no real reason for refusing him, since, in exchange, he would present me with a plan. There and then we came to an agreement: my money for his ideas.

'We must invent a mythical chap,' he said. 'Give him a name, position, money, and a home. Tell her he's looking for a mate ... something along those lines. I'll work on it later. And I'll work on Dee. She's getting a bit near the jolly old tether, so it shouldn't be too difficult. She knows we're all washed up, and she's dead scared of solitary. Literally terrified. Quite a thing to be homeless at forty-six, isn't it? Look at it that way and it takes on a new meaning, doesn't it? None of us likes to be alone, do we?'

'Some of us have been alone for a long time.'

'Don't make me laugh. You enjoyed yourself, I'll bet. I'm just wondering if you weren't the one getting the most pleasure out of it all. I'm still not sure.'

'I achieved a certain emancipation of the flesh denied to the rest of you.'

'Well put. But a bloody lie all the same. Now this situation's going to require a lot of brain work. We might have to call in extramural help.'

'Not James, please.'

'Oh no, not him. He'll be standing on the side-lines. No. I'm thinking of someone I know who'll be only too willing to assist, at a price. You see Dee's packed her bags, mentally speaking. So she's ready to leave as long as we can persuade her it's to her advantage. Now this fellow could do just that: fix her up with this mythical chap. The whole thing could be a work of art. I'll go and see this fellow and arrange the details. He's used to affairs of this kind, so he won't ask too many questions, not if there's plenty in it for him. And you'll see to that side of things, won't you?'

'Why not tell Dorothea that I want her to stay?'

'Are you mad? She wouldn't believe you. Why should she? But she'd believe a contract now, wouldn't she? She'd believe the sight of a piece of paper committing her to someone else. Of course she's not to know the someone else is you. That will come later, when the whole thing's settled.'

'What if she doesn't agree?'

'Of course there's a risk. There always is in any business deal. But this third party idea of mine is brilliant. Almost a guarantee of success itself. You see, she'll have turned the whole thing into a business proposition, and honour will be satisfied. Money and contracts will have changed hands. She'll be eager to settle the affair. You'll see.' Slowly he rose, stretching himself, and made for the door.

'My job's going to be the difficult one,' he said. 'I've got to persuade her to see this friend of mine. She mayn't like it very much. Still, he's very discreet. You'll have to see him too, of course. I think you'll like him. Great sense of humour. I did one of his flats last year: magenta and black, with mirrors. No taste, but expensive.' Before opening the door he adjusted his tie. 'It should be interesting to you both, carving out a new life from the husk of the old. You may put that down in your diary!' With a loose wave Max sidled out of the door, and gently closed it.

8

He sits in his room as he has always done, waiting for things to come to him. Perhaps that was the mistake: not to have gone out himself and looked for what he wanted. Others have been paid to do the job, and until now they have never failed. Drawer upon drawer, high to the ceiling, is filled with his desires: Terebrae, Mitridae, Olividae, Haliotidae, Volutidae, specimen after specimen, no two alike, marked and catalogued and counted. But he has never really known the battles that went on to secure for him certain specimens. Often when the price was far too high, with it would come a hair-raising tale that sounded fictional. He hasn't wanted to believe the possibility of escape for anything he'd ordered. Looking at the great Strombus gigas lying like a frozen fountain underneath its dome, he cannot bring himself to believe that once it burrowed speedily into the sand to elude its captors, or was capable of leaping wildly to freedom. The shell was empty of its animal when it arrived, its pink perfection hardly equitable with something as mundanely alive as a sea-snail whose eyes could see piercingly, whose tail could power somersaults, and whose nose (if nose it can be called) could smell so keenly. He would have liked the opportunity of preserving everything: eyes, nose, and tail, so that the shell was less hollowly perfect. He would have liked to see his shells in action: the fragile Ianthina drifting across the ocean on floating islands of Gulf weed: the Pectinidae flapping like multi-coloured butterflies through the waves, or tumbling towards the receding tide before it left them stranded. Then he might be able more easily to ascertain the chances of an escape or flight, and guard against it. He read of the escape of quite a large Trigonia which leaped suddenly into the sea before anyone could halt it. Was this sheer carelessness on the part of the fishermen, or is the animal's instinct for flight so strong? Some shells seem to possess a cunning hardly credible when one considers their exteriors. Some bivalves bury themselves deep in the sand, sometimes as much as five feet down, defying those who go in search of them.

It wasn't pleasant looking for Solen siliqua: wading through the cold water to reach the sand bars; trousers rolled, ankles chilled; eyes dazzled by the stippled sea, hands set stiffly round the bucket handles and iron rods with which we hoped to catch our prey.

I never liked to face the elements in such a way, neither did Max whose loathing for freshness in any form did him credit. But Dorothea's enthusiasm carried us along; forcing us both to go on what she described as a 'change of scene'. She said we had all been getting stale and bored in the confines of our mansion. Now that the days were long and the sun as hot as it would ever be later in the year, we should all go down to the sea again. Max only accepted on condition that I was included in the plans 'for the sake of the collection'; but I knew he wanted me to bear with him the burden of Dorothea's new-found gaiety. She felt that a crisis had been passed, and wished to celebrate, while at the same time removing Max from further temptations. He could only acquiesce, and keep his nose clean. It was Dorothea who booked the tickets and packed the bags and settled details about our reception at the summer house. She made Max put away his scissors and delegate responsibility for two whole weeks. She pushed me into locking up my room, and threatened me with someone coming in to dust if I should complain of its neglect. Telling her that Time was precious to me only helped her case: she said that I could spend my holiday searching for native shells as I had done when young. She said it would be just like old times again. Max pulled a face.

Due to Dorothea's care the house hadn't changed so very much since I had last been there. Someone from the village was regularly employed to keep it clean and free from moth. The gardens, on Dorothea's instructions, had been attended to. If there were signs of lawns and hedges hastily cut, and borders newly weeded, then who was I to complain, not having visited it for many seasons? Flaking paint and falling tiles were to be expected in a building of its age, so closely swept by salty winds and winter gales. The white road down to the house had more the appearance of a dried up river bed, its stones washed in grey heaps and ridges. The gate was off its hinges, almost overgrown by luxuriant growths of nettles. The front step had a tendency to rock when trod upon; lizards ran as we opened the front door. How small the rooms were to me after so long away, and how the sun had faded everything to the same muted shade of parchment. The creaking stairs set me wondering about the presence of wood worm, as did the shaky banisters; but there was no smell of mould in any of the rooms, and only pale patches on the walls to show where past rains had penetrated the outer bricks. Dorothea greeted these signs of dissolution like long-lost friends, dragging Max by the arm to point out what had happened in their absence. Judging by his embarrassment they had, since my last sojourn there, been back together. Pinned on a wall in one of the rooms upstairs were several sketches. Dorothea greeted them rapturously. 'There I am!' she cried, waving at the poor smudged renderings of an earlier face. 'You have such talent, Max.' He paid no attention to the work: his eyes had fixed on something else. Quietly he went over to a small sketch on the farther wall and surreptitiously tugged it down. While Dorothea still reminisced he hastily crammed it into his pocket. The action made me curious: the sketch wasn't of a female form. A small search of the other rooms provided evidence of another visitor: James' sand shoe came to light, lodged beneath a wardrobe: his spotted kerchief lay forgotten in a drawer.

Quietly I handed my finds to Max who stuffed them into his pockets with a murmured 'Thanks'. 'Now you can sort out the sleeping quarters,' I told him. 'With the minimum of fuss.' He portioned out to us a single room each, which arrangement Dorothea accepted with nothing more than a sly smile for him. I didn't ask how he'd persuaded her.

The days were long—too long for some of us. Max spent his (when he could) in writing lengthy, surreptitious letters which he found difficult to post. I spent mine, when the winds allowed, in wandering the half-forgotten shores among the summer visitors—more numerous than in the past. Children desecrated the sand with their digging or ransacked the rock pools for loot. When I came across their buckets filled with Littorinae I wondered if there would be any specimens left to preserve from their savagery. Motor cars had invaded the coast road, bringing with them armies of intrepid campers whose loads of litter spotted the sand and brought the seagulls down. Up on the cliffs their bright tents shook, and the noise of boisterous games dimmed the constant sound of the sea. Flowers still bloomed on the remoter sides of the shattered cliffs; grass kept a precarious hold on the crumbling verges; but a general slipping of the land was in progress, a falling away before the onslaught of the elements. Slides of rock had buried the upper parts of the beach and the water was coming to claim them. Slowly the land was being eaten away by processes quite plainly visible to a discerning eye.

'The cliffs are smaller,' I said to Dorothea.

'Bother the cliffs.' Already in her bathing suit, out of which she bulged in fat folds, she struggled against the wind to lay down a towel for Max. The strong sun wasn't reason enough for him to remove his jacket; he stood hunched, collar up, back towards the breeze, not trying to hide his dissatisfaction with such a foolish outing. The towel was put down and anchored with stones, and Max lowered himself with a groan and, 'I'm too old for this kind of lark.'

'Nonsense, Max. You're as young as you feel. Look at me.'

'Can't,' said Max. 'The sight's too horrible.'

Dorothea laughed. She sat down beside him to take off her shoes. 'Don't be such a cross-patch. It's a lovely day. You couldn't possibly catch cold on a day like this. Could he? Fancy wanting to stay at home! He needs a break. I always tell him he works too hard. He's been in the house for days, poring over those beastly papers.'

'Some people have work to do,' he said. 'They can't just take off with no thought for anyone but themselves.'

'Meaning me, I suppose? Next you'll be saying you didn't want to come. You were eager enough when I suggested it.'

'You've hit the nail on the jolly old head. You didn't stop to consider whether I really wanted to come, did you? Oh no. You just barged ahead and made all the arrangements, to suit your little self.'

'You said you'd love to come. Didn't he?'

'I may have *said* it, but how did I say it? With enthusiasm? There was no discussion, was there?'

'Of course there was. You asked if *he* could come too. And I said "Why not?"'

'There you go, damning yourself out of your own mouth! You thought of nobody but yourself, did you? Admit it.'

Several digging children raised their heads as the voices grew louder. A dog began to bark at us. Dorothea shivered and got up. She took a few steps across the sand. 'I'm going in,' she called. 'See you later. Mother's waiting!' Quickly she threaded her way through the lounging bathers, having to sidestep and back-track before she could reach the receding tide. At the water's edge she waved, then threw herself down with a mighty splash which won her applause from the groundlings. 'What did she mean "Mother's waiting"?' Max asked.

'The sea. She meant the sea.'

Only the rhythmic rise of her arms could be seen as Dorothea swam out to where the sea was free of people.

'God, I'm so bored,' Max said. He eyed a sandy, leaping dog with distaste, then watched a group of youths play volley ball. Sand whipped our legs, covering the towel on which we sat with a fine film. 'Look at them. They're all right. Sweet and twenty, I'll bet. Can't even remember what it was like.'

'I believe I can.'

'Oh yes. You would. Got it all written down I suppose, in a nice fat diary.'

'Twenty-four, to be exact.'

But he had risen to retrieve the ball that the wind had sent bouncing across the rocks in our direction. A young man came running to fetch it from him, and stood red-faced while Max tossed it in a teasing way before throwing it back. The youth ran back to the scuffling safety of his own kind, and the game continued. They shouted and leaped; dogs barked; children ran: everywhere was movement. The waves swept in with white flurries all along the undulating line of their recession. Gulls sailed backwards on strong air currents. Even the sky seemed to be racing away in a streaming pattern of cloudy streaks that threatened to leave us with a void above our heads.

'I'm so bored,' Max said. 'My life is slipping away.' He fingered into place a stray, grey hair. 'Forty-two, and see what it's got me.' Briefly he looked towards the distant sea, swallowing cloud shadows in its turbulence. My books lay about us on the sand; he picked one from a pile and opened a random, fluttering page. 'For God's sake read to me,' he said. 'Read anything. I'll never survive this wilderness. It's getting me down.'

I took the indicated page and started in middle chapter:

> 'The simplest method to employ with bivalves is to cut through the anchoring adductor muscles, using a sharp knife or razor blade. Immersion in boiling water is adequate to ensure loss of life in any of the gasteropods, the animal then being removed by means of a stout pin. Nevertheless it is considered preferable in many instances to preserve the specimen intact by the use of industrial alcohol (or spirit). There must be a solution of at least 70 per cent, and care must be taken to introduce the animal to this gradually, working up from a weak solution of 30 per cent—increasing the percentage every few days—until the final solution is attained. Hardening may occur . . .'

Max stopped me. 'For mercy's sake! That may be poetry to you, but it's killing me. It sounds positively evil.'

'The book is incorrect. In actual fact there is flaking and fading if this course is followed. It may lead to Byne's disease. Sea water must first be used. . . .'

'Look at her! Just look at her!' Max had seen Dorothea far out where the sea was grey. She had her arms above her head, waving. Max waved back. 'Do you think,' he said, 'she's drowning? I read once of a chap who was out at sea like that, waving madly. He was drowning, but the people on the shore thought he was only waving. So they waved back. And he waved back, trying to attract their attention. They couldn't hear him, you see, so they didn't know he was drowning. They kept on waving and waving at each other, until finally he sank.' He settled on his elbows and Dorothea disappeared to surface nearer us. She swam back with strong strokes, and Max looked at the youths playing ball.

Not until the tide had reached its lowest point did we go in search of shells. Many bathers had quit the beach away from the chilling wind, leaving us, a solitary threesome, to brave the rock pools filled with floating rubbish, and walk out across the sand to where low tide was marked by a dark ribbon right round the curve of the bay. Heads down we marched, watching the fluting at our feet for signs other than the water's vibrations, ready with our sticks to probe for the speedy Ensis. It was a long way to the sea, distance made further by the sameness of each yard we trod over the uprooted tangleweed and hidden mussel shells that cut the soles. Flickering reflections strained the eyes, the flash of the water and splash as the feet disturbed it, hypnotised me into believing that we were walking into a wide nothingness where sand, sea and sky existed only as the vitreous matter exists that floats in one's vision but cannot be directly seen. Not until we reached the water line with its gently rocking debris did some sense of order return.

I pointed out the possible habitat of Ensis siliqua, the means and method of capture, and we began a systematic scouring. Dorothea, in great excitement, ran in front, her heavy step causing the loss of many specimens which, at the slightest movement overhead, sink down to safety. Several jets were sighted and dug before she could be persuaded to go more gently, allowing us time to creep up on the creature and haul it out. Max was the one who became expert at plunging his arm in to grasp the shell before it could dive. He was oblivious of its slimy sharpness or the stinging, salty grit that lodged in any small abrasion. Totally absorbed in his work—for once—he never noticed the diminishing light, or commented on the turn of the tide that was bringing with it a hint of worse weather.

'I'm cold,' Dorothea said. 'Lend me your jacket, Max.'

'No. Go and get your own. Want me to catch my death?' Her clothes still lay, a distant speck of colour, under the cliff's overhang.

'But I'm cold...'

'That's your lookout. Anyone else would have had the sense to put something on. But not you. You had to flaunt yourself in *that*.' The bathing suit did no wonders for her figure, leaving those parts exposed which ordinarily might have escaped an unkind eye. Her neck was wattled like a turkey cock's; her thighs strangely quilted.

'You look obscene,' Max told her. 'It is undignified for a woman of your age to go around in that kind of costume.'

She pulled at the brief skirt. 'What do you expect me to swim in? A greatcoat?'

'People were staring at you today. I saw some of them nudging each other. Damned embarrassing.'

She gave him a horrified stare.

It wasn't pleasant standing on the same spot for long, feeling the suck of the sand slowly burying our feet. Unless moves were made we stood the chance of being fixed forever, slowly solidifying as the cold crept up our bodies, congealing the blood. We would stand, three monolithic markers of lowest ebb. Digging had been abandoned. We began to follow the line of flotsam which heaved with each hissing sigh that the waves made.

Max and Dorothea trailed beside me, feet dragging, heads down, arguing desultorily. Occasionally he stabbed the sand, seemingly not caring whether he went through her toes with the iron bar. Out at sea, boats were beginning their slow swing, turning at their anchorages as the tide began its inward sweep. It lapped our feet and sent us gradually farther inland until, by the time we had walked across our bay, we were half-way back to the shore again. We rounded the headland just as the waves began to break on the first small stones. Ahead was the curve of another bay, empty and desolate now that the lowering clouds were threatening to swamp it.

'It will rain soon,' I said.

'How observant! Let's get out of this God-forsaken place.' Max handed me the can he had been carrying, and put his hands in his pockets. The iron bar was stuffed inside his jacket so that it protruded from his collar.

'I like it,' Dorothea said. Although quite mauve with cold, she strode on, forcing us to keep up with her.

'A few minutes ago you were saying how cold you were. Can't you ever make up your mind?'

She swung round at him, sending the water from the bucket she carried over his coat.

'Mind out! You clumsy fool!' With a gasp Dorothea rushed at him, ineffectually trying to brush the drops away. 'Get off, woman! Don't touch me. I don't want you pawing me like that.' She understood he meant it, and backed away from him.

'The sky's dissolving,' I said.

She stood among the heaving flotsam which tangled in her legs. 'You don't, do you?' she said.

'No.'

As she stepped backward, long lengths of wrack went with her. 'You're heartless.'

'I'm tired.'

Waves were coming in with greater force, sending us steps away from her. She took another step towards the open sea which was coming at us with a rushing sound. 'So am I.' A sudden larger wave made her swing and totter. Catching a handful of water she poured it down her leg, then turned to face the tide. 'I'm going out there,' she said. 'I think I'll drown myself.' She waded clear of the weed, striding the water until it was deep enough for her to plunge and start to swim.

Max did nothing to stop her. He merely stood looking as her strokes took her away. He watched her head rise with the first large wave, disappear beneath its spume, and surface again to breast the next.

'Silly bitch,' he said.

I asked him whether he thought there was danger for her. Since he could swim it seemed to me that the safest thing was to go out and bring her back.

'That's what she wants me to do,' he said. 'So I'm not. Spoil my clothes anyway. She won't get far, not in this. The tide'll bring her in eventually. Look how strong it is.'

'Perhaps it will win.'

'Not a chance. If you're so worried, why don't you go out and get her?'

'You know I can't swim. Not like that.'

'Quite so, and I'm not going to. So that makes two of us.'

We saw her head plainly visible in the khaki water, and the upright arms as she tried to make more progress.

'Come on,' Max said. 'Let's go home.' The can that Dorothea had been carrying lay at his feet. He pushed it with his toes, emptying my shells. One by one he kicked them out of sight and into the water.

'Come on.'

'I think I'll wait for a while.'

'Suit yourself. She won't drown, she's too strong a swimmer. Besides, she hasn't got the nerve to do anything so positive. You're wasting your time.'

'Nevertheless, I'll wait. You go without me.'

He shrugged and set out for the shore, stopping once to call over his shoulder that it was a long way home.

I watched him go, waiting until he was climbing the sand dunes, kicking up dust flurries with the speed of his steps. The light was poor and getting worse, but according to my meter there was still sufficient to try a photograph. The camera was in my pocket. Dorothea's head still bobbed on each wave's crest, her arms still flayed the water: she wasn't making progress. I turned the camera sideways and shot her small form, mid-way between the huge mass of water and sky, just as she threw out her arms to make the turn that would let the tide bring her back again.

I walked home the way that Max had gone, finding him in a deep fury when I arrived. The next day we all went back to London.

He sits in a large room, at his desk, writing. Although it is still daylight, the table lamp is lit, casting its glow directly on to his work. Dense foliage masks the windows that open to the garden, its growth so compact that there is no way in which to get through it to the outer air. Bushes that once grew neatly in separate borders are now spreading their branches in luxuriant growth, intertwining twigs and leaves to make a continuous blanket of green until they mingle with the distant trees. Some light penetrates the foliage, glancing here and there on fallen timbers—victims of last winter's gales—catching the cracked surfaces of paths where the stones lie at crazy angles, and the grass sprouts through. Small evidence remains of past care: a leaning dovecote still stands on the shaggy lawn, flowers in high profusion mingle with the grass, and there is no way of telling wild from once-cultivated. Strangulating creepers are beginning to spin their nets over the hedges whose height so effectively hems him in.

He has no wish to go out there and ponder nature, therefore the loss of exit is a welcome one. He can now shut tight his windows, double glaze them, seal up the draughts, hammer home the catches, no more a prey to any wanderer—whether insect, animal, or human—from that direction. The light's free entry is further hampered by the division of the room into partitions, or blocks. Shelves have been built across the room, almost from wall to wall, with only enough space left on either side for one person to pass. The shelves are of the open type, allowing the weak light to glance through them as through the bars of a cage. Ranged along the shelves are glass bottles, jars and tubes, each containing a single specimen and stoppered with wax. Each is labelled with its Latin and its vulgar name: on each there is a date, time and place of capture, exact position when sighted (whether on shore or under the ocean), and method of execution. Most were caught many years ago, when he himself went along the beaches of the Southern shores (for all are natives to this country) to hunt for living animals. Only the Ensis siliqua, Solen marginatus, and Pharus legumen are of recent date. There is too much pain in the world outside. He cannot tussle any more with the elements. He would rather receive neat parcels from abroad which can be unwrapped in the silent room, revealing the dry, encrusted cases on which he can work with methodical attention, undisturbed even by a ticking clock. He labours happily for days, alone in the sweet, acrid smell, with his sets of brushes. On his hands he wears rubber gloves so there is no risk of his nails turning yellow when he plunges them into the nitric acid. Carefully he has stoppered up the orifice with wax, and covered all the spines. There will be no damage done to the delicate turreting and nacre: long experience will direct him when it is time to withdraw the shell and place it in the water. He has never been careless with the pumice stone, or had to restore chipping done by himself with a too-rough rasp. And always he has tried to improve on nature, giving each arrival a heightened gloss; making perfect the imperfect, whether in colour or shape or symmetry. No one who could see him at work would say he didn't know his business. His world is the world of the shell: lined with a pearly phosphorescence, where he lives in the inner chamber, cut off by the secret septa, and attached to it as firmly as the siphuncle is to the Nautilus.

Every shelf, cupboard and drawer he has made himself, tailoring each piece to his needs, wasting no space. Collections are housed in special drawers along the length of an entire wall. Only he holds the key to them, and only he can gaze on his achievements. One of his greatest delights is to choose, at random, a certain section—the Cypraea, say—and creep up to the drawer to insert the key. With a quick turn the drawer is open, and he looks down: there, lying in regular rows, are the glowing shells, as brightly splendid and intact as they were when he last played the game. They never change; never once has he been disappointed; they have always been there waiting for him in the same crystallized magnificence. For this he has saved them. To this end he will always direct his energies. Rarely does he finger them, for that might harm their bloom. Others may want to hold them, running their hands over the enamel surfaces in an effort to satisfy some sensuous longing; but this, for him, is a spurious pastime as frivolous as wanting a rocaille grotto, or a trinket box of painted cockles. His collection contains no Nautilii burnt and fashioned as goblets, gem-encrusted and mounted in disguising metals. He has never wanted to cut his cowries into objects of utility. He has read of people who think nothing of wearing round their necks discs made from cone shells, or strings of mauve limpets ruined by gimlet holes. Surely this betokens minds so primitive that missionaries are needed badly to spread the word of Conservation in their midst? Acts of desecration like these will be the ruination of this world.

One side of his room is given over to what he calls 'the tools'. Behind the solid cupboard doors lie the bottles of acid, vats and jars, burners and magnifiers which keep him employed. Without them he would be as lost as the Egyptian embalmer without his natron and linen strips. Often he has thought how pleasant it must have been to have lived in those days when the embalmers and funerary furnishers were considered craftsmen of first rank, men of stature essential to the community. They were never outcasts, only met with out of necessity, speedily forgotten or distastefully remembered: great nobles paid them constant visits, coming with deep understanding of their work, not with a superficial curiosity bearing no relation to their aims. He would have been able to join in pleasureable discussions concerning processes by which the Egyptians' precious *ka* could best be served. There would have been journeys to the sites where workmen laboured for years making chambers strong and deep enough to withstand the sand's assault or the robbers' shovels. He would have seen the mighty labour that went on to haul the huge stone blocks to their resting place; the carvings being carried out to commemorate externally his work which would rest inside. Then there was no trouble too great or expense too costly in man's protection of his eternity. Now he works alone towards the same ends, doing his solitary best in the face of a community interested only in ephemeral things.

If, sometimes, he wanders his room disconsolately it is because he sees his task as incomplete. There is so much still to do. He can work away for days and weeks on a favourite project, enjoying what he's about, but at the back of his mind rests the unsolved problem. Often he goes to the long shelves that house his books, looking for an answer there. He takes down the volumes and the catalogues— all of them priceless to him—trying to find, in the engravings and photographs, in the printed pages, a satisfying answer. But again and again as he walks along the rows he finds himself back at the same section, facing the heavy sets of encyclopaedias that were his father's legacy. He has read through them many times, out of habit mainly, and a desire to find out what those strange creatures, other people, have done with their days. But there is only one section to which he returns with increasing interest, and rereads carefully in case he should have missed a word or line. If asked he could recite the passages by heart, but compulsion drives him to the shelves to take out a certain volume and thumb through the pages, searching for those which open easiest, and have their corners curled. During the past few weeks these pages have provided him with constant reading: he has been unable to pass a day without going to them to ponder what they have to say, and every time he has pored over the words he has wondered if he has found the answer:

EMBALMING.

This practice has improved well beyond the bounds thought possible by the earliest artisans who, in the days of the Pharaohs, only achieved modest success by means of drugs, natron and gum-smeared strips which Herodotus has described as being in use for centuries. Since dehydration of the body occurred, men's aim has been to remedy this fault, and many methods have been tried.

Not until the seventeenth century in this country were any notable advances made, experiments being carried out among the following: zinc chloride solution, biochloride of mercury solution and saturated solution of arsenic. In the eighteenth, and early nineteenth centuries it was often the practice to pickle the body by placing it in a casket from which all air had been excluded, and filling the casket with brine or alcohol. Not until later in the nineteenth century did a French chemist, J. N. Gannal, experiment with vascular injections using aluminium salts and arsenic. Today great strides have been made in the art of embalming, allowing complete preservation of the corpse. The fluid now contains a definite percentage of formaldehyde in formula, added to which are alcohol, salts, dyes, and penetrating agents to delay or prevent dehydration.

Several gallons of this fluid are injected into an artery located at any one of these points: the groin, base of the neck, or under the arm. By this method the body is cleared of blood, even to remote areas once never reached, and drained by opening a vein in the region of the original incision. All fluids and gases from cavities in trunk areas are released by means of a large, hollow needle, inserted at a site near the navel where the abdominal wall can be penetrated. The same needle is used to inject a suitable disinfectant into the cleared areas. Any body which has had an autopsy performed on it before embalming takes place is injected vascularly into the head and extremities with preservative. A large hypodermic needle is employed to inject the walls of back and trunk. The viscera are removed to be dealt with separately in the embalming solution. Before being replaced in the correct position in the trunk cavity they are first covered with preservant in powder form.

In the treatment of the face much skill is needed to make full use of the waxes, cements and cosmetics employed. This branch of the embalmer's art is one that requires extreme dexterity, and an assured knowledge of such things as cosmetology, sculpture, and plastic surgery. By today's methods a perfect resemblance can be achieved.

For many centuries people have been collected in this way; methods of preserving them improving with the advance of science. He has always, in his work, sought out the best means available to help him go forward. In his cupboards lies the evidence of years of research; there are the tools, some now not used at all, which in their time have been the very best and most advanced that he could buy. Not for nothing are the cupboards crammed with catalogues from this and that firm renowned for certain up-to-date instruments, their pages marked carefully in red to indicate his purchases. His magnifiers range from one to plus twenty, the microscopes live in their own teak cases, the brushes on a special shelf. An entire cupboard holds his cameras which he has changed as each new one marketed promised to be better than the last. True he has not experimented greatly with colour slides, or found the idea of moving pictures attractive: in this field he has much to learn; but the possibility of seeing his subjects move on film has little appeal for him. He would be for ever stopping the reel, afraid of missing a single moment. He could, if he wanted to, develop the most complicated of film, or set himself up with any new equipment that took his fancy. Already he has a beautiful dark room built of stout partitioning into which no speck of light can enter. There he can develop and enlarge, so why not become totally involved with film in all its variations? He could utilise (if need be) the floor space now given over to his bed. He finds the idea unappealing: it would mean shifting his sleeping quarters away from the comforting darkness that nightly surrounds him, and once out where the night still has a chance of penetrating the cracks in the blinds he might not find so sound a sleep. Often there is moonlight which, so he has read, can make a man mad if it shines directly on to his face. No, there must be no change of sleeping habits, for if this occurred who knows what changes might follow? Therefore there will be no cinema—the very word suggests the threat of visitors coming to view what he has shot, eagerly taking their seats in the dark, to be entertained. His room will never resound to the expectant whispers of invited guests, waiting and watching the blank screen. Dorothea must not be allowed the chance of socialising him and what he does, so he will never give her the opportunity of complaining that he never wants to demonstrate how good a film maker he's become.

But when he takes out his photographs from their files he looks at them a little wistfully, wishing they were grander and more truthful. As his eyesight fades he cannot see so clearly his past intentions. Now he finds some difficulty in spotting the changes in his wife which once were so evident. And is it imagination, or does he think the photographs themselves are fading, due either to the infiltrating light which, try as he may, he cannot totally obliterate, or to his own inferior workmanship? Some are changing colour, slowly slipping into sepia and violet like ships pulling away from the shore into a misty sea. Those that have a sepia tint resemble certain paintings which have been obscured by layers of thick varnish, but, unlike the paintings, they cannot be restored by any scraping. And if the photographs are fading, what about the negatives? Do they still lie as perfect as the day he made them? Or are they scratched, twisted, bleached so that any attempts to make them positive again would only meet with partial success? He has been many times to the folders to look at them, for he is a careful man who believes his time well spent in checking and re-checking what he owns; yet while he sits so quietly at his desk, writing his inventories, his valuable and unredeemable negatives may be in the process of vanishing, just as Max and James will disappear. They may take with them their remaining hours of survival, not knowing that what he has preserved of their pasts is rapidly coming to nothing. It is too late to warn them, but if Dorothea remains there may be a way in which she can be saved.

Doubts being in his mind as to whether he has wasted all these years on her behalf, he has to ask himself whether he has used his talents to the full. Surrounded as he is by so much equipment, he asks now whether he has been worthy of it. Or could he not see beyond the bounds of a piece of best card, eight by ten? Should he have used the enlarger more? Why couldn't he employ it to produce specimens big enough to see so clearly that any shadow of doubt would have been removed? He could, had he wished, have made his photographs three times as large, or even larger. Why not life size? He could have made them all as tall as himself, so that he could stand them up and look directly into their eyes. He could have stood them up and arranged them in rows, like soldiers ready for inspection. Rank upon rank he could walk through them in military style telling them to smarten up, hold up their heads and think of something other than themselves. The only argument against this course would be the size of his collection. He wouldn't like one day to be on parade and find himself totally surrounded by his own creations, hemmed in by the crush of a two-dimensional army, and finally forced out of his own door by cardboard.

Enlarging, too, can bring out imperfections undetected on the smaller size. A head that looks so perfect when a quarter of an inch can spread itself into a life-size rendering of nothing more than a few blurred spots of black and grey, bearing no resemblance to anyone familiar. He isn't aiming at lovely textures and delicate tints but at a likeness so true that its clarity is blinding. There must be not a solitary doubt as to the subject matter's age and condition. And Dorothea is ageing. When he sees her again she may have noticeably passed the point at which he photographed her lying in bed in the morning. While he prevaricates he may be losing her again to those little lines which are spreading like a disguise across her features. Every day the speed of her disintegration increases: it must do so since every day, as he grows older, he notices how Time is shortening between the morning and the night. When he was a child he wished his solitary days away, they seemed so interminable; now there is a scramble to save what is left between waking and sleeping.

He suspects that nobody but he notices the rushing days, or even remembers them. He at least has managed to keep track of their existence by keeping diaries. By going to the shelves and lifting down the volumes, he can always check that the years were really there. He can see the blue ink tracing the days in tiny words, so that they were filled, if not by wonderful events, at least by what he wrote of them. He can thumb through oceans of detail concerning his collections; he can tell you exactly when he was engaged on what. The pages are filled with his daily rituals of work and relaxation: if he wants to find out when he received his first set of Tellina from Florida, he has only to flick through the diaries patiently until he comes to '38, and there he will find it. If a doubt arises as to its truth, then he can look in the corresponding margin where he will find the number of the drawer in which the specimens are housed. He can go through the pages all the way, checking on facts, and if the facts sometimes look dubious there are always the photographs to back them up. True, the photos mark only occasional moments, but they are his one sure guide to what was happening to Dorothea. He observed her as much as he could, and wrote most carefully of what he saw: he was never careless in the task; every triviality was noted, for it is with trivialities that people pass their days. Apart from noting daily how she looked, he detailed her conversations, gestures and moods. She doesn't remember losing the bread coupons on a train in '44: no doubt she has forgotten what she was doing on the train. The diary would remind her of a visit, perhaps to Max, from which she returned in a black temper. But was it Max she really visited, or did she go to strangers? He never asked. Not once did he ask her what she did with herself when outside his ken. This was his mistake. Unless she told him of her own free will, he never knew. He was clever enough at watching her when she thought she was alone, and in that way reaped a goodly harvest for his pen. He often followed her to see where she went, but this meant hours away from his room and it was hard to decide priorities. It was easier at the summer house to keep track of her: their small seaside world precluded totally separate lives and he could be more sure of writing down a fair approximation of her days. She was more open then, telling him more freely of what she did, and the people she met.

She must have met people, thousands of them that he had never seen, or heard of. When the move was made to London there were more opportunities for her to use up the long days. She may have found a million things to do of which he was never aware. Just because he saw her domestically instated in a too-large house with a garden requiring hours of upkeep, it didn't preclude an extra-mural life. When she left the house how did he know where she was going? The fact that she was neither waving in her hands a hockey stick, nor tickets for the theatre didn't mean she had no taste for sport or culture. Hidden away inside her useless, pretty frame may have been an urgent desire for amusement and company. If he wanted to he could check to see exactly how many hours per day or week she spent away from his watching eye. Then he could work out the possible ways of spending them. Not that this would bring back the lost hours, but it might reassure him that Dorothea is not already lost, and he is waiting for nothing. He has never before seriously considered the possibility of her having friends, real friends who are strangers to him, but to whom she can go whenever she feels the need. She may have a female confidante (in the way that many women do) to whom she can spill out all her petty worries. This unknown woman may have been her wailing wall for many years, and followed avidly the turns of Dorothea's fortune. She may have advised her what to do; she may be advising her still. Dorothea has always needed the support of others, so why has she not drawn to herself the comfort of another woman's sympathy? This line of thought is one which brings with it a sudden agitation. He sees his prize precariously balanced on the knife-edge of someone else's decision, and he feels a momentary panic. Now there is no knowing what force she has gathered out there to thwart his plans. There may be dozens of women friends assailing her with conflicting sound advice, so that she cannot act at all. They may have removed entirely any shred of will she still possessed. Or they may be men! The hypothesis is sound. Dorothea's devotion may have spread itself in recent years to take in someone other than her familiars, so that she has only made a show of caring, while inside herself she has been laughing with pleasure and anticipation. A man may be in existence who cares for her with almost the same single-mindedness as the man who sits at his desk. The thought stops his pen. He raises his head to look at nothing, while the ideas rush upon each other in furious waves. If this man exists (and why shouldn't he?), then he too has heard the story of the plan, given his advice and had it accepted. Now that man may be nearing the end of his long wait, telling himself that she won't be far away; that she is soon coming to start afresh with him. The thought of a contract doesn't frighten him for he is sure she has torn it up, signature and all, in favour of his claim. She may be hurrying this instant to the spot where he stands, prepared to precipitate herself into his arms and future. The idea is intolerable. He throws down his pen and staggers to his feet.

So now the thought arises that she may not come at all. He goes over to the door and makes sure the key is turned. Next he checks the window fastenings and pulls together the curtain nets. Then he draws down each blind and fastens it to the sills. Only along the blinds' edges do lines of green light still show, but the rest of the room is in darkness. He makes his way back to the desk with a sureness of foot that comes from long practice. There he turns on the lamp. Then down come the diaries. He opens the first one and begins the task of checking the possibility of Dorothea's defection. He does it as mathematically as he can—having great faith in the permanence of numbers—putting into columns the days when she was in his company, when she was not in his company but under surveillance, and the days she never appeared. He has ten thousand nine hundred and fifty days to check before he reaches this year. And the days of this year that have already gone may be as important as all the others. He is looking for some clue to tell him whether she will come, but all the way through the closely written volumes he has only two items on which to base his answer, and those are conflicting ones: item one—Dorothea refused a gift of money six years previously, so it may be argued she had no wish to leave. Item two—Max has given his word she will come, and Max is a stranger to the truth. The diaries are useless.

Sadly he sits back and heaves a sigh. He must, from somewhere, produce a thing called 'Hope'—that quality he can only understand as a word on which texts are based: 'Hope springs eternal'; 'Hope and the world hopes with you'; 'All the world loves a hoper' and so on. He must sit and concentrate until he has convinced himself that Dorothea means to carry out the contract she has signed and come today, fully intending to remain with him forever. Forever, and forever and forever. Chant the words like a charm and she'll come. Look for passages in books that will invoke her. He runs his hand slackly along the calf-skin volumes on the shelf, pulling at one or two of them with limp fingers; not actually trying to extract them because he knows where his fingers will eventually alight, and which book they will pull from the shelf. The dog-eared pages open easily. There's a smudge on the word EMBALMING.

> 'This practice has improved well beyond the bounds thought possible by the earliest artisans who, in the days of the Pharoahs, only achieved modest success...'

At the end of the article though, it states clearly that a perfect resemblance can be achieved.

> 'In the eighteenth and early nineteenth centuries it was often the practice to pickle the body by placing it in a casket from which all air had been excluded, and filling the casket with brine or alcohol....'

No difficulties there, unless it be the air-tight casket. The lid would have to be transparent, like Snow White's; always his favourite fairytale. But why stick to an eighteenth century recipe when much better methods have been evolved?

> 'Today great strides have been made in the art of embalming, allowing complete preservation of the corpse. The fluid now contains a definite percentage of formaldehyde in formula, added to which are alcohol, salts, dyes, and penetrating agents to delay or prevent dehydration...'

Although he would like her to swim in a bath of brine (in which she would surely be at home), he must bow to progress and agree to follow.

'Several gallons of this fluid are injected...'

Gallons! How many gallons? And what fluid? It isn't enough to know that it contains a definite percentage of formaldehyde, without knowing accurate amounts. And how many gallons of any fluid can be injected into one reasonably sized woman? The questions demand immediate answers.

'All fluids and gases from cavities in trunk areas are released by means of a large, hollow needle, inserted at a site near the navel where the abdominal wall can be penetrated. The same needle is used to inject a suitable disinfectant into the cleared areas...'

The operation has about it a pleasant un-messy quality. He should be able, by a careful search and subtle questioning, to find out more about its details.

'The viscera are removed to be dealt with separately...'

A problem presents itself at this point: is he capable of carrying out the instructions? Not only will a cool head be needed, but a stomach strong enough to withstand the removal of someone else's. Physical contact has always been the hardest thing for him to tolerate: such closeness with Dorothea may prove more difficult than at first supposed. He realizes that for her sake he must make certain sacrifices, but doesn't see himself able for long to sustain the role of augur, even with the aid of nostril plugs and rubber gloves. It would be unfortunate for him if, when at last in sight of his ambition, he found himself unable to go forward out of mere squeamishness. It is the project's size he finds slightly daunting: he isn't used to the scale. When handling a specimen of such a size as this, it is ridiculous to suppose that the process will be as neat as with something smaller. It would be a great mistake to turn his lovely room into an abattoir, yet any process, save the pickling one, suggests this possibility. What to do? How could her lovely features be saved by such a primitive method? Imagine his disappointment, having gone to such lengths to save her, at discovering the face resembles nothing more than an encrusted sponge. Rather than have this happen he would prefer her to continue growing old until the time when some other process, more surely successful, presents itself.

What he lacks at present are detailed descriptions of ways and means of conducting this affair. Obviously there are books and pamphlets to be had on the subject, with which a beginner can learn. Perhaps there are also evening classes, although he would find it hard to mix with others, however close their interests paralleled his own. Somewhere are (surely) gentlemen only too willing to pass on what they know, only too happy to keep the craft alive. They might teach him happily enough, even allowing him to practise on their specimens, so that his knowledge will extend beyond the theoretical. This would be very much to his advantage, for one cannot expect to learn a craft and practise simultaneously on the prize specimen: no apprentice baker makes a wedding cake on his first day at college. There must be learning. So he will learn. He will apply himself with the same enthusiasm that he once gave to his first white-ribbed Cowrie. And if it takes time, then time he will give it, until the great day comes when he feels adequate to the almighty task. He will learn with speed, because speed is the essence of his job: his whole future will be given over to the learning. He feels a new energy coming into him.

The attendant sitting by the door has woken up. Now he stares at me with eyes like fish, while I surface to the bright, grey day. A distant bell begins to chime: one, two, three, four, five, six, seven, eight, nine, and on and on and on. I thought at first it was a clock chiming my departure. Pigeons cry on a distant building, disrupting my peace. There is a terrible smell in here, like the smell of spices kept in an ancient chest. Or is it the scent of my carnation growing stronger as it dies? Now is the time to rise and leave these poor pictures with their blighted surfaces; to leave the wooden bench on which the dust had already settled; walk past the attendant who sits wishing his life away in sleep and go back along the interior corridor. The sound of generators begins to rumble in my ears and the floor vibrates under the tread of the visitors. They make way for me as I pass but I don't look at them; nor do I look at the portraits hanging on the walls. If I look only directly in front, then the eyes cannot claim me nor visitors get in my way. Since all these galleries are inter-sectional then it is an easy thing to take a route almost directly back to where I first came in. It is best to ignore the staring eyes and go past them with head down, as soft-footedly as I can, not letting them see I know I'm being watched. I walk along the yellow boards as carefully as a cat, my feet aligned precisely so there is no danger of stepping on the cracks. By rights there should be no cracks at all, but someone has been slipshod in his work of filling them. There is no telling how long they will remain at their present width—it may be weeks, it may be only days—but someone will surely lose his job if he doesn't set about repairing them soon.

I am a very careful man: even when I pass over a section of the floor which is dazzlingly lit from overhead, I can still remember where my feet should be, and emerge without a fault. When I reach that section of the gallery where boards give way to wood blocks, the problem isn't difficult. Many would attempt to skate its glassy surface, quite unaware that each block, however solid-seeming its facet, is liable to tip slowly sideways (and not all the blocks tipping in the same direction), until the floor is a ruined, icy sea of sharpness on which the flesh will bleed. The solution is comparatively simple: it consists in turning right into a minor corridor, also with a boarded floor. By stepping sideways with the feet still parallel it is possible to move along the entire corridor's length unharmed, emerging in yet another gallery, still on boards and still facing them. A wall on which paintings hang has to be intercepted at snail's pace before the new gallery is reached, but if one stares at the abalone suit, then nothing can delay the return.

Now I can see the lines leading me towards the farthermost gallery where my queen is waiting. If I raise my head I can see the pale oval of her face and neck and the colour's strange repetition in her skirt. Not until I have advanced to the centre of the nearest gallery can I see how her hands are folded across her stomach; the fingers are so tightly clasped that no amount of wrestling would pull them apart. The jewels on her forefingers are there to stay, and she is surreptitiously feeling that everything is as it should be. A weight of pearls outlines her throat and the edges of her dress, forcing her to sit upright with a proud throwing back of the head. She may be a fabrication, but she shines in her artifice like a lit beacon, guiding me to her. I am forced to admire her as I go forward, watching each detail reveal itself again: now I can see the richness of her, the layers of paint under which she hides, and the way, now and then, a glimmer of her real self peeps through. She smiles her self-satisfied smile now, and keeps her eyes turned from me, as befits a rogue with a secret to keep. Encased in a frame, under glass, under varnish, beneath gold leaf, beneath layers of paint, lies the secret of her inception—the way someone saw her on the day she took her seat for the first time on the dais, settled her skirts and said, 'You may begin now Mr. Unknown. Pray be as quick as you can. I fear I will fade if you are not fast, and your hands will lose their elasticity. Catch me now, before it is too late.'

Am I too late? I walk towards a painted queen who herself had to go through the process of daily decay before she could be trapped in a blurred resemblance; and I wait for one who still has to have the operation performed on her, with all my knowledge and dexterity. Yet there isn't much to choose between them; I know as little about the one, as the other. They are both specimens in need of restoration, with the good fortune to have me at their service. And I have served them both to the best of my capabilities, never stinting my efforts on their behalf. I have almost worn myself out in their service, yet considered my time well spent. Often have I come here—even when occupied with other, important work—to check on the lady before me now. I have come to see that her surfaces were still intact: it wasn't only a simple matter of looking closely at the cracks and blurs, making sure there were no newcomers; I made a study of her, lest she should be suffering from some malaise not visible to the casual eye. I used my set of magnifiers and studied stress and strain. It won't be through any fault of mine that she doesn't last as long as she has already. She has been a demanding queen whom I have served with fidelity, but all she has ever done for me is allow me to gaze at her. For this I should be thankful: it is all I have ever asked of her. Her smile tells me she cannot help me beyond that point, she cannot help me to stop myself from decay. All the effort has to come from me, for there is no one who can save me. So I must reconcile myself to that fact and remove from my system the petty jealousy that might interrupt my work or even halt it altogether. What does it matter that I am diminishing, if what I do will last forever? Already I feel today settling like a film on my skin. I feel my legs shrinking inside my trouser legs, and my arms growing thin inside my shirt. The fingers shrivel slightly. Slowly I walk forward and see myself appearing in the glass: a dwarf who was once a tall and shapely man, now standing in an ageing suit and fading shirt, gently dimming over with the breath of his past. My clothes prop me up, for inside them I am dwindling. One day there will be nothing left of me but a dry shell, so twisted and withered that I will be mistaken for a fallen leaf or piece of stick. Then the leaf or stick will itself crumble away until nothing remains but a few grains, like pepper, which the first puff of wind will lift and carry over the airy seas. But what I have done will stay as my rocklike monument, and will last forever.

I hear the rattle of distant lifts and the sound of voices. If they are coming I must be ready. I hear slow footsteps along the outer corridor. I stand erect and look straight ahead, superbly patient, prepared and calm, almost as though I have no real wish for the moment to come when the waiting is over and I know the worst. She had better come soon, before my strength begins to give way and I find myself suddenly unable to help her. She must come now, or the waiting and watching will have been in vain. She must come. Now.

But so far I am alone.

www.ingramcontent.com/pod-product-compliance
Ingram Content Group UK Ltd.
Pitfield, Milton Keynes, MK11 3LW, UK
UKHW030927060425
457073UK00002B/112